Barbara J. Hancock
Ridge Mountains whe
edge of the wilderne.
isn't writing modern
shadows with a uniqu
be found wrangling twin boys and spo

For those that champion the silenced
and love the lost.

Chapter 1

Playground sounds made the danger beside Victoria so much worse. High-pitched laughter and conversations about make-believe seemed surreal. Across the mulched expanse, her sister, Katherine D'Arcy Severne, pushed Victoria's toddler, Michael, and her own baby, Sam, on the swings. She glanced toward Victoria and waved. Vic waved back.

Pay no attention to the madman beside me, Kat. Keep my Michael and your Sam safe.

The monk sitting beside Victoria on the park bench was in a businessman's suit, as if he'd dropped by the Baton Rouge, Louisiana, playground during his lunch break. He crossed his legs gracefully like a civilized man. Kat probably thought he was a father watching his child play instead of an evil man come to threaten their own. Victoria had been resting in the sun when he'd approached. She'd actually smiled at him when he'd joined her on the bench.

And then he'd revealed his true purpose.

"The Order of Samuel has proven time and time again that you cannot run. You cannot hide. You will learn this lesson or your child will join us. A half daemon brother would be unusual, but I'm sure we could train him, put him to good use for Father Reynard's cause."

"Stay. Away. From. Michael," Victoria said. Her voice cracked with emotion. Her baby was only two. Katherine pushed her nephew higher and he squealed.

Victoria's throat had yet to recover from the injuries she'd sustained in the opera house fire set by Father Reynard. They'd blamed it on an obsessive fan. He'd been obsessive all right. But not a fan. He was a daemon hunter and she and Katherine had been his reluctant bloodhounds. They'd been born with an affinity for Brimstone blood that inevitably led them to the daemons Reynard hunted. Violence. Blood. Pain. No rest. No peace. He had dogged their steps for as long as they could walk.

He'd died in the fire, but apparently his cause hadn't.

"I will leave your daemon spawn alone, only if you set my brethren free. This man is our greatest enemy. He must be stopped," the monk in disguise said.

He held a magazine in his hands and tilted the cover so she could see the man who graced it.

Michael's laughter floated to her ears as his doting aunt pushed him on the swing. Victoria had fallen in love with a daemon. Her affinity for the Brimstone in his blood had drawn them together, but it had been more than that. He'd been a stop to running. He'd been hope. He had died trying to protect her and Michael. The Order of Samuel said they were warriors for heaven. They lied. The members of the D'Arcy family were tools used by one faction of daemons to hunt another.

Politics.

The D'Arcy ability to draw and be drawn to dae-mon blood had placed them in the middle of an other-worldly civil war.

Love wasn't allowed.

Ironic that her favorite role to play had always been Juliet. She'd traveled around the world to sing the part of a tragic romance again and again.

"What do you want me to do?" Victoria asked.

The man on the cover of the magazine was a beauti-ful stranger in a designer suit. Behind him, a vineyard stretched in seemingly endless verdant rows. He stood with one foot on the threshold of a historic stone build-ing, a massive wooden door with iron hinges looking rough-hewn and craggy in sharp contrast to his polished clothes. There was a gleam to the black waves of his hair, but those waves and his sun-kissed skin seemed more in keeping with the door than his suit. Victoria had grown up in the dramatic world of the opera. She knew a costume when she saw one. The man's civilized suit was a lie.

"You will gain his trust. You will learn his secrets. Once you discover where he keeps his prisoners, you will free them," the monk said. "Once they are freed, they will use their combined strength to kill him. In this way, you will guarantee your son's safety."

Children laughed and ran and played all around them. Tears burned behind her eyes. But she forced them to dry. She waved again and this time Michael waved back, still laughing. Katherine was looking at Victoria closely now. As if she sensed something wrong. But the monk had already risen, prepared to walk away. He didn't need her answer. He could sense her defeat in her slumped shoulders and her trembling wave of reassurance to her child.

"I'm not a spy. How will I do this?" she asked his back. He paused and halfway turned back to reply.

"He has Brimstone in his blood. He's damned. Your affinity is the perfect weapon. His home is a fortress. You will penetrate his defenses. Seduce his secrets from him. Free our brothers. Capture him. Then, you and your family will be left in peace."

He lied.

She would never know peace.

"Who knows? You might even enjoy yourself. You have proven you have a taste for damnation," the monk said. His knowing laughter didn't blend with the innocent laughter of the children around them. It jarred. It condemned. Her cheeks burned. Not because she was ashamed of loving Michael's father, but because this man didn't deserve to pollute what they'd shared by mentioning it. Daemons were nearly immortal beings who lived in the hell dimension. They were different but, like men, they were only damned by their actions, not by their blood. Michael's father had been heroic in the end, sacrificing himself for his child even though he'd been a daemon.

The children on the playground seemed to sense the evil in their midst. They parted as the monk passed as if a snake slithered among them. One little girl began to cry without obvious cause and a kind woman ran to see what she could do to help.

The monk had left the magazine beside her on the bench. She picked it up. The man on the cover hadn't looked at the camera. The photographer had caught him in a moment of reflection, with dark shadows from the vine-covered building on his face. The photograph drew her as if the Brimstone in the man's blood could already sense her affinity. Yes. He had secrets. She could see them in his shadowed eyes.

A single tear did fall then. The monk had already walked away. His laughter drifted back to her on the humid Louisiana breeze. She had loved and lost, but she wouldn't lose again. Only one tear fell. It rolled down her cheek to fall on the back of her hand. It glistened there, useless.

She would do what she had to do to protect her son.

She willed the unshed tears to dry as she widened her eyes and clenched her jaw. The magazine crinkled in her ferocious grip.

Her son's vigilant protector, the hellhound Grim, wasn't allowed to materialize in the playground, but Victoria saw a shimmer of shadows near the swings, too dark to be cast by the blossoming grove of cherry trees that surrounded the park.

The wind blew and petals fell like pale pink rain. They settled on Katherine's dark hair and the children laughed. They raised their hands to the sky to try to catch the drifting blossoms. Near the shadow of Grim, the petals shied away in puffs of disturbed silk as the giant dog shook his sooty coat to maintain his disguise. She could imagine his movements because she knew he was there. No one else noticed. Just as no one else had heard the monk's threats.

During the fire, Katherine's husband, John Severne, had risked his life to give Grim to Victoria's son. His sacrifice had saved Michael. The fearsome beast had been Severne's companion for two hundred years. Now, he watched over her son.

But Grim wouldn't be enough.

Victoria had to do more.

Even if it meant continuing to be a servant to madmen whose evil requests damned her as if she'd sold her soul.

As the playground full of children continued to laugh and play, fear burned hotly inside her chest, exactly as she imagined the damning fire of Brimstone might burn in daemon veins.

Chapter 2

Few people had gotten close enough to see his scars.

Adam Turov sat with his chest facing the back of a wooden chair. He gripped the polished cherry slats with white knuckles, but he didn't flinch as he hunched his bare back for Dr. Verenich. The Brimstone in his blood wasn't always enough to heal the injuries he sustained hunting devils with no care for how much human blood they spilled.

"Live for a century, learn for a century," the doctor murmured under his breath as he plied needle and thread to close the dagger slash too severe to knit itself. "I have learned to use specially constructed thread in your treatment, *shef.* And yet you have not learned to avoid daemon-cursed blades."

"Without effort, you won't pull fish from a pond," Adam said. He could fight the doctor saying for saying. He'd learned all his Russian idioms firsthand before the Revolution.

"So, no pain, no gain?" The doctor chuckled grimly as he worked on the man he still referred to as his boss as his father had before him, even though Adam Turov had also become his friend. Gloves protected his hands from Brimstone's burn, but every now and then they'd sizzle and hiss, and smoke would rise into the air as he pierced Adam's skin with his needle and fireproof thread. "I'll tell you what you have gained, my friend…" He urged Adam to turn his back toward an antique mirror with a gilded frame. It was Tsarist, of course. The Turov family had brought a king's ransom to California during the Revolution. They survived by adapting, persevering. They had worked through the darkest hours. Sweat and blood had replaced diamonds and tiaras.

Reflected in the mirror, Adam Turov didn't look a day over thirty, even after a life-threatening battle with evil monks from the Order of Samuel and their Rogue daemon allies. On a good day, in fine clothes, he would seem even younger. Too young to successfully run the oldest winery in Sonoma, California.

"Wings. Over all these years, you've developed a macabre pair of wings," the doctor said.

Adam could see them. The scarifications the doctor pointed out by gesturing in the air above them. The tracery of scars swept down his back on both sides like folded wings. The irony caused a grim smile to curve his lips. There. That expression was older. Much more in keeping with his actual age.

"A dark angel indeed, Doctor," he said.

He could remember the initial beatings with a lash that had begun the "wings." And later, every hack and slash. Every stitch. Every battle. He could remember the face of every monk he'd delivered to hell. None of the monks in his memory were the one that most haunted him. Not yet. *Father Malachi had wielded the lash with enthusiasm. The younger the novitiate, the better.* The Order purported to be the last line of defense between hell and Earth, but they lied. In truth, the faction of Rogue daemons that wanted to overthrow Lucifer's Army and wage war on heaven had corrupted them. The Order of Samuel wasn't holy. They were as damned as he was.

He liked to think he escorted them to their just ends, one monk at a time. He might never reclaim the soul he'd sold, but he could face his own damnation one day if he delivered every single monk to hell before him.

"No, not an angel. You are more like the legendary firebird caught in a greedy prince's golden cage," the doctor said. "You will insist on attending the party, I'm sure. Movement will cause great pain. That was a deep wound. You should rest. Heal."

The doctor was already wiping Brimstone blood and ash from Adam's lean, muscled back in preparation for the evening suit that waited across the foot of his bed. It was a disguise. He used the expensive, tailored clothes and the carefully cultivated sophistication of a vintner to hide his true warrior's nature.

But he'd been hiding it for so long that his disguise came naturally to him now. He ran the Nightingale Vineyards as easily as he battled evil monks.

"I prefer the nightingale to the firebird, Doctor. The firebird was my mother's favorite. I named our best pinot noir in her honor. There's nothing golden about me. I'm far too dark for that comparison," Adam said.

"Ah, but you're forgetting how the prince was cursed by the firebird for his greed. Capturing the firebird was a mistake. It proved deadly. A dark enough tale, indeed," the doctor said.

"Nothing heals more than movement," Adam said, dismissing the fanciful talk. He rolled his shoulders to illustrate. The doctor hissed, but Adam ignored the agony that flared outward from his damaged skin. "We must keep moving forward."

He'd been damaged for a long time. Agony was a familiar friend.

He'd been nine when the Order had stolen him from his family. He'd been infinitely older when he'd escaped. In experience if not in years.

"Victoria D'Arcy is arriving tonight. That's why I completed a sweep. To clear the area so I could focus on her," Adam said.

The doctor busied himself, cleaning his instruments and packing his case while Adam dressed. His bag resembled a traditional black leather satchel, but it held the instruments necessary to be the private physician to a powerful man who'd sold his soul a hundred years ago. Dr. Verenich was the second-generation descendant of a physician who had followed the Turov family to America.

"You must protect her?" the doctor asked.

"Those are my orders. I haven't decided if I'll be able to follow them," Adam said. She'd been hunted by the Order of Samuel. They were her enemy, but she was their pawn. She wasn't coming to the Turov estate as his friend. Adam had been kidnapped, beaten, tortured, programmed to become a daemon slayer so that he could be used by Rogue daemons to overthrow Lucifer. But it had been a Loyalist daemon that had saved him. And it was the new Loyalist king that he now served.

A daemon that claimed Victoria D'Arcy as his stepchild.

He'd been warned by the daemon king that the Order of Samuel was sending Victoria to infiltrate Nightingale Vineyards and uncover his secrets.

The woman he welcomed tonight might well be the most dangerous threat he'd ever faced. He was supposed to help her even as she planned to betray him.

She was afraid. Fear always made her angry. She rebelled against it. How many times had she stood on an opera house stage bathed in light and draped in a character's costume—completely armored in powder, wig and an imaginary persona—to sing out in protest against her plight? She had fallen in love with a daemon. She'd gone against the Order of Samuel. She had survived. The father of her baby hadn't. The Order had killed him. She'd barely lived. For their baby.

Everything had changed when Michael was born. She was no longer a rebel. She was a mother. Now she had to be cautious for two.

Tonight, as she hurried toward Nightingale Vineyards, more than her voice was lost. It was as if her very heart had been ripped from her chest and it beat elsewhere. Slowly, steadily, but threatened; each beat might be its last if she didn't do as she was told. The new leader of the Order of Samuel, Father Malachi, held her strings and she was a puppet who could dance only to evil's song.

She'd flown into California in a plain summer suit of black linen. The gray shell sweater underneath the blazer stretched loosely to brush the top of her thighs. As she was only five foot three, it didn't have to stretch far. She'd pulled an oversize black fedora low over her eyes. Only her heels and handbag betrayed any personality. She'd grabbed them too hurriedly to think of disguise. Red. A holdover from a much bolder Victoria. That flamboyant woman seemed a lifetime ago.

Katherine had handled the other packing. She'd sent Victoria's bags ahead to the vineyard's estate house. Victoria hadn't told Kat about the danger Michael was in. It was only a matter of time before Katherine discovered her nephew was being stalked by the Order of Samuel. By then, Victoria hoped to have accomplished what she'd been sent to do.

Anything to save her son.

Katherine thought she wanted to visit the vineyards as a retreat to rest and recuperate. Her voice hadn't been the same since the opera house fire that had almost claimed her life. Doctors said she would recover. That she only needed time. Yet it seemed ages since she'd been able to sing.

She admitted to no one that it seemed ages since she'd *wanted* to sing.

She'd left her toddling son with his daemon nanny, Sybil, and his hellhound, Grim. Surely, they could protect him even better than her until she could arrange their freedom. One more task for the Order.

But wasn't it always one more, one more, one more?

She stepped into a coffee shop for an espresso after her flight. While she ordered, she noticed a thick-browed man in a nearby queue. He hadn't been on her plane, but he had been at the Shreveport airport. She was certain she'd seen him there. He wore a simple suit with a boxy cut and he was bald, stocky, his face smooth and plain, but he didn't move like a casual traveler.

Maybe he was an off duty soldier.

Maybe he was a ninja in disguise.

But Victoria suspected an even more nefarious origin.

She sipped her small, rich coffee. She even managed a smile for the barista who had boldly scrawled *bella* on her cup instead of *Vic*. His dark eyes flashed above a bright smile, but he didn't distract her from the suspicious-looking man who now placed his order at the register beside her.

She didn't catch the man's name. She didn't have to. Now that he was closer, she could see the movement of his muscles beneath his suit jacket. Its loose cut couldn't hide his extreme physicality.

Suddenly, the man looked up and met her gaze. He took his coffee from the barista, ignoring the tip jar with its yellow smiley face sticker. She glanced away. Why should she give him an intimate glimpse of her fear?

He had to be a monk from the Order of Samuel. His smirk and the black gleam of his large pupils seemed too knowing. The monks were following her to make sure she complied.

Victoria abandoned her steaming cup in the waste bin, no longer needing the caffeine. She was wide-awake. The whole shop full of weary travelers must see her heart beating in her chest. The Order didn't have to follow or threaten her further to make sure the job got done.

One threat toward Michael was enough.

Yet the look in the monk's eyes did quicken her steps. She hurried outside to the waiting row of taxis, and took the dark gaze with her. His eyes had held no sympathy, only the fire of fanaticism. That hateful glow had haunted her life. She refused to let it haunt Michael's as well.

* * *

The Turov mansion was a California Craftsman castle with hints of Imperial St. Petersburg in its columns and arches. The cab approached down a long, winding drive. Rather than the expected cedar shakes, the house was constructed of rough gray brick, its roof gleaming slate instead of Spanish tile. Several turrets were capped in domes of copper that glimmered gold in the sunset. The material was echoed in hammered metal on the mansion's gutters and window frames. She had time to appreciate the gleam as the car neared the entrance where the driveway ended in a circular loop. There was something that touched her about its design. It was art, not merely architecture. There was personality evident in every curve, passion in every turret.

But the hundreds of shadowed windows seemed to warn that the walls might shelter a difficult personality and a dark passion.

When she saw the main house, her first thought was *forever*. She'd traveled the world. She'd walked on ancient cobblestones. She'd sung on stages much older than she was. Nightingale Vineyards hadn't been here forever, but it seemed to proclaim that it *would* be. Maybe she was attributing Russian determination to its every brick, every line, because she knew its owner's heritage. It was natural to assume the house was a reflection of the man.

Since the house intimidated as much as it piqued her curiosity, she looked away.

The inhabited portion of the estate was surrounded by landscaped gardens that eventually gave way to rolling hills of endless cultivated greenery. The grapevines stretched as far as Victoria could see. The magazine hadn't captured the truth of the expanse. The setting sun bathed the vines in a warm russet haze.

The scent of roses enveloped her when she stepped from the car. Loamy earth, green vines and roses. She breathed deeply, reluctantly soothed. She'd paid the driver before she exited the vehicle. There were no bags beyond the purse she carried herself. The cab drove away and the night deepened as she paused. The garden beckoned, but the house waited, with only the windows on the ground level aglow. She would have to go in. She had to do what she'd come to do.

All around her, the vineyard grew. She swore she could almost feel the pervasive, steady creep of its tendrils. So alive. It was early in the growing season, but soon grapes would be plumping in heavy bunches. What was it like to choose a place, set down roots and thrive? No running. No hiding. It was all so beautiful and real. She could never give this to Michael, but she longed for it. The permanence.

For a while, she was alone beneath a sky gone violet and beginning to wink with waking stars.

And then she wasn't.

She tried to ignore the sudden pull of Brimstone, holding herself in place because if she didn't she would immediately move to its source. And its source was her enemy in spite of his allure.

Adam Turov.

It had to be.

"I can do this," Victoria whispered under her breath, the hoarse sound of her voice still a surprise, though the fire had been over two years ago. She shouldered her handbag and moved toward the portico over the front entrance.

"There's no turning back once you step through that door," a voice said from the shadows.

The glow from the windows did little to illuminate her welcoming committee. He didn't require illumination. She knew who and what he was before he came closer. As he approached, she instinctively inched away and looked over her shoulder.

The Order of Samuel had used her affinity to hunt daemons. She'd been a reluctant bloodhound since she was a young girl. She still was. It hadn't ended. The man at the airport was stalking her. He might be out of sight, but he wasn't out of mind. She reminded herself that this time she was here willingly. Her job was to uncover Turov's secrets and help the Order shut him down.

For Michael.

She forced herself to halt her retreat.

Adam Turov stepped into the light near the front door and he surprised her. He seemed nearer to her age than she'd expected. But she knew he wasn't. He was much, much older. Fear fluttered in her stomach and she tightened her impressively toned diaphragm against it. She was a welcome guest. A harmless opera singer looking for a restful vacation. She needed to act like he was her host, not her prey.

Her throat might not be up to par, but her core was as iron as ever. *For Michael.*

"Mr. Turov. It's nice to meet you," she said. She recognized him from the magazine she'd been shown. But that didn't matter—she could feel the Brimstone in his blood. He had already found her because that Brimstone drew him to her like a moth to a flame. The thought was heady as well as frightening. He was tall, sinfully attractive and powerful. Her temperature had risen. His would run hotter than 98.6. Her cheeks flushed. The earthy spring air was cool against her skin. It was the Brimstone, but it was also the man and her deception. Her job had always been to create beautiful, dramatic fabrications onstage, but she wasn't comfortable with lies offstage.

"Welcome to Sonoma. Are you ready to leave work and worry behind? I'll show you to the cottage where you'll be staying. You can freshen up and join us for a drink," Turov said.

"Do you always personally greet your guests?" she asked.

He didn't confirm his identity. He probably knew he didn't need to. He was famous. One of the most eligible bachelors in California. Of course she would recognize the Turov eyes, nose and chin that had graced his father and his grandfather before him. He couldn't know she was privy to his deal with the devil. He was the only Turov left and had been for over fifty years. Brimstone fueled his longevity. But it had come at great price. What kind of man would sell his soul for wealth and acclaim? Never mind the permanent feel of the estate around her and the rich earth beneath her feet. It would all be ashes eventually. The devil's due.

"No. Not always," he said. Only that. No explanation. Her flush deepened as he looked closely at her, one brow slightly raised.

The damned master of Nightingale Vineyards offered her his arm and she lightly accepted it. Little did he know her work—the most important performance of her life—had only just begun. Her heart pounded as they walked around a manicured lawn to a rose-covered arbor that created a dark tunnel. There was discreet outdoor lighting to show them the path. But would he need it if he'd walked this way for decades?

Her son had Brimstone blood. This was different. Turov was no daemon. He was a human who had sold his soul. His was not an innocent, natural burn. He was dangerous in spite of his tailored suit and his cultured accent.

Who was the prey in his garden? She was afraid the tables had been turned already.

"You've lost your voice?" he asked as they walked through rose-scented shadows.

"I've strained it. There was a fire a couple of years ago. I breathed in extreme heat and smoke. The effects have lingered. I can talk, but I can't sing. Not in my former way. I might never be able to sing professionally again," she said.

"That's a shame. I'm sorry. Never is such a long time and I'd love to hear you sing. Perhaps our pinot noir will soothe your throat," he said.

She was used to taking on roles, but she wasn't a spy. She might as well have "fraud" written on her forehead in scarlet. Her affinity was supposed to help her, but she was afraid it did the opposite. She couldn't be as tactical and distant as she should be. Her senses were completely taken over by the heat in his blood. His arm was solid and strong under her fingers. His warmth radiated outward to counteract the night air. It was as if she walked with a flame. Her feet faltered. Her throat reflexively opened. For the first time in a very long time she felt a song well up in her chest.

"For you," Turov said. They exited the arbor tunnel into a private courtyard ringed by high hedges. At first she mistook the cottage as a part of the hedge, but it was actually a stone building completely covered in lush vines of dark red roses. They tumbled and curved and twined, a profusion of color as the night came on, a riot of greenery and blossom.

"Oh," she breathed out. She risked no other syllable. Her chest was full. Her lips trembled. She wanted to sing. It was the Brimstone. Katherine had shared the truth about their affinity and how their gift for music responded to daemon blood. They'd used music to drown out the magnetic pull, but in special cases the music seemed to resonate with the power of Brimstone. She had to keep up her guard. She couldn't afford to allow this man to inspire her to song. Not if the song would bind them together. He was bound for the hell of the Order of Samuel's clutches. That was all.

The cottage would have been a perfect retreat if that was what she'd truly come to California to find, but the song bubbling up in her made it a dangerous place.

"Your bags are inside. I know you're tired, but join us once you're refreshed," Turov said. "I can't claim it will actually heal your throat, but the wine is excellent. It will help you relax after your flight."

"Thank you. I'll join you soon," Victoria said. Her voice was a classic film star's dusky tones. Accidentally throaty and seductive. This was the first time she'd heard it that way since the fire. Always before it had seemed scratchy and ugly.

He opened the door of the cottage and then stepped back to hand her the key. It was a skeleton key made warm by his touch. Her fingers closed around it. She didn't mean to fist them tightly, but tension betrayed her. He seemed to note her discomfort and watched her gather her composure. His gaze on her throat, moving as she swallowed, felt intimate—and intimacy with him would be dangerous. His many years of life left him too experienced and perceptive. If he got too close, she wouldn't be able to keep her secrets. *Yet she was here to get close. Close enough to fulfill a dark task.*

"You're safe here, Victoria. I read about the fire. How an obsessive fan caused it. Nightingale is a special place. Sacrosanct. We are older and wiser than most retreats. For a long time, I've insisted on privacy. I maintain this hideaway at great cost," Turov said. "Please accept my assurance that no one can harm you while you are here with me."

In the gloaming, it was too dark to read his eyes. But she recognized a greater danger in that moment than she'd previously acknowledged. She needed retreat. She longed for protection. And the last person she could expect to provide it was the man she planned to betray. His Brimstone blood coaxed her to sing, but it was his offer of protection that weakened her defenses.

"Forgive me if I don't relax. It isn't you. It's me," Victoria said.

"Yes. I see that. You hold yourself contained. Unusual for an artist," Turov said.

She hadn't stepped over the threshold yet. She regretted the pause as soon as his hand reached to tilt the brim of her hat up. Only a millimeter. Only the very tip of his fingers brushed the felt. But her expression felt suddenly exposed to his searching eyes. He lowered his hand. She held her breath. He leaned. Slightly. She might have imagined a lowering of his shadowed face toward hers. She backed up just in case, away from his heat, away from his discerning gaze.

"Join us," he urged again. "It's a small party. You'll be a welcome addition."

She nodded as she walked into the cottage he'd given her for her stay. The scent of roses would likely always remind her of this adrenaline-fueled retreat. For a few crazy seconds she had thought he was going to kiss her, and she'd recognized the pinch of disappointment in her chest with the realization that she couldn't have allowed it even if he'd tried.

Chapter 3

Her sister had packed four bags for her. Katherine had spared no effort. It seemed as if Victoria's entire wardrobe was in the cases as well as some of her sister's. She shied away from her usual vibrant choices. Instead, she chose a black cocktail dress—a simple silk sheath with a chiffon overlay, complete with satin collar and cuffs. The sheath itself was formfitting and fell to midthigh, while the overlay was longer, with filmy panels that fell to her knees and floated softly around her legs when she walked.

The outfit said she was an opera singer going for a sexy librarian vibe. It also screamed *not a spy*. Poor Michael. He might be better off if she could do this in a costume and sing the part.

Adam Turov had told her she was safe, but he must sense she was more than she seemed. Even though he had gone back to the main house, there wasn't enough distance between them to keep the affinity from pulling her toward him. He would be drawn to her too.

That knowledge was frightening…for many reasons.

Michael's father had been gone for two years.

She'd survived, but she hadn't thrived.

She'd been a patient, a mother and a sister, but she hadn't felt like a woman in a long time. She could blame the Brimstone, the affinity, the adrenaline, or she could admit Turov was incredibly alluring without all that. His slight Slavic accent was both sophisticated and somehow rough. She thought he'd rather dispense with polite sophistication and speak bluntly. The mysterious roughness made her long to hear what he had to say. They could never have truth between them, but the idea seduced her.

She couldn't allow that longing to thrive, so she took extra care with her party persona.

She freshened her makeup, brushed her hair and slipped on a favorite pair of shoes. She hardly noticed the faint light of a waning crescent moon or any movement in the garden as she left the cottage to follow the path to the mansion. She wanted to go to the party in spite of all the reasons she shouldn't. It was the first party she'd wanted to attend in a long time.

She'd been dressed in gray and black, but her hair and lipstick had been closer to the truth of who she really was. He'd been mesmerized by the mass of curls under her hat, bright even in shadows. And her lips in soft light had been flush and full and painted boldly. They hadn't matched the fear in her eyes. More than ever, he wanted to personally hand-deliver Father Malachi to the fires of hell and throw him in the flames. The Order of Samuel specialized in traumatizing innocents, yet they called themselves holy men. It was obvious they haunted Victoria D'Arcy. She was a bold woman shadowed by fear.

When he saw her enter the rooms he'd had arranged for her reception, his glass paused halfway to his mouth. The hat was gone. And her shapeless traveling clothes were gone too. She'd chosen bright crimson heels and she'd refreshed her lips in the same shade. Her hair was a richer, deeper auburn and more subtle in comparison. Against the black of her dress and her pale porcelain skin, those pops of color stunned. The myriad shades of red in her hair seemed almost iridescent in the shifting light.

It wasn't only him. She entered quietly, but many faces turned her way. She had stage presence. No actual stage necessary. The whole room subtly shifted within moments of her becoming a part of it. It was no longer a miscellaneous gathering. It was a party with an anonymous star at its heart. She wasn't a celebrity. She'd been away from the opera world too long and even before that her career had been held in check by daemon politics. She simply shone and everyone in the room unconsciously arranged themselves to bask in the glow.

This was the woman the Order of Samuel sent to bring him down.

He lifted his glass. He took a long swallow of Firebird Pinot Noir. He didn't savor. He gulped. Because he'd rather fight an army of monks programmed to destroy than this one intriguing woman.

He watched her. She could feel his attention while she spoke to other guests. There were wealthy travelers, politicians, a celebrity chef, an aging rock star and a billionaire philanthropist—it was a posh gathering for an opera singer that had never been free to seek fame.

They were here for Turov. He was sharing his guests with her. But he wasn't being hospitable. She reminded herself that he used his sophisticated persona as a disguise for his covert activities. By and by, she was swept his way. Time and tide and Brimstone. When she took the warmed crystal stem from his fingers, she realized she'd abstained from accepting a glass of wine until she could receive her glass from his hand.

She sipped. And the room fell away. The aroma was delicate black cherry accented with a spicy hint of cinnamon. The flavor was of fruit and earth. But it was the texture that slayed. It was liquid silk on her tongue, soft and velvety. She savored. She swallowed. The rich, full-bodied vintage did soothe her throat and her spirits.

She wasn't an expert on wine, but she savored this one with her eyes closed, well aware that it was one of the finest she'd ever enjoyed. When she lifted her lids, she met the deep blue of Turov's eyes. He watched her drink as if her reaction to his wine mattered more than fire and Brimstone. She lifted her glass for a second sip, to savor and swallow again while he watched. His gaze tracked the movement of her lips and tongue and her throat. His intensity made her flush more than the pleasure of the wine or the effects of the alcohol on an empty stomach.

"You like it," he said.

Though they danced a dangerous dance of deception, she was stripped to raw honesty by the expression on his handsome face. This. The tasting of the wine between them was not part of her mission or their mutual disguises. Her reaction must be honest and real. His art deserved no less.

"It's beautiful. Pure pleasure on my tongue. I want to sing—and that is high praise. I haven't wanted to sing for a long time," Victoria confessed. This time when she swallowed, she also swallowed emotion. The lovely black cherry flavor lingered as a reminder of her honesty. She hadn't told anyone the truth about her lack of desire to sing. Not even Katherine.

"You honor my family," Turov replied.

His voice was rougher. Not as polished. In this moment, his disguise slipped. His face was both harder and more vulnerable. The set of his jaw was a tight line, but one made of marble that could be chipped if she wished it.

This man was the man she'd been sent to harm.

She swayed on her feet as if she'd forgotten to eat before a major dress rehearsal under hot lights. Turov snapped out of his trance. He took her glass and set it on a nearby table, urging her to patio doors that were already thrown wide. They walked through together with his warm hand on her back. Solicitous? Was he the host vulnerable to her enjoyment of his wine? Or nefarious? Was he the damned man who had sold his soul for success? There was no way to tell. Victoria could only step out in the cool air and breathe deeply of rich earth and growing things.

They walked out onto the broad expanse of a decorative-tiled veranda, framed by stone columns and a black slate rail. She leaned against it for support, but also to look out at the vineyards that stretched far into the night. Better to look there than to face her host. How could she read him when she was too afraid of what she might see? She needed to turn him over to the Order. To free their brethren. If he wasn't a greedy man who had sold his soul for success, who and what was he? She couldn't afford to care and yet she was intrigued by him. It was as simple as that.

"The Turov family has grown grapes here since they fled the Russian Revolution in the early twentieth century," Turov said. He had come to stand beside her. His profile was strong and proud. Anyone unaware of the Brimstone in his blood would assume he spoke of history rather than from personal experience.

"And you've built on what they established," Victoria said, playing along.

"In Russia, there's a saying. 'You live. You learn.' I have found this to be true," Turov said.

It was a confession, but one that was revealing only if you knew his Brimstone secret.

He had refined Nightingale Vineyards's pinot noir since 1918. He. Personally. He had overseen the process of living and learning for one hundred years.

Michael's father had been much older, but he'd been a daemon, not a man. Standing beside Adam Turov was different. He wasn't an immortal creature. He was a human whose life had been extended by selling his soul. How? Why? It didn't matter. It would be wiser to see him as corrupt and leave it at that. She didn't need to understand him. She needed only to betray him.

"Sometimes I feel as if I've missed a few lessons along the way," Victoria said. "Opera is all-consuming. Life is more complicated. Reality is harder to navigate."

"You'll rest here. You'll recover. There's something about being surrounded by growing things. It rejuvenates. Even a jaded soul like mine," Turov said. "Complications fall away. Simplicity reigns."

She looked at him then. The house blazed with light behind him. The soft haze from a sliver of moonlight came from the cloudless sky. People laughed. A piano played classical jazz while glasses clinked and indistinct conversation whispered all around. She was most vulnerable when she was seduced into thinking it might be possible for her to relax. Always, after, she regretted her weakness. Her greatest enemy wasn't someone trying to sell her safety and protection. Her greatest enemy was her wanting what they were selling with all her heart.

Nowhere was ever safe. Any haven was a lie. Her life would always be too complicated to set down roots.

"I look forward to relaxing," she said. She'd played this role a thousand times. The ingénue. Young and naïve. It was impossible to tell what he thought of her performance.

A figure revealed itself, moving in the shadows of the grounds in between the house and the vineyard. From grass to walkway to grass again, the figure crept.

The transformation in Turov was absolute. In a nanosecond, he went from cultured host with a hint of the Carpathians in his voice to a no-nonsense ruler whose California kingdom had been breached.

"Go to your cottage and lock the door. Don't let anyone in except me," he ordered.

He easily vaulted over the rail, dropping a story below onto the manicured grass. The party continued behind her while Turov ran across the lawn. The atmosphere was no longer seductively normal. Now, she strained at noises and squinted at shadows.

Before Michael was born, she probably would have obeyed such an order. She was no spy. She was no warrior. Before the fire, she could sing. That was all. And now even that was in question. Instead of going back to her cottage, Victoria moved quickly to the stone staircase that led down to the lawn. She couldn't afford to be the woman she'd been before she'd become a mother. She'd longed for love. She'd longed for life.

She still longed for those things, but now she wanted them for her baby instead of herself.

She'd recognized the stocky figure of the monk who was following her. She needed to stop Turov before he confronted the careless man, or her mission would be over before it had begun.

What could be more innocent than strolling through the garden, softly humming under the stars? Her heart pounded. Her steps were hurried and clumsy. She'd chosen her shoes for the party, not for a walk on the loose pebbles of a dimly lit path.

Still, she hummed.

She needed to draw Turov away from the monk.

The tune was scratchy and unused. A few bars from *Romeo et Juliet*. "Je veux vivre." "Juliet's Waltz." Her hum was rough and unmelodic to her trained ears. She didn't even know if it would work. She could only try. And pretend her effort was only about distracting Turov from the monk stalking her. The tightness in her chest and the heat of her flushed cheeks against the night air mocked that lie.

She had to keep Turov from finding out why she was here and inadvertently uncovering her ties to the Order of Samuel. She couldn't allow him to confront or capture her evil stalker.

But she also had to know.

Would her music act as a conduit between her affinity and the power in his Brimstone blood in the same way that Katherine's cello had called to John Severne?

From the moment when she'd first heard his voice tonight, she had to know.

She'd loved Michael, but his power as a full-blood daemon had completely overshadowed any she might possess. Their relationship had been fast and entirely based upon his fire. She'd been eclipsed and consumed by his daemon light.

And then that light was gone.

She walked and hummed in the darkness because she suspected there was a different sort of light to be found.

To be reclaimed.

Her own.

The night was silent as the soft noise of the party faded behind her. It was foolhardy to go too far into the darkness without telling anyone where she had gone. She wasn't dressed for a hike. In addition to the handicap of the heels, her dress was thin and the air was chilled. This wasn't the stage. If something failed, there wouldn't be a props manager to fix it. If she forgot her lines, there was no prompter to help her. She'd had no rehearsal to prepare for confronting an evil monk alone in a deserted garden…or a damned man for that matter. What if she encountered Turov on the starlit path with no one else around?

The idea frightened her, but not only that—there was also a hint of awakening in her quickened heartbeat and her rusty hum. Its tingle felt like an adventure waiting to happen.

A hard figure crashed into her and a cry replaced her hoarse hum, cut short prematurely by a cruel hand over her mouth. She was held in the hateful grip of the monk who had followed her to Sonoma. She recognized his stocky build and bare head in the moonlight.

"I have a message for you, D'Arcy. From Father Malachi. You met him in Louisiana. I bet you didn't realize you were talking to the best and brightest of us all. Father Malachi has chosen me to deliver another warning. We are always. We are watching. Do not distract or

delay. Free our brothers before Lucifer's Army comes
with the waxing of the moon. You have one month. Or
your son will pay the price." His spittle-fueled voice
dampened her ear. She was crushed breathless by his
powerful arms. His words and the physical abuse of his
bruising hold made her recall the madness she'd seen
in his eyes.

"Release her and die," Turov ordered from the shadows.

Gone was any hint of sophistication.

This was his truth.

He stepped into the soft glow of garden lanterns and
starlight. The seriousness of his face was revealed.

Hard.

Fierce.

His jaw was no longer marble, but iron.

Adam Turov reached behind his shoulder and with a
metallic rasp he drew a small sword that glinted, sharp
and deadly with purpose.

"Remember what I have said," the monk growled.
He flung her away and Victoria fell, but even the sharp
sting of gravel against the side of her face didn't distract from the monk's surprised scream. It gurgled in
his throat and was cut off as his stocky body fell heavily,
dead and headless. She heard a light, sickening thump
as his decapitated head hit the ground and rolled to rest
several feet away. She'd lived a much more violent life
than your usual run-of-the-mill opera singer. Would a
normal woman have recognized the sounds in the dark?

"I said release her *and* die. Not *or*," Turov clarified
softly, as if the dead man might question his semantics.

Victoria shifted to look toward Turov without being
obvious. He wiped the blade he'd used on the monk
with a pristine white handkerchief, rolling the silky
cloth to cover the blood before placing it back in his

pocket. Then he sheathed the blade at his back beneath his jacket. When he had finished the practiced moves of cleanup, his sophisticated costume was in place again. He straightened his cuffs and rolled his shoulders before he reached to help her to her feet. The monk didn't move at all.

"Is he...?" Victoria said, although she knew the answer. The monk was dead.

"He gave up the right to your consideration when he hurt you," Turov said. "My people will take it from here."

The Order of Samuel was violent and ugly and murderers, all. And the man she was supposed to best had just dispatched one without a blink of effort.

Turov took her hand and led her back toward the house. She didn't resist. Suddenly, her bold humming seemed reckless. This was a man with Brimstone in his blood. She couldn't afford to play games with the affinity that even now made her tremble near him. That awakening in her earlier hadn't been about anticipating an adventure. It had been a warning.

Adam Turov had killed the monk to protect her. But what would happen to her when he discovered she was on the Order of Samuel's side against him?

A little over an hour ago she had left the cottage for a party. Now she returned with blood on her shoes. She didn't notice the blood until they were inside, and even then not until Turov knelt to take her shoes from numb feet.

"I'm sorry. I'll replace them," he said. "I didn't mean to spoil your shoes." He tilted one shapely pump this way and that, as if appreciating its curves in spite of the blood. "From several years ago, I think, but I'll manage."

She backed away as he left the room to throw the shoes away like some bizarrely opposite Prince Charming. And, yet, he did have charm. Out in the dark, under the stars, with blood dripping from the blade he'd used to save her, he'd been charming as hell.

"You followed me into the garden even though I told you to come back to the cottage. Why?" Turov asked when he returned. He didn't stop inside the door. He continued with purposeful steps all the way to her. When she backed up at his continued advance, he followed until she bumped up against a bookcase. The scent of aged leather bindings filled the air to pair with Turov's Brimstone heat.

She wasn't afraid. Not of him. She was afraid because she refused to be a damsel in distress. No matter how distressing her life became.

"You may not be able to sing, but I heard you humming. I felt it," he said. "I've never felt anything like it before."

He didn't touch her.

He didn't have to.

The heat in his blood did.

The Brimstone that sealed his deal with daemons sang its own song to her music-starved ears. He'd made the choice to barter his soul. He wasn't a knight in shining armor. Too bad for her that she seemed to prefer much darker heroes.

"It won't happen again," she promised.

He leaned down to catch her whispered words. She was sure the breath that propelled them from her lips bathed his. He was close enough to taste with only a tilt or a sigh. She held very still. Apart. Contained. While her former nature urged her to boldly tilt, sigh, move to join him.

She ignored the urge to sing. She refused the desire to touch her mouth to his.

He looked into her eyes. His were brilliant blue, so bright to have seen so much, so clear to have just killed in her name. Where was his damnation hidden? Where was his shame? He looked undaunted and strong and so damn noble it made her ache.

"I hope that's a lie," he said. His gaze dropped to her open lips, but he didn't close the distance. The warmth between them flared until she tasted salty perspiration on her upper lip when she moistened it with her tongue.

His eyes moved to watch the pink flick of her tongue tip. For a second, he seemed almost as if he would dip to claim it. He seemed mesmerized. But he straightened up and backed away before she made the fatal mistake of wanting his kiss enough to make it happen herself.

He blinked. The move was gloriously slow, as if he really had been in a trance and had needed to force himself to lower his lids. When he opened them again, his jaw had hardened and the expression in his eyes had cooled. She could still feel his Brimstone heat, but he was no longer controlled by it.

"Good night, Victoria. I told you that you'd be safe here and I meant it. From every danger," he said.

He was shaking with it—anger, desire, the willpower it took to not pick her up and carry her away from the life she'd been forced to lead. His men were already discreetly cleaning up the mess he'd left them in the garden. It wasn't the first time he'd had to kill one of his "brothers." The Order was twisted, obsessive, and they never stopped. There were times when it had been kill or be killed, although his primary mission was to capture them and turn them over to the justice of Lucifer's court. One of the reasons his body quaked from adrenaline overload this time was that capture had ceased to be an option as soon as the evil monk had hurt Victoria.

He was supposed to be a sophisticated vintner with her. No more. No less. But she stoked the fire in his blood until his disguise went up in smoke.

He checked on his men. They had standing instructions. When he saw all was in hand, he turned away to seek sanctuary in his own rooms. What the guests would make of his and Victoria's early disappearance from the party wasn't his concern. He needed to wash away the blood and forget the look of fear in her eyes.

She'd pretended not to fully understand what had happened, but a darker knowledge had been in her hazel gaze when she'd trained it on his face.

A spiral iron staircase provided an outside entrance to his private retreat in the house. It was almost hidden by his mother's roses. She'd loved the climbing vine varieties and he'd continued to have them tended after she was gone. They'd become a profusion of tangles near the staircase where he'd instructed the gardeners to allow them to grow unchecked. In this back corner of the house, he had a bed, bath and study that were completely separated from guest bedrooms. Guests were rarely invited to stay longer than a night. He didn't run a bed-and-breakfast. He only allowed visitors at all in order to provide an alibi for his actual activities beyond wine making.

As he climbed the familiar treads of the staircase, it wasn't the Brimstone in his blood that made him see red. His memory called up the image of the petite opera singer in the grip of a madman trained to be merciless. His anger came from the same sense he'd always had of a wrong that needed to be righted—magnified by fury at an innocent's pain.

Victoria was caught up in a war that wasn't her making. Just as he'd been as a child.

Adam shed his ruined clothes and left them for a housekeeper he could count on for stoic discretion. She'd seen worse. All his people had. The small sword he wore in a specially made sheath that fit close to his body between his shoulder blades he placed in a hidden compartment in the top of his mahogany dresser. He would clean it later after he'd cleaned himself.

He couldn't afford empathy for Victoria, this sense of connection to her that shook him to his cursed core.

He told himself this even as he recalled the tense moment when he'd almost given in to the temptation to taste her lips.

Steam filled the bathroom when the cool water hit his Brimstone-warmed skin. Clouds of it rolled and swirled, disturbed by his movements as he scrubbed his hair and his hands. Beneath the soap, he felt his scars as he washed. A familiar reminder of what he'd been through and what he still needed to accomplish with the long life the Brimstone had given him.

Father Malachi was his objective. Finding him, capturing him, delivering him to Lucifer's court. It wasn't revenge. It was justice. Not only for the abuse he'd suffered at the obsessive monk's hands—all in the name of "training"—but also to keep him from harming other children.

This dance with Victoria added another element of challenge to his mission. If she knew he was aware of why she'd come to Nightingale Vineyards, she might become even more determined and reckless to find and free his prisoners before Lucifer's Army came to claim them. The Loyalists came when the moon was full each month. On that night, he held a party to provide cover for the prisoner delivery. The full moon galas were much larger than the occasional dinner parties held at other times. The gala was a coveted invitation, never more so than in June. To commemorate his mother's birthday each year, he brought in an orchestra, dancing and a Firebird theme. He needed to keep Victoria in the dark until then, or longer if possible.

And while he kept her in the dark he needed to keep himself under control.

The water became superheated to the point of pain as it ran down his skin. Paired with the stitched wound on his back, the discomfort distracted him from the lush, full red lips he saw every time he closed his eyes. They'd been slightly open, welcoming, even though she'd seen him at his most ferocious.

He'd been trained to be a ruthless killer. Though he'd turned those skills on the men who had made him, he was pretty sure that didn't negate the fact that they'd created a monster.

It had been dark in the garden and she'd been thrown to the ground with her face in the grass, but she'd seen the blood on her shoes.

And a monster had no right to kiss a woman with the voice of an angel, even if she'd temporarily forgotten how to sing.

Chapter 4

Dressing for breakfast with a man who had decapitated an evil monk for you was more challenging than you might think. Adam Turov had secrets the regular world wasn't privy to. He'd showed her his true nature for several violent seconds. Now, she either had to pretend she'd been disoriented enough to not fully realize what she'd seen, or she had to risk more honest discussion.

Honesty wasn't possible between them. Not as long as Michael was in danger.

She'd had wine on an empty stomach after a long trip. She'd been accosted in the garden and her host had helped her. She wouldn't mention the sword. She wouldn't mention the blood on her shoes. It would only work if he wanted to maintain his disguise enough to play along.

So, she dressed in a light dress with a soft cashmere sweater and sandals. Very holiday. Much innocent.

She matched her outfit to the embossed invitation that had arrived with a fragrant coffee tray at her cottage door that morning. Semicasual, but elegant and nothing that said, "I saw a man lose his head in the garden last night."

Her sundress was translucent georgette in white with fine satin polka dots sprinkled in black across the skirt. The dots lessened in number until they disappeared completely at her cap sleeves and the cut flared out softly from a pinched waist and tight bodice. She gathered up her hair in a soft chignon with a clip that allowed wayward tendrils to brush her cheeks.

She couldn't help it if her expression didn't match the swingy skirt that swirled against her pale legs as she walked out to meet her host. She couldn't help that her eyes looked wide and dark, much greener than the usual soft hazel that had to be lined with kohl to show brightly enough onstage.

She followed the directions of the invitation to a—thankfully—different part of the grounds, where a table had been set among the wildly abundant roses. Her low-heeled sandals crunched on the path. The silky rose petals were soft and dewy against her fingers when she reached to brush the blooms as she walked by.

Victoria had to present herself at the table as a regular guest even as she decided how best to explore the estate in secret. So far she'd seen no other evidence of Turov's activities involving the Order of Samuel. None beyond his aiding her against the monk last night.

She had to pretend she hadn't seen him in the pale moonlight with a bloody sword or that afterward he hadn't courteously offered to replace her shoes. How else could she proceed? She knew who and what he was.

He might have suspicions about her. But she had to pretend innocence over toast and orange juice.

Luckily, Adam Turov had been living a double life long enough to cover for them both.

He sat at the table sipping his juice from a cut crystal glass. His suit was tailored tight to his broad, lean chest. His black hair was as dark and gleaming as the shine of his jacket's gabardine. He was freshly shaven. Not a wave of his hair was out of place. His blue eyes glittered mildly in the sun as she joined him.

"Just us?" Victoria asked. She took the only other seat at the table. It was on the opposite end from Turov, giving her a reprieve from his Brimstone heat.

"Yes. No one else is staying with us at this time," her host said. He used a silver knife to spread butter on a toast point as he spoke. Its blunt blade winked in the sun. The larger sword he'd used last night was a secret best kept in the moonlight.

In the sun, Turov was the picture of sophisticated ease.

Victoria blinked and reached for the pristine linen napkin on her plate. Its swan shape dissolved in her fingers.

"I have a meeting that will tie me up until this afternoon, but I hope to give you a tour at some point during your stay," Turov said.

"Thank you," Victoria replied.

Swords and winery tours. She doubted the tour he offered would give her the access she needed to find the monks he'd captured and set them free.

Father Malachi had said that they would use their combined strength to kill Adam Turov once they were freed.

The table was a long rectangle of polished glass with

hammered copper legs, but she was still closer to Turov than she should be. She looked away from his direct gaze, uncomfortable with the truths that they weren't free to discuss that were revealed with eye contact. She noticed movement in the vineyard. Dozens of workers in coveralls were obvious among the greenery. She could see their hands busily tending the vines. Occasionally, they would call out to each other, but mostly they focused on the work of their hands.

"Are they pruning the grapevines today?" she asked.

"It's time for shoot thinning. Every spring we refocus the energy of the plant. Some of the leaves are removed and most of the buds to encourage uniform flowering. They'll leave windows in the canopy to allow filtered light to hit the cluster of grapes as it grows. We take great care to ensure proper color development," Turov explained.

His whole demeanor changed when he talked about his vines. Gone was the sophisticated businessman. But the warrior didn't take his place. Instead, he was all vintner, an artist who worked with nature to sculpt an exquisite harvest.

"I had no idea the process was so complex," Victoria said. Her mouth had gone dry. No Brimstone heat necessary. His honest passion for his work was seduction itself.

Oh, she could feel the pull of Brimstone. The table was only eight feet long. Her skin flushed in the sun, but not from its rays. Yet it was more than Brimstone that called her to Turov. He was an artist. And like calls to like.

"We have numerous parcels—vineyard blocks—they all produce a different crush. Different altitudes, different soil types, slightly different sunlight…all influences the flavor of the grapes. I'll be thinning the shoots of the hillside block later this evening, before dinner. Those vines produce the crush we use to create the Firebird Pinot Noir. If you'd like, you can ride over with Gideon to see how it's done," Turov offered.

"Yes. I'd like to see you work," Victoria said.

Be interested in the grapes and the growing process. God, do not make it about his hands or about seeing him completely honest as he labors in the sun.

She couldn't avoid him. She had to engage in an odd dance of following him around and keeping her distance. She needed to discover his secrets without revealing her own. But now she had even more to worry about because she was pretty sure natural chemistry was as much a part of her reaction to him as the Brimstone.

She hadn't meant her gaze to linger on him, but when he abruptly rose and broke eye contact she knew it had. He tossed his napkin on the table and approached her. Her temperature rose with every step. Maybe because of the Brimstone. Maybe not.

She held her breath when he paused beside her chair, but she released it in a shaky sigh when he reached to take her arm gently in his warm hands. He tilted and lifted until the underside of her arm was exposed. Only then did she see what had caught his attention the length of the table away.

Her arm was bruised. The monk's hands had bitten painfully into her skin. She'd noticed a scrape on her cheek and she'd covered it with makeup, but had missed the marks on her arm, a reminder of the evil fingers that would never pinch and hurt again.

Turov had noticed.

His brow had gone heavy. His jaw hardened into a chiseled stiff line. A hint of his hidden warrior returned.

"You're hurt," he said. His thumb brushing her bruised skin was incredibly gentle. A whisper. Shakily, she breathed in and held it as the unexpected sensation of tenderness claimed her.

She looked up at his face. The move was a mistake. Sunlight fell full on her cheek, revealing the mark she'd tried to cover. He lifted his other hand to cup her cheek. Her eyes went wide in a sudden reaction she couldn't prevent. Her whole body stilled. The magnet of Brimstone urged her to rise and press against him. She had to resist that pull and the added allure of his touch, his concern. Every ounce of self-control she possessed held her in place.

"I promised you safety," he said. His accent had deepened and strengthened. He traced the scrape on her cheek with his fingers, whisper soft. But she wasn't fooled. Battle was in his eyes. It waited to be released on anyone who deserved his wrath. She shivered. The warmth of sun and Brimstone didn't negate the potential for ferocity she'd already seen.

"No one can promise me that. Not even you," Victoria said.

Her reply broke the spell. He dropped his hand from her face and stepped away. Her body swayed an infinitesimal bit toward him, but she corrected herself before he'd seen. She couldn't gauge what he'd felt. She could only feel her reaction to their connection. And her control over herself felt tenuous at best.

"You're probably right. Safety is an illusion. And, yet, I insist it will be so. No more bruises. Your skin…some of us have scars we can never erase, but your bruises will fade and your skin will not be marked again," Turov said.

He didn't speak of killing the monk. She didn't have

to pretend she hadn't seen the sword or heard the head roll away. She covered the bruise on her arm with her opposite hand.

"Please. Don't bother with pledges. It's nothing," she said.

"A line in the sand is everything. It's how a man is defined. By the limits of what he will allow or withstand. By what we can endure. The mark on your cheek is nothing to you. It's heresy to me," Turov said. "If you'll excuse me, I'll let you finish your meal in peace. I'm no fit companion for a civilized meal."

He fisted his hands as if frustrated he couldn't kill the monk again for her slight injuries. He turned and walked away, his body in tight lines beneath the tailored suit and his posture determined. She'd been hurt before. Daemon hunting was risky business even for the hunter's bloodhound. But she couldn't remember anyone reacting to her bruises the way Adam Turov reacted.

Victoria cooled when he left. The flush in her cheeks drained away until her face chilled. Her entire body cooled until, bereft of his Brimstone heat, she sat shivering in the morning light.

After she left the table, Victoria returned to the cottage. She changed out of her sundress into more practical celery-green pants that she cuffed above sturdy canvas sneakers. She paired the pants with a snug black T-shirt and a soft loose sweater in complementary green. She wasn't supposed to care how she looked for Turov. Meeting him in his favorite vineyard block wasn't a date. To prove it, she did nothing with her hair, leaving it clipped up. She planned to wander around the house and grounds during the day until it was time to meet the vineyard manager at the equipment shed Turov had pointed out to her while they ate.

Victoria expected to encounter servants and staff in the main house, but cool and quiet darkness greeted her with hushed shadows instead. Age showed in the house's walls, where darkly stained teak wainscoting was topped by richly tinted wallpapers. Upon closer inspection, the textured papers had the faded sheen of silk or satin. Green, pale gold and burgundy tinged with scarlet were prevalent in the varying designs from room to room.

She stepped lightly. Her heartbeat felt obvious in her chest. She hadn't been invited to tour the house. Around every corner, she expected an unpleasant reaction to her presence. The coolness of the air seemed deserted, empty of any living warmth, but it also held a hint of wood smoke scent that reminded her of Turov. This had been his home for a long time. His scent and the aura of all she touched and saw that belonged to him made her jump at every creaking floorboard and the whispers from each well-oiled door.

She wandered with no interruptions through hallways and rooms filled with framed memorabilia and photographs. Awards, newspaper articles and family photos all in black-and-white. Adam Turov wasn't in many of them. When had he realized his longevity meant he shouldn't be photographed?

Victoria found only a few solid hints of him. His tall, lean back and dark cap of black hair were in one photograph with a couple that was probably his parents, although they seemed like his grandparents. The man was in an old-fashioned suit with wide lapels and cuffed trousers. The woman was in a shirtwaist dress with a fabric belt. On her chest was a brooch. Vic leaned in close enough to see that the gem-encrusted pin was in the shape of a bird. They were seated at a table in the garden. She wished the photograph was in color because a large bouquet of dark roses was placed in the center of the table. She imagined they must have been lush and red. The couple looked at Adam with great affection. Not like he was a monster. They'd loved him in spite of the Brimstone.

And he had been all alone since they'd passed away?

An army of servants who seemed to wait on him without direction wasn't the same as a family that adored him.

Added to the photographs and memorabilia was a vintage collection of birdcages of varying sizes and shapes. Some were quite elaborate, created from a twining of fine metals such as copper and brass. Others were simple and crafted of wrought iron. All of the cages were empty.

All had their doors opened wide.

From the delicate and small to the large and ornate, the cages were so prevalent that they were obviously a beloved collection and not simply a decorative theme. When she saw the myriad of cages in the main house, she remembered that there were several in the cottage as well and she promised herself she'd look closer at them when she returned to her rooms.

It was fitting, actually, for Nightingale Vineyards to have a collection of birdcages, but there seemed to be more to it than that. Especially when she leaned closer to one or two and saw the open cage doors could easily swing close and latch if someone hadn't decided to keep them open, as if to be sure no bird was ever trapped inside.

The upper stories of the house were silent and still. Hallways branched from the main staircase in a labyrinthine confusion. Occasionally, she heard footsteps and doors open and close. She assumed Turov had many maids in his employ, but she never encountered one. The solitude suited her clandestine intrusion, but it also made her avoid silent shadows that seemed darker than they should be. The house was too big. Too empty. It seemed almost like a museum or mausoleum. Turov had lived long beyond his natural time. There was obviously a price to his longevity beyond the damnation he ultimately faced. Isolation. Loneliness. He lived in a house that must once have known love and laughter, but was now dusty with all humor long forgotten in gray photographs.

Finally, she found a room that drew her curiosity even more than the birdcages. At its heart was a large glass case—the glass waved with age—and within its protection sat a Russian tea service decorated with an elaborate design. The wallpaper throughout the house must have been chosen to complement the tea service with its antique pot and dainty cups. The motif on the porcelain featured an exotic bird with boldly colorful feathers outlined in glimmering gold. The gold also accented the handles and the rims of the cups as well as the curved spout of the pot. The whole service rested on black velvet that was faded and dusty even within its case. It hadn't been used in a long time. She chose not to disturb it now.

But she did note that an open gilded birdcage was a part of the background design.

On a card table nearby she found a copy of a book with illustrations similar to the tea service. She picked up the volume and found it delicate from frequent use and age. Its spine was cracked. Its cover was worn. It wasn't dusty under glass. No children lived in the house, but the book wasn't forgotten. The title page was translated, *The Firebird*. The rest of the book was in Russian.

Again, she noticed an open birdcage featured on one of the pages.

She would look up the tale on her laptop when she had a chance. For now, she reluctantly put the beautiful book down after quickly skimming through the illustrations.

Victoria explored the rest of the room with more urgency. The book wasn't abandoned. That meant the room wasn't as abandoned as it had first appeared, although the chairs were covered with linen sheets gray with age.

Low on an otherwise empty shelf, she found a wooden box carved all over in a design of grapes. She almost glanced over it, but something in its rough, dust-embedded surface called to her. When she opened the lid, she felt more intrusive than she'd felt so far. This had been someone's keepsake box. It wasn't meant for her eyes or fingers. Inside, nestled on a bed of scarlet velvet gone pale and worn, she found a ring of keys much like the one Turov had given her for the rose-covered cottage. In fact, exactly like. Her key must have been taken from this set. Only now did she realize the swirled design in the key's grip was another firebird.

Suddenly, she remembered the woman in the photograph with Turov. His mother. Firebird Pinot Noir was named in her honor. Now, Victoria saw the meaning behind the name. The Russian fairy tale must have been a treasure to her. She'd worn a firebird brooch in the photograph. The tea set had been hers and this must have been her sitting room. The dust everywhere but on the book indicated Turov visited at times to mourn or recall.

Had the birdcage collection been hers as well, and was it somehow tied to the firebird fairy tale?

Her fingers shook when she placed the keys back in the box and put the box back on the shelf. Tears pricked her eyes and shame colored her cheeks. She shouldn't be here. She might as well have desecrated a tomb. How horrible to outlive the family you loved by decades and more to come. They might be the only people who ever understood his dark secrets. Turov's mother had loved him as she loved Michael. And Victoria had disturbed the room where he came to sit with long-dead memories.

Briefly, she'd even considered taking the keys.

She should. If one fit her cottage door, the others would unlock other places, maybe even the secret prison she sought. But she couldn't. Not now. It was too intrusive to contemplate.

Instead, she looked long and hard at the whole room. She adjusted the book on the card table to more closely assimilate its previous position. She couldn't help the disturbed dust. Best to leave it as it had been found. A place for a son who'd been left behind to grieve.

The middle-aged manager introduced himself as Gideon. His friendly sun-crinkled eyes and informative banter eased her disappointment after a fruitless day. She'd seen or heard nothing to indicate a clue about where Turov might be holding crazed monks for the devil. His house was cool and shadowed and overwhelmingly empty.

Except for the firebird keys.

Of course, she hadn't ventured into his private apartment. There were many places she wasn't free to explore. But the whole dark house had made her feel guilty for her snooping. Especially his mother's sitting room.

"Please, climb aboard, miss. I'll drive you over to the hilltop," Gideon said.

The vehicle was an ATV designed like a miniature pickup truck. It had large tires with deep tread and two rows of side-by-side seats. The small aluminum truck bed currently held a cooler and what seemed to be gardening equipment—rakes, gloves, shears and buckets.

"I'm sorry to add to your chores," Victoria said. She was glad she'd changed out of her dress into practical clothes. Gideon's coveralls were belted neatly but she could tell he'd put in a long day.

"I've overseen the thinning for years, but I don't often get to drive such pleasant visitors through the rows. Happy to do it," Gideon said. He grinned and Victoria couldn't help smiling back.

"You must have known Mr. Turov for a long time?" Victoria asked as the ATV bumped along. Gideon was explaining that the cover crops grown to fight erosion between rows had been recently mowed. The rainy season was over. Drier weather and approaching summer meant moisture needed to be directed toward the grapevines instead.

"No. No one knows Mr. Turov. He's a private man. But he's a good man. I haven't always been a grower. My life before I came to Nightingale Vineyards was a very different sort of life," Gideon said as he cut the wheel so that they were bumping over different terrain. "I owe Mr. Turov a great debt. I'm honored to repay it every day in these rows. He gave me the sun. I give him my hands and my back in return."

He spoke so warmly of Turov that Vic was taken aback. She tried to absorb what he said and what he'd left unsaid. How had Turov given him the sun?

They left the gentle roll of the main vineyard behind

in order to curve up and around a rise. The sun was low on the horizon. It painted everything it touched in a gold wash of color. Other crews were finishing for the day. She could see them piling into other ATVs and tractors in the distance.

"You'll ride back with Mr. Turov. He has his own vehicle. There he is now," Gideon said.

She could see the tall outline of Turov's form silhouetted by the glow of the sun.

"Most of the maintenance on the hilltop is done by hand. There isn't room for equipment. Mr. Turov oversees much of it himself. This was his mother's parcel. The Firebird is named after her," Gideon explained. "From her favorite Russian tale."

He stopped at the base of an even steeper slope. The vineyard rows extended up in diagonal alleys from the path where he parked beside another ATV long enough for her to exit. Turov didn't come to meet them. After raising his hand to salute his foreman, he bent to continue his work. Victoria climbed from the mini truck and thanked Gideon.

"Please, take the cooler. Cook sent some refreshment. Mr. Turov never rests as he should. He's a driven man. These grapes are his obsession," Gideon said.

Victoria didn't argue. She suspected Turov had much darker obsessions, ones that would shock Gideon and Cook.

"Good night and thank you," she said. Gideon waved as he drove away.

Victoria stood for a few moments as she noticed several large windmills spinning on steel posts. There didn't seem to be enough wind to make the red blades move. The air was rapidly cooling and still. She placed the cooler in the last remaining ATV and climbed the hill toward where Turov was working. He didn't look her way. He continued to tend to the vines with flying fingers.

That's what she noticed. Deft manipulation of small pruning shears had leaves raining down at his feet.

She'd seen a Japanese bonsai trimmed once at a garden show. This reminded her of that meticulous attention to detail on a grander scale. The vines seemed perfect to her. Not a stem out of place. And yet tendril by tendril across hundreds of acres would be carefully groomed to maximize and perfect this year's harvest.

"You can see the flowerings. Those will be our grapes. I'm making sure each bunch will receive optimal filtered light. There was a rainfall and a heavy mist this morning and temperatures will fall tonight." He paused and glanced at her, his nimble fingers stopping their work. "I saw you looking at the fans. They'll dry the moisture to ensure it doesn't freeze."

"I thought they were spinning too quickly to be windmills," Victoria said.

"Windmills would need to be taller to catch the breeze. These fans are motorized and low enough to optimally dry the vines. We've made it almost to the end of the rains. That's always a relief. You probably noticed Gideon was happy. We didn't lose any crop this year," Turov said.

How could this man so proud of his vines be in league with daemons? Had his passion for grapes come before or after he sold his soul?

Unlike Gideon, Adam Turov wasn't dressed in coveralls, but he wasn't in a suit or tuxedo either. He wore a flannel button-down shirt that he'd rolled at the sleeves. If possible, his chest looked broader and his bare arms were as muscular as she'd suspected from the athletic grace of his movements. A ring of keys attached to his belt rattled as he worked. They looked solid, worn and timeless, like the man they belonged to. They were much simpler than the firebird keys she'd seen when she was exploring the house, but she suspected the two sets unlocked many of the same doors around the estate.

The keys drew her attention again and again. Her instincts were much better at espionage than she was.

She'd watched him kill a man, pour wine and swirl a crystal glass, and now she watched him coaxing abundance from a growing thing. Would the real Adam Turov please raise his hand? Her chest tightened because it didn't matter. She was uncomfortable lying to all three.

"Would you like to try?" he asked.

He'd paused again. Victoria took the pruning shears he offered. He watched her mimic his movements on the next section of vine. More tentative, but she'd watched what he did and he nodded when she did well.

Snip-snip-snip.

He was right beside her.

The soft wind from the fans blew his scent to her face—soap, sunshine, clean sweat and a hint of wood smoke. The hair that waved at the nape of his neck was damp.

"My mother tended this parcel. It was hers. She preferred the low yield of the hilltop. The hand manipulation. She was from a simpler time. To do a job right, you must feel it. Get your hands dirty. There's a density to the crush from this hilltop. It's tannic in youth, but becomes intensely smooth with age," Turov said.

"Like velvet on the tongue," Victoria added.

She shouldn't have. Her voice was huskier than usual. Influenced by his nostalgia, his nearness and the Brimstone pull between them. He reached for the shears. The sun had almost fully set. They stood in the twilight. It was too dark to work now. In this light, you might cut off more than you intended.

"I asked Gideon to send a bottle so you could taste the Firebird, here, where it's grown. There's nothing like breathing the air that has infused it with flavor as you taste the wine itself," Turov said. He dropped the shears in a bucket and led her back to the path.

She dusted her hands off and followed. She tried not to obsess about the keys on his belt and what they meant she had to do. Hadn't she known even when she'd left his mother's keys in the box? She wasn't free to choose between right and wrong. Respecting his mother's sitting room meant leaving Michael in danger.

He placed the bucket of tools in the back of the ATV and retrieved the bottle of wine from the cooler.

This was intimate. The wine he'd made surrounded by the vines he'd tended with his own hands. When he released the cork with fingers stained green from his work, Victoria felt a pull stronger than Brimstone. And her intentions toward the firebird keys burned her cheeks.

"Doesn't it need to breathe?" she asked.

He reached into the cooler and handed her two glasses.

"This is perfectly aged. Its tannic levels are low. Pouring correctly into the glass is the only aeration Firebird needs," Turov said.

He poured into the centers of the glasses, allowing the rich, red liquid to fall from a height of eight inches. She was holding her breath. She allowed it to sigh from her lips as he placed the bottle on the tailgate and reached for the glass in her right hand.

"Now. Enjoy," he said.

She couldn't help it. She watched him first. The swirl of the liquid in the glass. The deep inhalation as he enjoyed its bouquet. Then the pleasure that suffused his face when he sipped from the glass and savored the wine on his tongue. She allowed his enjoyment to distract her from her duplicitous intentions for the keys hidden back at the main house.

The pleasure he took in his first sip was incredibly sensual.

Her knees went weak with his obvious care and pleasure. So like he might be in bed savoring other things. She copied him with less finesse, but as she'd experienced the night before, even a novice could appreciate this spectacular pinot noir. Its fruity, velvet spice exploded on her tongue.

The Brimstone burn of his blood was a constant seduction of her senses, but she was as seduced by the vintner as she was by his daemon heat. She sipped as the darkest night settled around them. The full moon was a month away. She had only a few weeks to save Michael. Turov turned the headlights of the ATV on and they were oddly illuminated in brilliance and strangely cast shadows.

The wine didn't mellow the burn. It softened her resistance to the Brimstone's pull. She couldn't deny the answering coil of heat low in her stomach that had nothing to do with rich grapes and everything to do with damnation. Her affinity for Brimstone damned her to be drawn to the one man she couldn't afford to desire.

But the desire was so warm compared to the cold fear she'd been running on for too long. She was able to push thoughts of keys and what they might unlock from her mind too easily.

The bold Victoria she'd been before the fire stirred

deep in her breast. That Victoria would have taken one wine-flavored kiss in the green-scented night. That Victoria would have taken much more from this mysterious, dangerous man. Not in spite of his darkness, but because of it.

She'd lived a dark life plagued by the Order of Samuel. Never simple. Never free. Was it any wonder she was drawn to a man who could match her shadow for shadow? A man who had still managed to root himself in the rich California soil?

As if he read her mind, Turov took her glass. Their fingers didn't brush, but she could feel the warmth of his even without contact. Hers tingled, but she didn't reach out. She fisted them instead. He didn't offer her another glass of wine. He put the bottle and the glasses back into the cooler. They hadn't touched the chocolate or cheese.

"I need to drive you back to the house. I have more business to attend to this evening. I won't be in for dinner," Turov said.

There was no door to open, but he stood by the side of the vehicle as she took her seat instead of crossing around to take his. He placed both hands on the roll bar frame above her head. Her body recognized his pause as he lingered. Her heartbeat sped up. Her breath quickened. The warmth of her affinity to his Brimstone caused her skin to flush. She looked up at him. In the odd light, her high color might be disguised. Could he feel her body temperature rise even as the night cooled down around them?

"Velvet on the tongue," he said softly.

She nodded. Not to confirm her earlier thoughts on the texture of pinot noir. The slight affirmative tilt of her head was a bigger confession. Even in this light, she could see the direction of his gaze. Her lips.

Turov leaned in and she held very still. He continued to hold the roll bar above her head, but he allowed himself to move just enough to softly capture the lips he focused on. The press of his mouth was no more than a sigh against hers. He held himself back. She could sense his control. The warrior was caged, the damned man was daunted, the vintner was striving for an air of casual pleasure the other two would belie.

His lips were soft, as gentle as his hands had been when he'd touched her that morning. But the second they grazed hers once, twice, teasing tastes, his lips slightly open so his moist, wine-sweetened breath met and mingled with her sigh of reaction—that second of contact caused her entire body to tense.

Her diaphragm tightened. Her lungs expanded. Her vocal cords tingled with unsung notes. He brought something to life in her with the barely there kiss. With the slightest pressure, with the slightest contact, he awakened something so long dormant she'd thought it might be dead and gone.

Her whole body trembled as she parted her lips to meet the next brush of his and he noticed her quickening. He still held the roll bar, but even in the deepening night she could see his knuckles begin to whiten as the strength of his grip increased.

He didn't pull back, but he didn't touch her with anything other than his lips. He didn't take more though he could have. He didn't deepen the contact. A deepening would have scorched them both. When her tongue lightly touched his, offering an instinctive invitation to take more, they both stiffened as Brimstone heat flared between them with the sudden arc of electric shock.

He did ease back then. He looked down at her with shadowed eyes. The headlights illuminated the path in front of the ATV, but it cast the seats and their bodies in garishly outlined shadows now that night had fallen.

"I promised you'd be safe. This isn't safe. Far from it," Turov said.

His accent had thickened, as if emotion affected his ability to control it. Suddenly, she wanted those Russian inflections murmured against her ear while his body pressed against hers.

As if he read her mind, Turov let go of the roll bar and stepped back. His longevity hadn't moldered his emotions or his passion. If anything, he was filled with a concentrated need for human contact that had been distilled from years of being isolated from normality. Victoria licked her sensitized lips, tasting the hint of per-spiration he'd left there from the moist swell of his upper lip. The heat that radiated from him touched deep to her core and spread outward, but it also called forth energy within herself. All from the slightest taste, the merest touch. She could only imagine what deeper kisses and less controlled embraces would…no she couldn't imag-ine. She wouldn't allow her aroused senses to go there.

"I should go back to the house," she said. It was as much a confession as a request. She could see the war in him. The stiffness of his broad shoulders. His clenched fists. He held himself back even though he'd let the roll bar go.

Michael's father had swept her defenses away. This was different. This was mutual. Her sensual power rose up to meet Turov's. Their bodies were drawn to each other.

"You should. I should," he agreed.

And still they paused under the glittering stars that winked to life in the blue-black Sonoma sky. Her affin-ity and his Brimstone blood were held at bay by sheer force of will. She was grateful for the shadows. Sunshine would have revealed how badly she wanted to succumb. She wanted to touch, taste and sing in his arms. To revel in the forbidden awakening she'd unexpectedly found on a mission that was cold as ice.

Would she see an answering hunger in his eyes? To forget his daemon deal in her arms? It was best if she didn't know.

Finally, he broke the standoff. He chose the best course for sanity and retreated to the driver's side of the ATV. While he slid in behind the wheel, Victoria tried to calm her breathing. She willed her heartbeat to slow. She needed to take advantage of this weakness she'd found in Adam Turov. He desired her. Of that she was certain. The connection between them didn't lie. But how could she seduce him into revealing his secrets before she was seduced herself?

Chapter 5

Turov drove through the darkening vineyard. They were in shadow while the lights of the ATV cut a wavering swath ahead of them, illuminating the path between rows. Only the edges of young greenery were distinct in the light, the rest of the vineyard was only a thousand acres of dark twining mystery around them.

He didn't speak again. No doubt he regretted the kiss and was focused on whatever his plans were for the night ahead. Meanwhile, Victoria burned. It wasn't until he pulled into the pebbled drive as near to her sheltered cottage as the riotous garden allowed that she saw his hands on the wheel.

The soft garden lights revealed a white-knuckled grip.

The ATV came to a stop and she was caught in a pause created by the emotion his grip betrayed. He was a dangerous man, but she was a danger to him as well.

For seconds, the potential for exploring that danger hung hotly in the cool air between them.

"Good night, Victoria," Turov said, his accent thicker with strain.

His decision to resist prodded her to break temptation's trance. She tumbled quickly from the vehicle to make up for her telling pause.

He pulled away almost as soon as her feet hit the ground and her answering "Good night" was lost in the crunch of rock beneath tires. He headed back toward the equipment shed where lights revealed the activity of evening after the vineyard's busy day. The bustle there only served to make the garden path where she stood seem too deserted and quiet.

The main house loomed darker than ever now that she'd explored its age and emptiness. She was glad to walk toward the smaller cottage and the welcoming scent of roses.

But she wasn't alone.

She hesitated between one path and another, uncertain which would lead her in the direction she needed to go, and during that hesitation she heard a furtive step. Only one. The other person in the garden had stopped mere seconds after her. They waited somewhere behind her. And waited. The quiet seemed to swell, impregnating the atmosphere with unease. A normal garden visitor would have continued to walk, would have said hello.

Victoria resumed her walk because she didn't want to reveal her fear. She acted unconcerned. She tried to move at the same speed. She didn't look over her shoulder. But she did pause suddenly when she came through the hedge to the cottage's clearing. Once again, she heard what might be the shuffle of a follower who hurriedly matched her movements, pause for pause.

She slowly fished the cottage key from her pocket to excuse her stop, then she proceeded to the dimly lit stoop. If she hurried, if she didn't fumble with the old skeleton key, if the antique latch didn't drag, maybe she could get inside and lock the door back against whoever was behind her.

But that plan evaporated when she reached the stone stoop of the cottage. Someone had left something there in a scattered pile. She pulled her phone from her pocket and illuminated the stoop to find a profusion of pale, dried flower petals that a breeze disturbed just enough for her to recognize because she'd seen ones like them in the park in Louisiana. Someone had left a pile of crinkled cherry blossoms for her to find. These had gone to a darker pink as they'd withered and dried.

She didn't look over her shoulder. She could feel a malicious presence there. Perhaps a presence brazen enough to have come out of the cover of the hedges to stand boldly in the clearing. If she turned, she might see another monk from the Order of Samuel sent to deliver this threatening message of flower petals.

"I haven't forgotten why I'm here. I don't need the reminder," she said.

Still she didn't turn, but she did kneel and gather up the petals because she had lied—she did need the reminder. She'd been too easily swept up in the dramatic story of Turov's past, his family, the obsession he had for his vines—a thousand acres of roots when she'd never managed to put down a single one.

Sybil and Grim hid and protected Michael, but for how long? She could blame the affinity for the distraction from her mission, but she wouldn't. Turov would be seductive to her, affinity or not. Now that she understood this, she could fight temptation.

Once she'd gathered the dried petals in the hem of her shirt, the step on the path resumed without subterfuge. This time her stalker moved away from her with loud crunches of gravel on the path. The loud movement seemed a mockery of her fear. She used her key, and if her life had depended on using it quickly she would have died on the stoop. Her fingers were clumsy. She clutched the flower petals in her shirt and unlocked the door at the same time so neither move went well. Dried bits of blossoms fell all around and the latch protested as she clanked and clanked the key, trying to find the sweet spot for the tricky tumblers. Finally, she made it into the cottage and closed the door. She slid the bolt home and leaned against it. But her tension didn't ease. Because now she knew what she had to do while Turov was away for the evening.

She placed the dried cherry blossoms in a jar on the vanity in her room. She needed the constant reminder. She wasn't on a luxurious Sonoma vacation where she was free to sympathize with her dark and dangerous host. She had a job to do. She had a son to save. Turov had beheaded the monk who had followed her from Louisiana, but there were more where he came from. The Order had an endless supply of zealots.

She might never be free, but she had to try.

For Michael.

Turov had said he had plans for the evening. Before he kissed her. And the kiss was irrelevant. She had to focus on her mission. He had left the estate. She'd picked over a dinner tray sent from the kitchen while she'd waited and watched. Finally, she saw his low, lean luxury sedan—a vintage one—pull away to be swallowed by the night highway that led to Santa Rosa.

She wasn't here to play.

She'd already changed into black jeans and a dark gray long-sleeve T-shirt to better blend with shadows. She intended to make her way to the sitting room that held the box full of firebird keys and then get back to her cottage before anyone, especially her host, was the wiser.

The garden was ghostly, lit by a sliver of moon and ambient lanterns turned low at midnight. She tried not to wonder if her stalker still lurked behind bushes that had taken on eerie animal-like shapes in the night. There a hunched antelope leaped and beneath its belly was a man-size black hollow. Here a grotesque ape with arms raised high could easily hide a man behind its enormous back.

Straight to the sitting room. Straight back.

The door opened at her touch and her first fear— that of being locked out—faded. The only activity she discerned as she entered the back passage was in the distant kitchen where the cook cleaned and prepped for the next day.

She held thoughts of Michael close as she hurried to the stairs at the front of the house. She crept up them, unable to prevent the occasional creak. A few lamps had been left on. Their Tiffany shades disbursed the glow in jewel tones that matched the walls and the firebird tea set no one had touched for decades—green, gold, amber, burnt red.

Victoria tried not the think of love and loss when she made it to the room again. Only then did she risk her cell phone light to penetrate the gloom.

The book had been moved.

Somehow she'd known. Maybe it was a daily habit for Turov to come here and flip through its pages. Had he noticed anything amiss? Was it foolish to stage a repeat visit so soon?

It was too late to back out now. She hurriedly scanned the room to make sure an angry Russian didn't lie in wait to capture her. Then she bent to open the box and grab the keys. She was too quick. The keys rolled together, making a noise that seemed thunderous in the quiet house. She closed the box and shoved the keys into her pocket.

A mother would understand.

She had to pass Mrs. Turov's photograph on the way out. She was sure the woman who had watched her son burn would have understood why Victoria had to tiptoe into her memorial to take the keys. It was wrong to take them, but to save her son she would do worse before the month was over.

The estate was massive. Finding where Turov held the monks would be a needle-in-the-haystack task, but the keys were a start. Seeing Turov's set and finding the cherry blossom warning had showed her the course she had to follow.

Though she'd only been in the house fifteen minutes, it seemed to take far longer to make her way out than it had to make her way in. A whistle down one hallway caused her to hold her breath and crouch for long moments on the first landing. A maid passed, carrying a basket of folded laundry. Victoria moved again when the woman turned the corner away from her. The stairs seem to protest her downward path even more loudly than they'd protested her upward one.

But she made it outside without running into a soul.

Unfortunately, before she could even take a relieved breath of night air, she ran into a man who had sold his soul long ago.

* * *

Turov wasn't wearing a tuxedo or a suit. His casual work clothes were gone as well. He wore black as she did, and she suspected for the same reason. Only a glimmer of eyes and teeth showed well in the garden light. Unlike the dark clothes she'd found from an ordinary wardrobe, his outfit looked made for the night. His black uniform was strategically fortified with leather quilting in vital areas such as chest, abdomen and thighs. It hugged his muscular form like a second skin.

She'd suspected he was athletically built and she'd been right, although she couldn't have guessed how lean and hard because she'd never seen this kind of body in real life. Not even her sister's husband, John Severne, who was obsessively fit from two hundred years of dae-mon hunting could possibly be this lethally made.

Victoria took in his appearance in seconds. The broad shoulders and hard arms above a trim waist and equally sculpted legs. He took in her appearance just as fast, just as well. Did her outfit scream cat burglar? Did the bulge of keys in her pocket show in the shadows?

"I thought you were going out for the night," Victoria said. Her voice was too breathless. Adrenaline robbed her lungs of their usual power.

"I did. I finished sooner than I expected. I didn't have to travel as far as I intended," he said.

She risked a glance at his face, but he didn't meet her eyes. Was that blood in his hair?

They'd been moving quickly enough that he put up his hands to catch her arms when they almost collided. Through the light material she could feel each of his fingers scorch. She looked down, surprised they didn't glow with Brimstone embers. Then she looked up. His eyes were closed, almost as if he was in pain.

"You should be inside. It's safer," Turov said.

"Safer than here? In the garden? With you?" Victoria asked.

He held her, but not close enough. The wide expanse of his chest was a foot away. She wanted to press against it, to feel his Brimstone heart beat against her cheek. Only with effort did she swallow the hum rising in her throat like a morning dove that sensed the dawn.

"Yes. Definitely safer. You should keep a locked door between us," Turov murmured, almost to himself. He relaxed his elbows. Her body immediately swayed toward him of its own volition. He allowed it. She allowed it. Long, heated seconds of her body leaning lightly against his. In forbidden time, it was an eternity. In real time, it was less than a minute. But it felt like the most intimate thing she'd ever done because he wasn't a man that allowed any intimacy at all.

She tried to soak in his Brimstone heat, his hardness, his smoky masculine scent that was somehow also green and earthy and fresh. A song rose within her, but it was a song she couldn't allow herself to sing.

Victoria stepped back and he let her go.

"Good night, Adam," she said.

She retreated several steps and then she turned to the warmly lit cottage. She assumed Turov moved away as well. She didn't look back to watch him go. She concentrated on placing one foot after another. She walked away. It was a triumph of willpower. She made it into the cottage and shut the door behind her. It was a testament to Turov's heat that the cozy fire that greeted her seemed cold.

Adam strode to his spiral staircase and climbed to his rooms. Every step felt like a lie. Victoria beckoned.

She called to him, a siren in a storm-tossed sea, and it would be just as disastrous for him as an unwary sailor if he heeded her song.

Damnation.

Adam braced himself as unbidden memories assailed him.

He'd had a taste of spring that morning so many years ago. He could recall the crisp bite of it still. It had expanded his lungs with a chill that shivered happily along his spine. Outside the Order of Samuel's compound, the mountain had been coming alive with tender green grasses and wildflowers. He'd walked around the struggling patches of color, inspired, but also frightened by their precarious hold on new life. A killing frost or a late snow at this elevation would end their struggle.

He had identified.

How many times had he tried to run away from the Order, getting a taste of life and freedom only to have it cut short when they dragged him back to the enclave?

Malachi said he'd been taken in too late. Most novitiates were stolen from the cradle or gathered in before they could barely walk and talk. But Adam had been nine when he'd been "adopted." He'd been stolen on a market day by a monk who'd taken advantage of the chaos and crowd to snag a healthy youth. Adam had been old enough to remember his mother and father and the lessons they had taught that had been so very different from the lessons that the Order tried to supplant them with.

He remembered one failed escape more vividly than all the rest. That morning so long ago he'd breathed the fresh air deeply into lungs that were weakened from a long, damp winter. He'd known he might fail again, but at sixteen he'd been ready to try rather than be buried alive beneath evil zealotry. Malachi hadn't been able to beat away the memory of his mother's face or his father's strict but fair hand. Malachi's lash was cruel rather than strict. And there was nothing fair about being pressed into an Order of merciless killers.

The mother's milk of this mountain orphanage was blood.

This time he hadn't escaped alone. He'd carried another, weaker novitiate with him, but Thomas wouldn't be with him long. Adam sat with the frail younger boy near the flowers while he drew his last breaths. Thomas was only five. He'd never known another life. Spring hadn't come soon enough to the dark confines of the monk's conclave. Dampness had settled into the tiny boy's lungs. He'd never been strong. Even Adam's sacrifice of most of his winter's gruel from his own plate hadn't been enough to strengthen Thomas and help him withstand the chill. Adam's kindness had probably only prolonged his suffering.

In the end, hot with fever and dreaming about the sky, Thomas had begged to be taken away from the compound. Adam had heeded his prayers because they echoed the longing in his own heart.

Every moment outside was a reprieve, even if it meant his suffering would increase once he was dragged back to the Order.

Adam had held the boy's hand while he gasped the fresh air. Each pause between gasps became longer and longer. And something had darkened inside Adam. He'd seen so many others come and go. He'd seen and shared their suffering. One more. One more. One more.

They tracked him down again, of course. He'd stood on the crest of a rise when they came for him, looking toward the south where his parents' village may as well have been a different world. He hadn't fought them. The monks who reclaimed him were not boys. They were full-grown men who had embraced the life of the Order. Their flesh was steel. Their hearts burned with hell's fire. He was no match for them.

Yet, even when Malachi lashed the skin from his back in punishment, an ember of hope remained kindled in his breast. They hadn't found Thomas's body. Adam had hidden it deep in a crevice so Thomas could at least be free of the monks in death. Adam had taken care to be sure that the small body had fallen faceup to the sky.

One day he would be strong enough, quick enough, smart enough to defeat these men he refused to call his masters. Then he would return to his true home. For now, he endured the lash and, later, the punishing chore of mucking out the filth from the deepest, darkest dungeon beneath the main keep.

In these tunnels that wound in a seemingly endless maze, wafts of sour air carried with them the defeated moans of the dead and dying. He knew Malachi wanted him to dwell in the atmosphere of stinking defeat so it would permeate his soul. The jailer had laughed when he'd left Adam to his broom. He'd even dropped his heavy iron ring of keys on his chair before he walked out, mocking Adam's earlier efforts at escape.

As Adam worked, his rough robe rubbed raw the scars and fresh wounds on his back that spoke of all too frequent beatings. The pain was severe. The memory of the monks as they crushed the wildflowers beneath their feet was worse. He needed flowers to grow unharmed, somehow, somewhere. The thought helped him endure this darkest of hells.

"The love of your master drips cruelly down your legs, son." A coherent voice from one of the cells startled him. No one spoke in this place. Ever. Words took energy and effort. By the time prisoners came here, they had nothing left but the basest animal instincts.

Adam didn't need the smoking light from flickering torches to see that the wounds on his back bled dirty rivers of blood down both of his bare legs. He could feel their sticky trails. He could smell the metallic bite blended with the disgusting scents of filth and decay around him.

"Not my master, sir. My captor. Although I'm not in chains, I'm bound like you," Adam replied.

He cautiously moved to the bars of the cell until he could see the creature within. Creature, not man, because the torchlight revealed the nightglow eyes of a daemon when its head tilted this way or that. Manlike for sure. A tall, well-made masculine figure with broad shoulders and a proud stance in spite of the manacles and prayer-scribed chains that bound it to the wall. Other than the eyes and obvious strength despite its circumstances, the creature looked like a man and a noble one at that.

No ordinary man could look so well in these dungeons.

Adam had grown up around daemons and he knew they had fallen from heaven by choice to rule in hell. He hated the Order, but the very idea of a creature who would choose damnation caused his knees to go to liquid in the being's presence.

But even the dark land the daemons claimed and ruled could not be as hellish as this dungeon—Adam's hell on Earth.

"You are a novitiate of the Order of Samuel. You wear the robes. You do the work they set you to do," the daemon noted.

It moved closer to the bars and Adam didn't back away, although he did grip his broom tighter until his knuckles showed white beneath grime and dried blood.

"My mind is my own. My heart is my own," Adam insisted.

His body was marked forever by Malachi's lash. Even now, his blood continued to drip on the floor. The daemon's eyes flashed as it looked him over from head to toe.

"Release me and I will free your body from this place to join your heart and mind," the daemon said.

In the flickering torchlight, embers, ash and dust sparkled as suddenly suspended motes in the air. Adam had to exert effort to expand his lungs in the thickened atmosphere. His heartbeat slowed.

"I've been warned against such bargains with daemons," he said.

The daemon in the cell stepped fully into the light. Though he was smudged with dirt and his long hair was rumpled in clumps, the disarray didn't seem to touch his proud angular face. Him, not it. Adam could no longer refer to the creature as a thing when he was obviously a man, whether he was human or not.

The daemon turned his muscular body, clad only in dark leggings and no tunic. The torchlight revealed savage scars on his shoulders, cruel and deep.

Adam took a step back and a gasp escaped his grimaced lips. The daemon was old. One of the ancients who had actually walked in heaven. The scars on his back revealed where he'd once had wings.

"My heart and my mind are also my own, in spite of the scars," the daemon said.

Adam's knees were barely supporting his body and his head was light. Surely empathy with a daemon damned him, but his raw back would allow no other response.

"We are their prisoners, but if you free me from these chains, I will free you from this place," the daemon promised.

"Freedom isn't the only thing I seek. I want to stop them. To make them pay for what they've done," Adam said. The words came from a deep, dark place inside him, darker than the dank dungeon. It was the place he'd discovered while he sat beside Thomas as the tiny boy lay dying.

The air hardened and thickened even more around him until his chest was compressed by the pressure. The daemon's chains rattled as he straightened in response to Adam's proclamation. He might have been shocked. Or he might have given the words the respect of a soldier standing at attention. But when the daemon nodded to affirm that he heard and accepted, his nod was the nod of a king.

"If you will free me, I will free you. If you serve me, I will help you achieve the justice you seek. You will be bound to me until the Order falls," the daemon said.

"Yes," Adam said. He forced the agreement through petrified lips. "This I pledge."

"I accept," the daemon said.

The thickened atmosphere held Adam in place for the space of several long moments. He couldn't breathe. He couldn't move. His heartbeat thudded sluggishly in his ears. He was a statue painted with blood.

Then all returned to normal around him. Torches flickered. Prisoners moaned. The daemon waited.

Adam placed the broom against the wall as the daemon watched. He turned and traveled back through the corridors to the jailer's chair, where the heavy ring of keys waited. He could have chosen a different kind of slavery in that moment. He could have walked away. He could have accepted the life of the Order of Samuel. Instead he chose to barter his soul for freedom and the chance to fight. He couldn't save Thomas. He couldn't save himself. But there were countless others he might be able to save. Even if the price was his soul.

It was in that moment that the deal was really made.

He didn't pause.

He didn't pray.

He picked up the keys and carried them back to the daemon's cell.

The walk was dark and long, but elsewhere wildflowers struggled up through the snow and parents waited and wept.

The first key fit the lock on the cell's door. His heart pounded quickly, no longer sluggish, as he approached the daemon who waited within. Once the chains were removed, the daemon might easily crush the life from him and leave him to rot.

"A daemon is bound by their bargains as surely as a human. I will stand by my promise," the daemon said.

Adam tried key after key. His fingers fumbled beneath the daemon's fierce stare. How had he felt they had anything in common? He was a grimy, scarred failure of a boy, kidnapped and forced to train as a merciless warrior. While this daemon had once had angelic wings! But he found the right key and opened the manacles, prepared to risk death to be free.

He wasn't prepared for the burning agony that suffused his entire body when the chains fell free. He collapsed to his knees, crying out against the fire that claimed his veins until nothing but Brimstone-tainted blood remained.

"I should have warned you that the irrevocability of a daemon's word is something every mortal should fear. There are always ramifications and complications to every daemon bargain. The Brimstone mark is only the first of many hardships to come, I'm afraid. A deal with the devil is not something to enter into lightly. But I knew as soon as I saw your face and your bloody scars that you might be able to withstand the burden. Might. We shall see. We shall see," the daemon said. "You are no longer merely human. You are more. Stronger, better, faster, smarter. Only time will tell if it will be enough to give us victory over the Order of Samuel and the Rogue daemons who use them. The Brimstone will give you time."

Adam remembered the daemon picking him up as he'd picked up Thomas that morning. He remembered the Burn of Brimstone searing away the pain on his back, cauterizing his wounds.

Once free of the sanctified iron, the daemon had carried him out of the compound, too fast for anyone in the Order to stop them. But he could also remember how the struggling wildflowers had gone up in flames as he and the daemon had blazed past, more ferocious and terrible than any spring sun.

Damnation.

It seared his veins. It fueled his cause and kept him warm at night when he eschewed companionship. Now it was nothing but ash. He'd captured two of the Order's monks on the estate tonight. Even though he'd swept the area clean before Victoria arrived. They were moths to her flame. Both had Brimstone in their veins because they'd sold themselves to the Rogue sect.

He stripped off his clothes and tended to minor injuries that wouldn't need the doctor's help. Most were so shallow the Brimstone had already cauterized them.

But his hands shook.

He wanted to go to her. He'd fought like a fiend to protect her. And he refused to imagine how his daemon masters might be drawn to her. She'd loved one of them. An Ancient One who had actually walked in heaven before he chose to fall to a new autonomous land with Lucifer. They had reigned in hell until the Rogues had overthrown and killed Lucifer. The Rogue sect was made up of younger daemons who resented the fall. They wanted to wage war with heaven and reclaim their "rightful" place in the stars.

A revolution in hell hadn't ended well for the Rogues. The Loyalists had reclaimed the throne and set a daemon named Ezekiel on it. A daemon king who considered Victoria D'Arcy his adopted daughter.

She'd loved one of them. She might love him still.

Adam could certainly use support from Loyalists to handle the extra influx of monks and daemons that Victoria's affinity seemed to be drawing to Nightingale Vineyards, but he couldn't stand the thought of Victoria drawn to Loyalist blood, even as he refused her affinity himself. He recognized the gnawing teeth of jealousy. He couldn't pretend he was only interested in keeping her safe from harm.

Damned for a hundred years? He hadn't known true damnation until now.

Once he was clean, he stretched out on the bed and replayed every expression, every breath, every sigh, every taste until finally the torture of the present became entwined with the mistakes of his past.

She'd been hounded by daemons her whole life, but

she was still beautiful. The hope and determination in her heart was more powerful than the Brimstone in his.

It was another mistake, but he reached for the earbuds beside his bed. He'd managed to find an amateur recording of Victoria before she'd arrived. It had been a mere curiosity, easily satisfied by unlimited resources, but it had turned into something more once he'd heard her hum the same song in the garden.

He stretched out again once he'd tabbed the icon for the song to resume. He'd had it on Repeat for a long time.

The song had soothed away his nightmares before she'd arrived. Now it fed his dreams.

Chapter 6

She should have been content to hide in the cottage and catch her breath after pilfering the keys, but an odd restlessness gripped her after her near miss with Turov in the garden. He'd returned to the house. No doubt he was now sound asleep, having completely forgotten about the kiss. Her affinity didn't seem to seduce her host as easily as Katherine's had seduced Severne. Either that or Adam Turov resisted more successfully.

She should be glad. Her resistance to the pull of his Brimstone was shaky at best.

When she returned to the cottage, instead of hiding, she used her laptop to chat with Michael and Sybil. She needed to ground herself in the reality of her situation once more. She wasn't here to seek contentment or romance. Michael was happy to see her. He pressed his chubby hands to the screen and she'd pressed hers against his. He was still too young for conversation. His excited babble had included definite words such as *ball* and *Gim*—her son's name for his ferocious hellhound Grim—but much of what he tried to tell her was indistinguishable syllables.

Sybil filled in the blanks of how her son was spending his days in the Cape Cod vacation house in Massachusetts, far away from their home in Shreveport, Louisiana. Grim filled the screen behind the boy and his daemon nanny, a hulking black shadow with glowing eyes and gleaming white teeth that shone against his smoky fur.

As Sybil spoke of sandcastles and swing sets, Grim settled down in the background and Michael settled with him. Her son fell asleep against the hellhound's flank, using his hell-spawned guardian as a pillow.

"I'm not sure I'll ever get used to that," Victoria told Sybil.

The smooth-faced daemon nanny was hundreds and hundreds of years old. Older than Severne. Nearly as old as Michael's daemon father, who had been one of the Ancient Ones who had once had heavenly wings. She looked Victoria's age, but she spoke like a wise woman with many years of experience under her belt. She'd raised John Severne when his mother died. She'd mothered him for two hundred years while loving his father, knowing that one day John's father would die and leave her to go on without him.

"Grim is the nanny. I just do the cooking and anything else that requires opposable thumbs," Sybil said.

Sybil had also been the seamstress at l'Opera Severne for a couple of centuries. No big. The dress she wore was old-fashioned, but lovely. Each stitch perfectly placed. Victoria was certain that Michael's pants had also been hand-sewn by Sybil.

"Thank you for keeping him safe. I know you miss the opera house. I hope you'll be able to return to it soon," Victoria said. Her sister and brother-in-law had rebuilt the opera house after it burned to the ground. Sybil had been welcomed back to an even more cavernous costume warehouse where she still preferred to use large wheeled iron ladders rather than the electric revolving racks, shelves and bins that Severne had custom-installed.

"This is a nice vacation. Which I well deserve after a couple of hundred years," Sybil said.

"He loves you," Victoria said. "They love you." She spoke of Michael, but also of Kat and Severne. It was complicated. Sybil had almost hurt them with her daemon manipulations, but she had acted out of long-standing love and loyalty to Severne's father and Severne himself.

"Love is dangerous, Victoria D'Arcy. Remember that. Love requires sacrifice. Sometimes it seems as if it craves our very blood to sustain it," Sybil said. "Be careful. Be wary. Guard your heart."

The daemon woman didn't know all the details of what Victoria was doing in Sonoma, but it was safe to bet she knew ten times more than she'd been told. Besides her Brimstone blood, her perceptions were heightened by nearly immortal experience.

"Michael is my heart. You and Grim are guarding him. The one that beats in my chest went cold when Michael's father died. It's as worn-out and unused as my scratchy voice," Victoria said.

"You're too young to speak of wearing out," Sybil scolded.

"I feel ancient," Victoria confessed.

In the background, Grim had closed his eyes and

Michael's soft snores indicated he'd fallen into a deep and peaceful sleep. Victoria ached to be there with him. To pick him up and rock him while he slept as she had when he was much younger.

"He is well. He is cared for. Even if there was no danger, you needed to take some time to heal yourself. You haven't had a moment alone since the opera house fire. You have been sister and mother…you need to find yourself again," Sybil said. "Reclaim Victoria's voice."

"I don't know how," Victoria said. On the screen, she could see the smooth porcelain of Sybil's lovely forehead wrinkle slightly as the daemon frowned.

"I have sewn something for you. You'll find a red dress packed in your luggage. This is a gift freely given. Or perhaps in exchange for your acceptance of me after I….after I threatened Michael and Katherine to try to help Severne. I warned you about love being dangerous, but I offer it to you. I am a daemon and we feel differently, but deeply. More deeply than we can comfortably express."

Victoria left the laptop open and turned away to rummage through her luggage. She found a tissue-wrapped parcel she hadn't noticed in the bottom of one case. She picked it up and brought it over to the vanity to open it in front of the screen.

The string and pristine white paper came apart easily in her fingers and deep red silk fell into her lap like a bright waterfall. She lifted it and drew it to her cheek to feel its liquid softness. She immediately loved and feared it. The old Victoria would have jumped up to put it on right away, but the Victoria she was now hesitated.

"I give you this dress to wear when you will. When you need it, you will have it on hand," Sybil said. "And now I will bid you good night. There's a small boy who needs to be carried to bed and Grim doesn't have the arms necessary to perform this service."

"Thank you, Sybil," Victoria said, but the screen had already gone dark.

Thick with emotion, she hung the dress in the closet without trying it on and then went out into the garden. The fans were still in the distance. The rows and rows of grapevines were peaceful and unthreatened on a dry night in spite of the slight spring chill in the air. The main house was dark. No windows glowed. Her footsteps crunched along the path as if she was the solitary being on the planet who was awake and about.

Only the growing moon kept her company and illuminated her way. It was slightly more than a sliver now. Its growth was like her hourglass in the sky.

She didn't hum or sing. The effort not to express her longing for—something—in song was great. She bit her lip. She clenched her fists against a stomach that swirled with unexpressed lyrics.

The smoky quality of her voice wasn't unpleasant. It was changed, and while not suited to opera there were other types of music she could still sing. If she would. If her heart wakened and quickened and allowed her to reclaim what she'd lost when she'd lost Michael's father to Father Reynard's daemon blade.

Adam Turov woke her affinity. He sparked possibilities with his Brimstone blood that she'd thought lost forever. It wasn't the red dress she was afraid of. It was the song Turov woke in her heart. The need to sing that he loosened in her breast. That need twined inexorably with her need to feel like herself again and to be a passionate woman, not just an automaton surviving day by day in desperate times.

Michael's safety came first. His future was paramount. She refused to lose sight of why she was here and the mission she had to fulfill. But Adam Turov was more than just a mission. She couldn't deny that. He drew her. Oh, how he drew her. And not only because of his Brimstone blood.

But if she freed his prisoners, Turov would die.

While she walked, thinking of the red dress that hung so full of potential in the cottage's closet, she was suddenly interrupted by a sound in the garden. Victoria stopped. She listened, trying to distinguish what she'd heard when all she heard now was the roaring of blood in her ears and the thump of a quickened heartbeat in her chest.

The sound of metal rasping against metal came from the distance as a breeze lifted tendrils of hair on her cheek and tickled her skin. It sounded like a rusted hinge of a gate. She waited for the clank and latch of the gate being closed, but it never came. The drawn out *screeeee* had come from somewhere in front of her on the path.

The slowness of it bothered her. It seemed clandestine and sly as if someone was opening a gate that was supposed to remain closed. She stayed still and silenced her breathing. If she approached the sound, she didn't know what she might find. If she returned to the cottage, the gate opener might follow her. They might intercept her from behind. Victoria was suddenly more conscious of the darkened main house. The desolation of the night garden around her. If the sound had been caused by a monk, she might face an ugly fight.

Working for Malachi didn't automatically protect her from other monks from the Order of Samuel; she would be seen as a valuable commodity for any monk who wanted to grasp for power now that Father Reynard was

gone. And there was always the possibility that a daemon would be drawn to her affinity.

It was also just as likely that the sound had been
caused by the breeze that stirred the hair around her
face as she stood still, trying not to breathe as if she'd
run a marathon.

"I'm not going to run from the wind," Victoria told
the garden.

She made her decision. There was no way she could
make it to the cottage if a threat was right around the
corner. She decided to face whatever had made the
sound head-on rather than flee.

The first step was the hardest. After that, she took
step after step toward where she'd heard the sound.

When she came to a branch in the path that led to
a large wrought-iron gazebo, she realized she'd found
the origin of the sound. The gazebo was covered in ivy,
but she could see that it was shaped like a birdcage. The
door hung open. She paused for only a second before she
forced herself to approach and take the cool iron in her
hands. The door to the birdcage gazebo was too heavy
to be stirred by a breeze. It protested against movement
when she tried to swing it closed.

But the sound was definitely the metallic sound of
hinges rasping she'd heard earlier.

All the birdcages in the house and the cottage had
been arranged with their doors opened. It was as if someone had let all the birds they might once have held free.

She suddenly didn't want to close the gazebo's gated
door. She opened it wide instead. The screech of the
rusty hinges was loud again in the silent night. The
shadowy interior of the gazebo was clearly revealed by
the crescent moon. There was no one inside. But there
was something. Victoria stepped just inside the door to

lean over and pick up a single dark red rose. The skin between her shoulder blades tingled and the hair on her neck rose. She turned to survey the garden behind her. The path was empty. She could see all the way to the edge of the main house, but there were many places she couldn't see. Buildings and hedges and vines, trees and bushes and deep dark shadows—all of those things were blanketed in midnight mystery.

The rose was different than the dried cherry blossoms. It felt more like a gift than a warning. The garden was filled with roses. She remembered the rose centerpiece in the black-and-white photograph of Turov and his parents. His mother had loved to garden and grow—grapevines and roses.

In the moonlight, the rose in her hands took on the same gray color as the roses in the photograph that had moldered long ago.

Who had opened the gate? Who had left the rose?

Often, particularly after bloody nights, he made his way to his mother's study. He wasn't immortal. He could bleed. He could die. But those he'd loved had been nothing but ash for years. How many times had he seen his mother serve tea from the prized firebird service she'd brought with her from Russia? Yet all of those days had been the blink of an eye. Beneath glass, the vintage set was cold. He hadn't preserved the warm memories as easily as he'd preserved the gilded porcelain.

He sat in his father's chair and paged through the fairy tale book. The language and art on its pages soothed him. The pages had remained more vibrant and alive with memories than the tea set.

His mother had always loved the firebird tale, but they had been poor. Peasants. It was after he made his bargain with the daemon when he returned from the Order that he had changed their lives. He had refused to speak about his experience. His injuries healed. His scars were noted with stoic, if concerned, silence. It had been a blessing to be able to provide them with a luxurious life while he lived with the curse of Brimstone in his blood. The Revolution had driven them to America, which had been another blessing in disguise. It had distanced his family from his far more dangerous business of hunting the Order while giving them the vineyards to focus on instead.

His mother had been too observant. She'd known he was somehow not his own man. That's when her fascination with her favorite fairy tale had grown. She'd filled his home with images of the firebird and a plethora of empty, gilded cages.

She had hated his continued imprisonment even after he'd escaped the Order, but she had loved him all the same.

He missed the family that had loved him before the Brimstone and accepted him after. But he was also conscious of the allure of Victoria. She could never love him, but she was drawn to his Brimstone rather than repelled by it.

See me.

Know me.

It burned him with possibility more than the Brimstone burned.

He paged through the beloved book, but as he did something niggled at the edges of his perception. Time gave a person heightened senses. Like time-lapse photography, a millimeter of movement in a room you'd visited every day for fifty years stood out like a scream. On the shelf, he saw the wooden box his mother had owned before he'd been taken by the Order. She'd made her own wine even then. He remembered the flasks of simple red so unlike the sophisticated pinot noir Nightingale created now. The box was simple. His father had carved it from a dead walnut tree. It was no treasure for a burglar to disturb and yet someone had disturbed it.

Only a nearly immortal person would have noticed the difference in its placement after seeing it one way for so many years and then seeing it tilted ever so slightly another.

He placed the book back on the table and stood. Even before he approached the box and picked it up, he knew what he would find. His mother's firebird keys were gone. And he knew the beautiful burglar who had taken them.

Victoria had a mission. And now she had discovered the tools she would need to fulfill it. He held the empty box for a while trying to recall the way it had looked in his mother's hands. It was a distant memory. Hazy and indistinct. He visited the room the way one might visit a cemetery. To pay his respects. To grieve. His mourning had been disturbed by a nightingale who had forgotten how to sing.

He could show her how. He could feel the inspiration he could provide burning in his veins. But he hadn't been seeking justice for so long that he'd forgotten the lesson of the wildflowers. Burning and burning until they were nothing but ash in the sun.

Chapter 7

Victoria was smudged and covered in dust and grime for several days as she explored the main house from the attic to the basement, where centuries of detritus was stored in boxes and chests. Every day she watched and waited for Turov to leave, but she'd had many close calls with the master of the vineyard as well as his employees. She wasn't barred from the house. Far from it. There was a library she'd been invited to use and the kitchen was always open for her to graze or order a tray of tea or snacks brought to the cottage.

But she was sure she was the only guest who crept around trying vintage skeleton keys in every locked door. She hadn't really expected to find a wing of rooms filled with evil monks. But she had hoped for clues to point her in the direction of where Turov might hold his prisoners.

Mostly, she'd intruded upon memories of days gone by.

She had discovered that none of her keys fit the lock on Adam Turov's office door or the door of his apartments…the most likely place for secrets to be found.

It was late afternoon by the time a vacuuming maid had caused her to give up on locked doors for the day. She'd almost exhausted the doors her keys would unlock anyway. She'd asked for tea in the rose garden and the cook had been happy to oblige because she'd made very few requests so far.

Once Victoria had washed her hands, she discovered the cook had even asked some of Turov's men to carry a chaise longue and a small table into the clearing in the center of the garden where an ivy-covered arbor provided shade. It was a spot that would have been perfect for a fainting Edwardian woman who needed to loosen her corset and guzzle some tea after a long morning of social calls.

Victoria sat in her dusty jeans and smudged flannel shirt and put her feet up. In spite of the thick rosebushes all around her, she was able to eye several buildings in the distance that might be worth investigation.

"Your hair in the sunlight rivals the roses," Turov said.

She looked from the buildings with a start. The intensity of his blue eyes rivaled the Sonoma sky, so vivid against the white clouds and green surroundings that his gaze made her chest ache.

But she wouldn't tell him that.

She wouldn't tell him how exploring his house and the memories he'd carefully kept for a hundred years made her itch to reach out and hold him. Even now, though he walked into the clearing in a suit cut so tight and sharp that its tailoring perfectly mimicked his cheekbones and angular jaw.

Untouchable.

But his Brimstone burn said otherwise.

She was exhausted from her search and from the tension of snooping where she didn't belong, but as he approached she still bit her lip against a song. It was one she didn't know how to sing. New and different, throaty and sweet, it rose from her gut in a sultry curl like smoke.

"Esther told me you'd asked for tea. I thought I'd join you, if you don't mind," Turov said. As he spoke, a man carried another chair into the clearing and placed it beside her chaise longue.

It would be a mistake to have tea with a man who once made a deal with the devil that still burns in his veins.

"Of course. Please," Victoria said. She didn't sing.

But she did feel faint when Turov settled close beside her as if they were going to enjoy an intimate tête-à-tête. She resisted the magnetic pull of his blood. She didn't resist meeting his gaze. She was a terrible spy. He must see her guilt swirling in her irises. Yet she looked because he compelled her to look, not with Brimstone, but with all else she might be able to see. Time. All the things he'd seen and done and endured. How had anyone ever imagined him to be in his late twenties when his eyes were so obviously much, much older than that?

"The tea might take a little while. I made a special request that might take them longer than the usual service," Turov said.

"I don't mind," Victoria said. In truth, her throat was parched, but more from dust and nervousness than thirst. Would he see her smudged appearance and wonder what in the world she'd been up to? "I've been hiking. It's nice to rest."

He raised a brow. Her wilted appearance could have been caused by a long hike around his estate. But when Turov leaned toward her it wasn't a leaf he plucked from her hair to hold out to her like a chivalrous offering. It was a telltale fluff of attic insulation.

She reached to take it from his fingers and allowed it to float to the ground where the yellow puff lay in the grass like a shout of accusation.

"The cook's name is Esther?" she asked. "I noticed everyone calls her by her title rather than her name."

"I knew her before she was a cook," Adam explained. "But she's very proud of her position and has earned the title most proficiently."

Victoria didn't mention that Esther was at least seventy years old. The rosy-cheeked, wrinkled woman had twinkling eyes and a spring in her step in spite of her age. She seemed years from retirement. She'd noticed that Adam was warmer to his people than most wealthy men. Did he remember what it was like to be less than he was today?

"She's been the heart of my home for many years. I'm sure you've noticed the air of abandonment in much of the house. Esther's kitchen is the exception. Before my mother died, she was also like Esther—strong, but all heart. My mother's name was Elena. She was born of the sturdiest stock. Her hands were calloused because she kept them in the dirt. That's what I remember most about her. The scent of soil and green and growing things. The scent of her roses," Adam said.

Two men carefully carried the firebird tea service into the rose garden on a silver tray. Esther must not have trusted one alone with the task. They each held one end of the tray as if they carried a great and precious burden. The extra time must have been spent washing the pot, cups and saucers until they gleamed. How frightening it must have been for the cook to be asked to take on such a task.

"It's beautiful," Victoria said. Tears burned at the back of her eyes and her throat tightened. Her voice was huskier than usual. She had disturbed Elena Turov's sitting room without permission and now Adam Turov had the firebird tea service brought into the sun for the first time in decades…for her.

"The service was a gift from my father. My mother loved the firebird fairy tale. She was one to hold on to the old ways and old tales. Russia was settled by Slavs in the early sixth century. It's from these ancestors that the Slavic firebird tales were passed down to us from generation to generation. My father gave her this fairy tale in so many ways. He said she was his firebird because she had escaped the Russian Revolution and taken flight to America," Adam said. "She would have loved your hair. The flames in it. She only grew scarlet roses because she said they reminded her of the firebird's flight."

Adam stood to pour the tea. When he handed her a cup and saucer she was very careful to keep her hands steady. The tea was piping hot in spite of its journey from the house. Her host wasn't as calm as he appeared. This offering was significant. As a former opera singer, she understood myth and metaphor. She understood symbolism. But she didn't begin to understand the complexity of this man who had lived so long with damnation burning and burning at his heels.

"It catches fire in the sun," she said, lifting her gilded cup up so that the sunlight hit the firebird's tail.

Adam's cup rattled against his saucer.

"Everything does," he responded when he had settled the delicate porcelain in his strong hand.

Did this firebird tea in the rose garden mean that her affinity had seduced him? And why did that idea make her cringe?

As she sipped from the vintage porcelain cup decorated with its lovely gilded bird that was more legend than reality, her own emotions were even more elusive than a bird sought by princes and principalities.

She was supposed to get close to Adam Turov. Her stolen keys were worthless if she couldn't discover what they unlocked. The trouble was that she *had* gotten closer to him in the last few days as she pilfered through all of his memories and personal treasures from a hundred years of life and love.

She wanted to enjoy the tea in her firebird cup as a generous offering of burgeoning attraction from a man whose kisses she craved. She didn't want to plot his downfall.

Victoria watched Adam sip his tea quietly surrounded by the roses his mother had planted. And then she thought of Michael guarded by a hellhound and a daemon nanny while she struggled with tea and roses.

She didn't have the luxury of enjoyment or the freedom to appreciate the attraction that burned between her and Turov.

He had lived forever and a day, but Victoria D'Arcy would be the death of him. He'd survived the burn of Brimstone so long that he'd forgotten there were worse burns. Like words spoken lightly that cut like swallowed shards of glass. He played with fire. Not only the way his blood bubbled and boiled with need for Victoria's kiss, the song of desire she'd yet to allow herself to sing for him—he allowed her to search for his prisoners with no interference.

He served the daemon king to earn back his soul, but he also served to bring the Order of Samuel to hell where they belonged. Victoria was a song that woke him from decades of sleepwalking; a song he wasn't free to taste.

Victoria D'Arcy couldn't be allowed to interfere with that mission. Not only because he brooked no interruption, but also because she was very wrong to believe that freeing the monks he'd captured would protect her son. He knew Malachi. The corrupt man could not be trusted. If he was interested in Victoria's son, he wouldn't rest until the child was in his clutches.

He carried the firebird tea service back to the kitchen once Victoria had excused herself to wash attic dust from her face and hair. Oh, she'd said to freshen up after her hike, but he knew the dust of his house's nooks and crannies well. Nostalgia was a hobby he indulged only rarely, but it surrounded him powerfully and painfully, always.

Esther met him at the door of the kitchen and he allowed her to take the service from his arms. She'd never known his mother, but she reminded him of her often. She'd also been born in Slovakia although her birth had occurred long after his mother's, so Esther's stories were of Czechoslovakia.

"I was happy to bring this out of its case. So sad to see something so beautiful shut away and unused," Esther said. "The young lady is very like it—I suspect she's shut herself away. I can almost see the shimmer of a glass case around her when she talks. So careful. So quiet. And I don't think it's her natural way."

"No. I have a recording of her that's not careful or quiet at all. The fire caused damage beyond her voice, I think," Adam said. "And the Order has stalked her since she was a child."

The cook held on to the side of the sink where she'd carefully placed the teapot to wash. Her calloused hands were white-knuckled from her grip.

"I'm sorry. I shouldn't have mentioned the Order," Adam said.

"They have stalked us all for too long, Mr. Turov," Esther said with her head bowed and her shoulders taut and stiff. "I know you'll help her. You always do."

The words seared him even though the Brimstone in his blood protected him from fire. He wasn't sure if he would be able to help Victoria D'Arcy without losing a battle he'd waged for a century.

"Always is a long time, Esther. A very long time," he replied.

The cook who had once been something far fiercer turned to look at him. Her eyes usually twinkled with humor, but now they glimmered with tears. Her cheeks were ruddy, but not from an oven's heat.

"I have appreciated every second of the normal life you've given me. I expect she'd do the same," Esther said. "But you're only one man. An extraordinary one, but *they* are many. Take care of yourself too. Don't lose sight of your own salvation."

For a hundred years, taking down the Order of Samuel had been a clear objective in his mind. But that objective had become clouded as soon as Victoria stepped onto the soil of his vineyard. Saving his soul had always been secondary. But there was salvation in her song. One he wasn't exactly sure how to claim.

It was much later that evening when Victoria decided to brave the kitchen for a late dinner. She'd washed all the evidence of her snooping from her face and hair in a long, hot bath, but while the soak had eased her sore muscles and cleansed her body, it had also allowed her too much time to think of Adam Turov's kisses. It had been torturous to watch him sip tea that afternoon. He so composed and she so discombobulated. Perhaps he simply had more practice than she did at keeping secrets.

He should have looked out of place in the rose garden, in his tailored suit that gleamed as darkly as his hair in the sun. He hadn't. He'd looked perfectly comfortable while she had worried over the yellow insulation he'd found in her hair.

She was surprised to find someone in the kitchen when she pushed open the swinging doors that led from the back hallway into the most beautiful room in the house. The kitchen complemented the house with crafts-man elements, like a huge rock wall boasting an open fireplace that was still actually used for roasting on a spit. But it also hinted of a Slavic influence with its mosaic-tiled floors and the red-painted cabinetry. On the door panels of the cabinets were accents of folk art designs in hues of soft blues and greens. There was also a Slavic-style bread oven in the middle of the room made of stone but smoothly plastered with beige stucco. From the ceiling, iron fixtures hung like folksy chandeliers each fitted with a rope and pulley so that the candles could be lit. Stubby chunks of melted wax gave evidence to the fact that Esther still cooked by candlelight when she wished.

Esther was the crowning touch. Even now, well after other servants had left the main house, she sat at a heavy polished oak table in a colorful apron that could have been in a textile museum.

"I wondered if you would venture out for sustenance or if I was going to have to tap on your door with a tray," the smiling cook said when Victoria came into the room.

"I'm so sorry. I didn't mean for you to wait up," Victoria replied. Her face was as rosy as Esther's, but while the cook's face was red from constant exposure to the fire of her oven, Victoria's was red because she'd been caught trying to avoid her host.

"I just finished baking a batch of pagach bread. You'll try it and tell me how you like it," Esther said.

She rose and ushered Victoria into the chair she'd vacated. Her tone and enthusiasm brooked no resistance. Besides, the smell of yeasty bread filled with cheesy potatoes filled the whole room and caused Victoria's mouth to water. She'd had pagach before, but in the shape of a fancy crinkled-edged pie in a restaurant. Esther brought her homemade pagach to the table on the long wooden paddle she'd used to lift it from the baking sheet in the oven. Her pagach was a circular mound of dough much thicker than a pie pan that had been cooked a perfect golden brown.

"This was worth the wait, yeah?" Esther said as she cut into the pagach with a long knife she'd taken from a hook on the wall near the table. Aromatic steam rose in the air, causing Victoria's empty stomach to growl.

There was a stack of heavy ceramic plates and a basket of utensils already on the table along with a napkin holder. While Esther served a generous piece of pagach onto a plate Victoria held, she noticed that beside the napkin holder stood a quartet of dolls made from knotted twine. One had a long braid of twine down her back. Another had two pigtails on either side of her head. The last had a tiny peasant bonnet on her head. All three had brightly colored glass beads woven into their strands of twine and dresses as colorful as the one doll's bonnet. None of the dolls had faces.

"They are wishing dolls. Toys from my childhood.

Every time we want for something, we add a bead. Like a prayer. I find that even though I'm too old for wishing I like to keep the tradition," Esther said. She twitched the braid on one of the dolls.

Victoria chewed and swallowed a piece of heaven. The flavor of cheese and the texture of the creamy potatoes melted on her tongue.

"If one of those beads was for perfect pagach bread, the doll definitely delivered," Victoria said.

"You make me happy. Eating. Enjoying. I love to see this smile on your face. I live for smiles," Esther said.

Victoria ate several more bites while Esther went to the refrigerator and poured a glass of milk from a pitcher. The thick white creamy texture could only be whole and Victoria cringed when she realized her late-night snack was going to necessitate an early-morning jog tomorrow. Still, she couldn't resist. She anticipated the ice-cold treat before Esther made it back to the table. When the cook set the tall glass beside Victoria's plate, the sleeve of her dress rose up several inches.

Victoria's fork froze several inches from her mouth and she slowly lowered it back to her plate. Esther's wrist was badly scarred. Deep ridges cut into her flesh all the way around her arm. The scar was wide, but it had several raised areas that had been spared from the cut of whatever had dug into her skin. Esther drew back and pulled her sleeve into place, but it was clear that the cook had been cruelly bound at one time in her past.

"Eat. Smile. Don't ask. We don't talk of some things. It is better to forget," Esther said. She walked over to a rack where herbs had been hung in bunches to dry in the corner. From the rack, she lifted a small blue linen bag. She brought it over to the table and placed it near Victoria's plate.

"It's filled with juniper needles. Helps to rid one of bad thoughts. I keep one nearby always. Another one of our Slavic traditions. My gift to you," Esther said.

Victoria's curiosity was at its peak, but she was also empathetic to Esther's pain. She didn't want to pry into private nightmares the other woman wanted to forget.

"Thank you. For the bread and the juniper," Victoria said. She reached for her glass and drained the decadent milk. When she set it back down, she was sure she had a mustache. Esther smiled and her tension eased. "And thank you for the half a mile I'll have to run tomorrow morning to work it all off."

They both laughed then and Esther fussed about putting meat on her bones whether she liked it or not. The kitchen was a refuge. She'd known it from the start. Adam had given the kitchen to Esther. He'd given the sun to Gideon. It wasn't up to her to find out why. She had another mission. But there were more secrets at Nightingale Vineyards than she'd been sent to find. Her job was to unlock the hidden prison and free the monks Adam had captured, but more and more she wondered if unlocking Adam himself would be the true prize.

Chapter 8

Too much time had passed. She could feel the end of the month approaching. Every night more of the moon illuminated the garden. Every day and night, she searched for the hidden prisoners she was supposed to free. She was trying to save Michael, but her maternal instincts fretted over the amount of time she'd been gone. Even with modern technology, touching his face on a laptop screen wasn't the same as tucking him in at night herself. She missed the sloppy toddler kisses and his chubby arms clenched around her neck. She missed the scent of his towheaded curls when he was sleeping and his high-pitched giggles when Grim inadvertently tickled him with hell-spawned fur.

Her mother's heart pulled her in the direction of her child. But she was pulled in another direction so fiercely that she ached with the necessity of refusing the call.

Adam Turov.

He was everywhere. The whole of Nightingale Vineyards was Adam. From the decades of memorabilia in the main house to the grapes plumping on the vines. From the shadowing garden pathways to the sunny bustle of workers helping him to care for his vines. From Esther's Slavic kitchen to Elena Turov's birdcages. From dusky roses to the rich, red beauty of his Firebird Pinot Noir. She was surrounded by Adam even when he was mysteriously absent, day after day.

She should be glad that his actual presence had been scarce for the past week and that she'd been left mostly unobserved to skulk about the entire estate trying her keys. But her true feelings were more complicated than that. When he was gone, she missed his burn. Having basked in its glow, she was...bereft. Not relieved. She was cold. The farther away he ventured, the colder she became. Last night she'd had to burrow under the covers and light a fire in the small fireplace of the cottage.

She'd found nothing while he was gone. No hints of activity that might indicate prisoners being cared for. No sign of the prison itself. But rather than focusing on her failure, this morning she could only feel relief.

Adam was back.

She could feel his magnetic presence, but she had no excuse to seek him out. None at all. She'd taken to the sunlit garden to warm her bones and wander near the house without giving in to the desire to find Adam and seek the much greater heat she craved in his arms.

The affinity had never ridden her so hard. She'd never had to resist it to such an extreme that she was left shivering.

The sun helped. She wrapped her arms around herself and willed the soft, early morning rays to soak deeply into her. She could see the sprawling roof of the main house through the trees. The estate was old and empty. It existed in a tangle of roses and ivy that counteracted the orderly rows of grapevines, but all of the green growth served only to highlight how dead the main house had become. Only Esther's kitchen remained a place of life and laughter. The rest of the house was a tomb, a memorial for what had been.

Adam burned with Brimstone blood, but had his heart grown cold?

It didn't matter. His emotions were none of her concern. She wasn't here to cultivate an actual relationship. Yet she found herself less able to contemplate coldly seducing information from him now that she'd tasted his lips.

She found Adam in the doorway of the birdcage gazebo and stopped in the middle of the path. When the sunlight fell on his face it suddenly seemed as if she hadn't seen him for years.

She should have known the affinity would bring them together even as she tried to stay away.

"My father had this gazebo made for my mother. But she didn't spend much time here. She loved her birdcages, but this one was too big. She said it made her feel like a poor trapped bird even with the door open," Adam said. "I like it myself. I sit here at times and then walk out whenever I please. It reminds me that I'm free in so many ways. I can step out of the cage. I can grow my grapes and talk with a beautiful woman as she walks in my garden."

She knew his soul wasn't free. She could see that truth in the shadows of his eyes even as he blinked in the sun. But some cruel truths didn't have to be said. Instead, she moved again. They could ignore his bartered soul for just a little while. Nothing could have stopped her from approaching his warmth. Not when she'd suffered through colder and colder days—and nights—without it.

Adam watched her come toward him. He straightened and his expression grew more serious. His jaw hardened. His eyes shone like blue diamonds in the morning light.

"I saw smoke coming from the cottage's chimney this morning," he said.

She continued to move closer to the gazebo where he stood. He didn't step down the wrought-iron stairs to meet her. But he didn't move away. In fact, he'd wrapped one hand around the rail and she could see that it was the white-knuckled grip he'd used before. The question was: Did he hold himself back, or stop himself from walking away?

"I've been chilled to the bone since you went away," Victoria said. Her voice was husky and low. There was a cadence to her words that was almost, but not quite, a song.

Adam closed his eyes and swallowed. He opened them only when she'd climbed the bottom two steps leaving only one empty between them. A wrought-iron tread of possibility. She could step up. He could step down. The choice was theirs to make. Nothing to do with a hellish civil war or an evil monk. Only him. Only her. Only a response to the separation that had left them both looking for each other this morning.

"I'm never cold, but it was very dark where I traveled and I missed your song," Adam said.

Adam was the one who took the last step. She had raised her face toward him, but she hadn't been able to risk the last tread. He risked it for them both. She closed her eyes against the nearness of his Brimstone fire as if it flared bright enough for her to see. It wasn't visual, but her body could feel the aura of heat around him grow stronger. She could feel when they were close enough for his heated aura to encompass her. He reached to wrap his arms around her back.

Her eyes were still closed, but she wasn't surprised when his warm hand touched her face. He traced the outline of her cheek and jaw and then, as she thought the soft tickle would kill her, he allowed the pads of his fingers to trail over the outline of her lips. She drew in a breath and released it in a shaky sigh. Her nipples peaked. A rush of adrenaline flowed to her legs then drained so that her knees were left weak and trembling.

"I'm fascinated by your mouth. But I know it isn't where your song starts. I know it starts lower," Adam murmured. His fingers left her lips to move down to her throat where he gently cupped them near her voice box. The move from a different man would have felt threatening, but his hand was light around her throat. His palm was hot and soothing against the skin that hid her damaged vocal cords. The doctors said she'd breathed fire trying to save her son. Sometimes she dreamed about a dragon flying from the burning opera house with Michael on its back. She didn't open her eyes. She focused all of her senses on Adam's touch. It wasn't Brimstone that made her throb intimately when his hand left her throat to trail down to her chest. It was his touch and the slight tremble of contained desire she could feel in his fingers as he moved his hand to her diaphragm, as if he traced the path her song would take if it ever decided to fly.

"I can feel it in you. The music. The melody. Its grace fuels your every sigh," Adam said.

He'd moved his face down to hers and he spoke against the lobe of her ear. She shivered in response to his Brimstone-heated breath. She wanted to feel it everywhere. When he moved his hand to nudge her T-shirt up so that he could spread his fingers against her bare stomach, her respiration went shallow and quick. She could no longer remember being cold. She was molten inside and the flow of lava seemed to have settled in the V between her legs.

She startled as his lips touched hers, and her eyelids fluttered open enough to see Adam's eyes close in a savoring swoon. Hers drifted closed again and she opened her mouth in welcome as his tongue teased against hers. She wrapped her arms around his neck to keep from falling. She buried her hands in his hair. They kissed and she forgot all about keys and Malachi. Her chills were erased. Her loneliness and worry forgotten. Their bodies didn't care that they weren't allowed to explore their connection. The affinity and the Brimstone, once loosed, were nearly impossible to restrain.

Adam's body burned. She pressed against him as close as their clothes and position allowed. It wasn't close enough. He groaned deep in his throat. She hummed in response. Her skin began to tingle wherever it touched his. She was more than willing to hold him until she burst into flame rather than let him go.

His hand moved from her stomach to trace the zipper of her jeans all the way to the juncture of her thighs. She cried out into his mouth when he found the heat he'd kindled and pressed it firmly beneath the palm of his hand.

It was an ATV rumbling along the garden pathway that broke them apart. They stood, each trying to regain their equilibrium as the gardener passed. He waved at them and Adam raised his hand in reply. Victoria stumbled down the steps to put distance between her and the damned man she craved. Her affinity ached. Her unsung song left a cold knot in her chest.

"I wanted to ask you to dinner. Only that," Adam said. He pushed one hand up into his hair and smoothed it back from his forehead. She stared at the droplets of sweat that glistened on his upper lip. She resisted the urge to step back into his arms and lick them up.

"Only dinner," Victoria said. She pressed her hands against her stomach and breathed in deep as if she was centering herself to step onto the stage.

"You'll join me?" Adam asked, sounding surprised. He stepped down the stairs, but walked a couple of paces away as if he didn't trust himself to stand near her.

She had no choice but to join him. He was back on the estate and she needed to increase her efforts to find his secret prisoners. But that justification didn't fool her affinity. It sensitized all of her nerve endings so that every touch they'd just shared replayed again and again with arcs of feeling that shook her to the core.

"Yes. I'll join you," Victoria said. She lifted her chin to face him. His gaze tracked over her from her eyes to her flushed cheeks and swollen lips to her chest that still rose and fell more deeply than it should. "For dinner. Only that."

He was far more experienced at control than she was. He no longer breathed too deeply. The Brimstone blush on his skin had already faded. The perspiration on his lip had dried. Only the swollen curve of the lower lip she'd nibbled indicated that they'd shared a passionate kiss moments before.

"Until then," Adam said. He was back to the sophisticated host who would seem completely untouchable to someone who hadn't tasted his fire.

Unfortunately, she had and those tastes only made her burn for more.

Chapter 9

She wore the red dress Sybil had secretly packed for her.

The fabric slid over her body like shimmering liquid once she'd decided to pull it from the closet. She shivered beneath its silky touch negating the idea that she'd ever intended to wear the black dress at all. The red had been sewed for her, each stitch placed to complement her curves. She was slightly bustier now than she'd been before Michael, but Sybil never missed by a millimeter.

The dress seemed to love her new figure. Her fuller bust and rounder hips seemed to suit the simple cut of the flowing skirt and soft draped bodice. She had more cleavage where the V neckline dipped. She turned full circle to survey the effect and was surprised how feminine and sultry a figure she cut in the floor-length mirror. She wanted to wear this for Adam Turov. She wanted to see his hard, angular face soften in appreciation. She wanted to see if his color heightened, if his breath quickened. For long seconds she thought of how those things might happen in an intimate setting where she might see his paler skin, untouched by the sun, become flushed from her touch. But that was getting far too carried away.

The keys were her top priority. She had to find every locked door on the estate. But she couldn't help if her imagination found Adam a locked door in many ways as well. Surely he was well beyond a mere mortal woman's reach. Yet she had seemed to reach him. Again and again. In intimate ways. He hadn't wanted to kiss her, but he had. Almost as if he couldn't help himself. She wished she could pretend there was no allure in that.

She placed the keys in a small clutch embroidered with pavé crystals. Hiding the keys in plain sight was a bold move, but the clutch complemented her sandals perfectly, both glittering against the red simplicity of her dress.

She expected one of the vineyard's ATVs to pick her up, but when she left the cottage and walked down to the pebbled drive she discovered a gleaming black vintage limousine instead. Its rounded fenders and narrow wheels looked like a vehicle that would take her to a speakeasy instead of a modern dinner. She could see her reflection in the glossy fender as she approached the liveried driver who also seemed out of a different time.

"Good evening, Ms. D'Arcy," the older man greeted her as he opened the rear door.

"Thank you," she replied as she sank down into buttery tan leather.

She'd thought Adam might be riding with her, but the backseat was hers alone. Only a fluted glass of pinot noir waited for her. The driver closed the door behind her and she reached for the glass to sip as the car smoothly pulled into the night. The tinted windows were so dark she couldn't see their route.

Would her appearance hide her true intentions as well as the tinted windows hid the world outside the car? She had to admit one of her intentions was to look attractive for Turov. Actually playing with fire—his Brimstone blood and her affinity for it—was bolder than she'd been since before Michael was born.

Her skin flushed with the idea of enjoying their attraction in spite of her mission. She could still recall with total clarity the press of his lips and his white-knuckled grip as he'd held himself back from more. It was too bold to want him to release the grip he had on his control. But imagining how it would be between them if he did caused her breath to quicken and her pulse to jump.

She had a dark mission to fulfill at Nightingale Vineyards, one that made any relationship between her and Adam Turov impossible before it even began. But he drew her. Oh, he drew her. His lips could soften…for her. His eyes could focus on her with laser intensity as the rest of the dark world fell away. His pinot noir—so rich, so rooted in heritage and heart—could ripen and sweeten when shared between their lips and tongues.

Victoria closed her eyes and swallowed the last of the glass the driver had prepared as the car slowed and came to a smooth stop. She waited for the driver to exit and walk to her door. He opened it with a flourish and offered her a gloved hand. She accepted his help more to linger over the old-fashioned procedure and slow her arrival than because she needed help. She needed a pause. She needed to catch her breath. She needed to decide if she was experiencing anticipation or dread.

"Mr. Turov is waiting for you inside," the driver said.

Victoria gathered herself and squared her shoulders. She held her clutch tight in her nervous fingers while she looked around. The car had stopped in front of a hillside slope where a massive set of double oaken doors was set into a curved semicircle wall made of stone block and concrete. Moss and grass grew on the stones, turning the wall verdant green in ever increasing patches. It was surreal to approach and take a hammered copper handle in her hand, as if she prepared to enter a fairy mound while the driver watched, stoic and still. He was another one of Adam's loyal people. Did he often deliver unsuspecting women to a fey master?

It was a fanciful thought when she knew it wasn't a fairy realm, but a hell dimension that Turov served.

The door opened easily, but she could see where a key would fit below the handle, more conscious than ever of the keys hidden in her clutch. Cool, earthy air met her as she stepped inside a long, lofted space carved out of the ground, lined with large, familiar stones. This man-made cave matched the main house down to the hammered copper fittings.

She paused as her eyes adjusted to the artificial light and as she paused her attention was drawn up, up, up where a giant chandelier made of twining branches dominated the room. It curved down from the stone ceiling glowing at each of a thousand tips in an artistic tangle of twinkling vines.

"I had it custom crafted from roots taken from some of our first vines," Adam explained. "It's a fitting reminder of our humble beginnings."

The first vines. The first roots. Victoria could only absorb the idea of a chandelier created from beautiful twisting and twining grapevine roots preserved forever with lustrous varnish that glowed brightly with a thousand tiny bulbs. She could almost imagine the elaborate fixture was still connected to plants far above that fed its light directly from the sun.

"It's perfect," she breathed.

The chandelier drew the eye from the cavernous space that once must have held hundreds of barrels of wine. Now it was a banquet space complete with a highly polished dance floor that glowed with a sheen from the light high above it.

Adam had risen from the seat at the head of a large oak table. Its surface was smoothed by generations of use, but there were only two place settings beneath the chandelier. Hers and his. She walked beneath the chandelier's glow to meet him. He watched her approach. The look in his eyes was hard to ascertain, but more than the appreciation she'd hoped for. Much more.

This place wasn't meant for a casual dinner.

This was a place meant for family and celebration, for large gatherings of loved ones full of warmth and home. Yet he'd invited her here. He moved to hold out a heavy chair that matched the table. Much used. Much loved. The plain, enduring oak was the perfect complement to the delicate complexity of the root chandelier above it.

She looked from Turov's face up to the light and back again. The glow and shadow from its coils painted his handsome face in mysterious ways. He was both young and old. Passing time was apparent in the depth of his eyes and the stone of his jaw. Even though his skin was smooth.

He was no daemon.

He wasn't immortal.

But he seemed ageless and forever beneath his vineyard roots. Too planted for someone like her to understand.

"I'm glad you came," he said.

As she sat his hand brushed her arm.

Just that. The softest, inadvertent touch and she hummed in response. Out loud. And they both froze as they burned.

"I should confess how I long to hear you sing," he said.

This time, when he touched her arm, it was on purpose, the lightest caress. The heat of it flowed down her spine to liquefy everything in her—all resistance, all caution, all intention—until nothing was left but instinctive reaction.

"I'd like to sing…for you," she replied.

It was an answering confession. One that caused him to take a step back. His retreat was a reminder that they weren't free to explore the connection urging them otherwise.

Victoria sat, far too weak in the knees to stay on her feet, and he moved to take his own seat. Though they were at a giant table, the length of it wasn't between them. Their place settings of delicate vintage china were close together. His chair on the end was only separated from hers on the side by a couple of feet.

"This is a lovely pattern," she said. She traced the familiar crimson-and-gold firebird on her plate with a trembling finger.

"Do you know the story of the Russian firebird? There are several versions. My mother's favorite was the one in which the firebird escaped a prince who had imprisoned it for greed and gold," Turov said.

He watched her closely for a reaction. Too closely.

"I've noticed the birdcages. There are several in the cottage and the main house…" Victoria trailed off.

"There are dozens upon dozens. Hundreds. All open.

All empty. My mother loved the symbolism of an empty cage," Turov explained.

"And the firebird with its flaming feathers," Victoria said, tracing the gilded scarlet tail.

"Yes. I hadn't thought of that, but all the firebird art she favored was the flaming image. The glow of the free firebird in flight," Turov said.

Victoria looked at the man beside her, at the glow of the chandelier on his face. He looked at her in the same moment and the blue of his eyes was vivid in the backlight of shadows.

"Did the firebird ever sing in the tales?" she asked.

"Burned mostly. I think singing is left to nightingales," Turov said.

Several servers interrupted then, carrying food from an anteroom she hadn't seen. Turov noticed her surprise.

"This was one of the original wine caves that we abandoned when we constructed newer ones in the '50s because of more modern construction methods and better technology for temperature control. But I'm a nostalgic man. I didn't want to give up on this first one completely. We reclaimed it as a dining hall. Although since my parents died I'm afraid it's been mostly abandoned again," Turov said.

He'd said "we" in the '50s when he shouldn't have been born. She didn't correct him. The keys she'd borrowed were on the table in her sparkling clutch in plain sight. His near immortality was also in plain sight. Neither of them acknowledged their secrets, known or unknown.

After the food was served and the servers withdrew, Adam spoke quietly while she picked at the filet mignon.

"I found a recording of one of your performances as Juliet. I enjoy it. Immensely," he said.

Her eyes moistened, but she didn't allow any tears to fall. She cleared her throat, but she could still feel the scratchy tightening that had been with her since the fire.

"I would sound very different now. My voice is changed. I'm no longer the singer I once was," she said.

"Your vocal cords may be different, but your expression, your emotion, your depth? Those would be the same," Turov argued.

Victoria forgot about keys. About daemons and monks and filet mignon. Her fork paused in the air as she looked at Adam. She could feel the truth of his words in her chest where emotion tightened and squeezed.

"There are different ways of singing. When one song is taken from us, there's always a new song. Every day," he continued.

Victoria thought about the years ahead of her. She was young. She had never made a conscious decision to never sing again. But she felt to her bones the impossibility of singing *opera* again. It was indelibly tied to her past and her loss even if she regained her singing abilities. The urge to sing she felt with Turov, her affinity to his Brimstone, was a new song, full of hope but not despair, full of possibility not tragedy. She didn't want to perform a part for him. She wanted to sing the truth from the depths of her heart.

And that's why it scared her.

She didn't understand it. She didn't know how to trust it. She was a nightingale firmly locked in the safety of its cage.

"I hope you'll sing for me one day. I burn to hear your voice live, smoky, sweet as I imagine it would be now. But even more I hope you'll sing for you. To continue to express all that you have inside. All that I can sense sitting here with you, though you don't make a sound," he said.

Victoria had gone utterly silent and still. She was afraid to breathe lest she sing. She was afraid to move lest she break out in a sultry siren's song that would break down all the protective bars of her cage.

She wasn't here to play with the affinity and his Brimstone burn. Especially when all that was at stake felt too serious to be playing at all.

"I can't," she said.

The meal carried on in silence until the servers carried the last of the barely touched food away. Adam rose and moved to pull out her chair and she stood although it brought her humming body too close to his.

They paused there. He didn't step away. He burned. She didn't sing, but she burned too. She could feel the heat coming off his lean body and wondered how his perfectly tailored suit didn't go up in flame.

Suddenly, one of the servers returned wheeling a large antique Victrola into the room. No. No. No. Not a good idea at all. Music, even music she didn't create with her own voice, couldn't be a good idea between them. But when the server started the music and the tinny sound of vintage jazz echoed from the fluted horn, she didn't resist as Adam Turov pulled her into his arms.

The man had learned to waltz a hundred years ago, give or take. His grace and style was smooth perfection in motion. But it was the controlled passion she felt in his hand on the small of her back that seduced. The ferocious grip he took of her hand, his strength contained, but still a harder grip than it should have been.

Her whole body trembled in response. Her clutch was forgotten on the table, and she allowed herself to be gathered so close that her cheek rested on his chest against the steady rhythm of his Brimstone-fueled heart.

They moved around the room beneath the chandelier in a cocoon of heated sound until everything in the room except the two of them was unimportant, an indistinct blur.

"Victoria. You're humming," Turov said. It was a warning. She could hear the strain in his voice. She could feel the tension in his body beneath her trembling hands. But she could also feel the Brimstone heat that flared in response to her barely uttered song.

The servers had disappeared. They were alone with the Brimstone and the music beneath the light of a thousand grapevine roots.

"I'm no saint, Vic. I've made denial and duty my life's work, but resisting your song is too much for even heaven to ask," Turov growled.

He stopped in the middle of the floor where patterns of shadow and light were created and cast by the chandelier above them. When she looked up, his blue eyes were bright with a fever her own body answered with a hum of need.

"What do heaven and hell have to do with us? We aren't caged. Who can dare tell the firebird not to flame and the nightingale not to sing?" Victoria whispered.

And for a second she believed it—that they were free.

Adam lifted her high toward the light and held her there. She braced her arms on his shoulders as if she would take flight, but he tilted his chin to watch her descend as he lowered her back down. She wrapped her legs around his hips and her arms around his neck and allowed herself to sink into his upturned lips.

Sweet, sweet wine so much the sweeter when shared between perspiration-moistened lips.

He cupped her silk-clad bottom to support her and met the gentle thrust of her tongue with a fierce thrust of his own. Then they hummed together, but it was a rough song of hunger and need.

She'd once loved a daemon who'd fallen from heaven to rule in hell and like the opera she'd also loved, he'd scorched most of her away until she was a vehicle of his passion and desire. She'd been a vehicle for the tragic stories she'd sung on the stage as well. Adam's was a mortal song. He burned along with her and they experienced the blaze together, supporting each other, very aware of every groan and sigh. It wasn't damnation Victoria tasted. It was a glimpse of heaven. She'd always been rootless and alone. She'd given herself to her craft because nothing else was allowed by the Order of Samuel. Then she'd been subsumed by Michael's father. In Adam's embrace, she was wholly herself for the first time. No role necessary, but more aware of roots than ever before.

But their kiss was interrupted.

Suddenly, there was another burn and it was an intrusive one. Victoria struggled to reject its pull. She cried out and Adam broke their kiss. She slid down his body and would have collapsed to the floor, but he held her until her legs firmed. She didn't pull away from the strong arm he kept around her back.

"You make a mistake coming here, Rogue. You're not welcome," Adam said.

Victoria had known it wasn't a man who had invaded the wine cave. She could feel the full force of the daemon's Brimstone heart before she turned to see him.

"She calls to me, human. And I've come for her," the daemon proclaimed.

He looked like a mortal man who had lost weeks of

sleep to a drug habit he couldn't shake. His clothes were rumpled and they hung on a body that was lean to the point of emaciation. But his red-rimmed eyes and the fiery glow in his pupils said that he wasn't weakened by his lust for Victoria's affinity. Rather, he was burned up from within by the desire to possess her as his own.

"Even a Rogue knows better than to threaten a daemon king's daughter," Adam said.

He had edged in front of her and now stood between her and the daemon who stalked restlessly in a pacing motion, back and forth across from them.

"What do you know of kings, human? You are a slave. Nothing more. I bow to no king. I answer to no slave," the daemon said.

He moved closer and Victoria pushed away from Adam, moving to the side to stand on her own. The daemon's words killed some of the pretense between her and her handsome host. Adam knew who she was and now she knew who he served. The daemon king was Adam's master. The daemon who had loved her mother and adopted her and her sister because of that love.

"You will answer to worse than a daemon king if you harm me, Rogue. The Order of Samuel will hunt you down. I am under the protection of Malachi," Victoria said.

At the name of the evil monk, the Rogue daemon and the man beside her stiffened.

"Trust me, *Malachi* is the least of your concerns if you harm this woman," Adam said.

But Victoria could feel him distance himself from her. There was only a foot between them, but it suddenly seemed an impossible chasm.

"Leave, Victoria. Now. Go back to the cottage and lock the door," Adam said.

"No," she protested. It was for her protection, but she could tell it was also a rejection. Go. Run away. There is no place for a servant of Malachi here. "Unless the lock on the cottage is sanctified I won't be any safer there."

"I can handle this daemon. Alone. Your presence will only drive him to greater madness. See how he paces? He's like an addict kept from his drug," Adam said to Victoria.

"I fear no man. Least of all men who have no souls," the daemon said. "Malachi is also a slave. A mere human seeking glory. Neither of you can stand between me and Samuel's Kiss."

Samuel had been a daemon hunter born with a natural affinity for daemons that he'd at first assumed was a call to hunt them. Later, he'd realized that daemons had as much a right to existence as humans. He'd gone against his fellow hunter, a man named Reynard, and Reynard had made a deal with Rogue daemons in order to kill Samuel. He'd sold his soul to defeat Samuel and afterward established the Order of Samuel to continue his quest for power. Reynard became Father Reynard, a self-proclaimed prophet. The Order's name was a mockery against the man who had once been his partner. Before he died, Samuel passed his affinity for daemons to a random stranger he met on a train. Victoria's grandmother was dying during a premature childbirth and Samuel gave her mouth-to-mouth resuscitation. His "kiss" not only saved her, but bequeathed his special affinity for Brimstone blood to her and her descendants.

Samuel's Kiss.

Adam was right. She'd seen daemons follow her to their death because of her affinity. Besides, the only way she could protect her son was to do as Malachi had commanded her to do. Adam didn't matter. Her desire for him didn't matter. She didn't wait to see the outcome of the fight. She moved to the table and grabbed her clutch as the daemon leaped on Adam Turov.

Abandoned caves.

Caves.

More than one.

Where better to craft a dungeon for evil monks than in an abandoned cave crafted of heavy stone beneath tons of earth? While Adam and the Rogue daemon fought, Victoria slipped outside. She paused for one look back. She swayed on shaky legs when she saw the blood and steam rising from the two writhing forms.

There was no happily-ever-after for her here with Adam and his acres and acres of roots. But maybe she could avoid the kind of tragedy she'd portrayed as Juliet again and again. If she refused to allow herself to fall in love. If she ignored the affinity and found the imprisoned monks, she could free them and Michael would have a chance for a life of no running.

He was the son of a daemon. He would always be different. And no one knew how the affinity would react when carried by a person who actually had Brimstone in his blood. But maybe there was hope for him if she could fulfill her mission.

Outside, she ran from shadow to shadow. She had no way of knowing if the daemon had traveled alone or if there were more of his fellows out in the darkness. She'd been right about the caves. Carved into the banks of the rolling hills where the limo had dropped her were multiple wine caves. The doors were mostly covered with fifty years of moss and grass. Several of the walls around the doors had deteriorated to the point of crumbling ruin as the tendrils from the greenery had eaten into the stone.

She'd hidden the firebird keys in plain sight in her pavé clutch. Had Adam invited her to dinner where he had hidden his secret prison in plain sight as well? Or were the caves all abandoned except for the dining hall?

She passed cave after cave. Three in all with entrances that had obviously been left to rot. But when she reached a fourth cave she found an entrance much like the one she'd entered to dine with Adam. The oak door was solid and firm in its frame. The stone was mossy, but not completely covered. But when she reached for the hammered copper of the door's handle she found it wouldn't budge. Not because it was faulty, but because it had been locked.

She tried key after key until she finally found the one that slid home. She had to use both hands to turn it, but when she did the latch clicked and the door loosened. She wasn't dressed for spelunking. Victoria opened the door just enough to see bright artificial light before she pulled it closed once more. Like the cave that had been renovated as a dining room, this cave had also been wired for electricity. For a more nefarious purpose? She would come back when she was better prepared to deal with what she may have found.

Suddenly, she heard approaching steps. She had just enough time to turn the key and lock the door back into place before Adam staggered into sight. She shoved the firebird key back into her clutch as her heart leaped. But she was dizzied by her heart's sudden fall as Adam collapsed to the ground.

She forgot about her mission. She put his rejection out of her mind. She hurried to his side and dropped to her knees, but the heat of his body covered in Brimstone blood drove her back.

"Dr. Verenich. Call Dr. Verenich," Adam said.

She crawled closer to better hear his voice, but an eternity seemed to pass and he said no more.

Chapter 10

The driver knew how to call Adam's doctor. He was one of Adam's loyal people as she had assumed. Victoria insisted on helping as a special fireproof blanket was pulled from the back of the limo to wrap around the unconscious man. By the time the driver took extra precautions to settle his employer into the back of the limo without setting the upholstery on fire, Victoria worried Adam was too far gone for help. His face was deathly pale. She dared to hold his head in her lap, risking burns because in the dark she couldn't ascertain where the blood was coming from as they sped back to the main house.

A man Victoria assumed was Dr. Verenich met them at the front door. At first, he had eyes only for his patient, but eventually he noticed her following.

"Ms. D'Arcy, I presume. I fear you'll be the death of him. I've never seen him so driven. He senses that his lifelong goal might be in jeopardy and with his long life that's saying something extraordinary. Come, come. I won't bar the door against you now. Too late for that," the doctor said.

They moved into the house and up the stairs. The driver carried Adam to a suite of rooms at the back of the house. Victoria would have followed with the doctor's permission or without. Adam had risked his life to protect her. Even after he knew she was working for Malachi. She wouldn't abandon him now. The monks could wait. Malachi could wait. Michael was safely hidden with Sybil and Grim.

She would help Adam. She would be with him now whether he wanted her here or not.

Her courage faltered when the doctor rolled him out of the fireproof blanket and onto a mat that had been prepared on Adam's bed. He landed facedown. His shirt and suit jacket had been mostly burned away by the Brimstone blood. The scarification on his back made her cry out in horror.

"It never gets easier to see. Such pain he must have suffered to carry the marks with him for a hundred years. The memory of Father Malachi and his whip is seared into his nightmares. Forever," Dr. Verenich said.

Victoria reached for Adam's unresponsive hand while the doctor worked. He cut away the remains of the shirt and jacket that still smoldered. He paused for only a second to note their clasped hands with an arched brow, but otherwise he focused on his patient. After he removed the clothes and let them fall in a smoking heap, he used wet towels to cleanse Adam, turning him to thoroughly saturate and wipe down his back and chest.

"The blood wasn't his. Most of the blood wasn't his," the doctor mumbled.

Victoria looked to confirm what the doctor said. Adam had nothing but superficial scratches. "The daemon. Adam was soaked in the daemon's blood," Victoria said. Relief flooded her, but along with it came a shiver of acknowledgment very like fear. Adam was a fearless warrior with decades of experience. He'd been trained by the Order of Samuel to be merciless and deadly. He'd been enslaved by a daemon king and bound by powerful Brimstone in his blood.

And he wasn't her friend.

They were destined to be enemies.

He served the daemon king and she served Malachi.

But she didn't release his hand.

"He passed out from the heat. It must have been extreme. Flowing straight from the daemon's veins. It's happened before. His body is mortal in spite of its unusual…additive. He lost consciousness as his body worked to cool itself," the doctor said. "There are only superficial wounds and they're already cauterized and healing. He'll be fine after some rest and hydration."

The doctor washed his hands and packed up the bag he hadn't had to use. Adam's ruined clothes, the protective mat and the blackened towels used to wash him were disposed of by a quiet maid.

Victoria hadn't released his hand. No matter what the doctor said, her once-vital host looked as pale as the crisp white sheets he rested against. His black wavy hair and brows were damp from the doctor's wet towels. His sculpted lips were dark against his lean cheeks.

She was struck by the sculptural lines of his face. His Slavic heritage was so apparent in his coloring and his angular bone structure. In repose, he was achingly beautiful, but when his fingers twitched around hers she looked away to avoid being caught in abject admiration. His hand immediately tightened as he sensed her shift.

"No. Stay. The cottage isn't safe. You shouldn't be alone. More daemons will come," Adam said, gruff and low. "More will come."

"Take it easy, *shef*. You need to rest. This lovely lady isn't going anywhere, although it would probably be better for you if she did," the doctor said. He paused in the doorway as if he waited for some reassurance that his patient wouldn't be disturbed, whether a daemon came and dragged her to hell or not.

Victoria settled back on the edge of the bed and allowed Adam to keep possession of her hand.

"I'll stay," she said.

"I'll leave him with you then. Call me if you need me, *shef*. You probably will, I'll wager. You probably will," the doctor said.

"Thank you, Dr. Verenich," Adam said, but he didn't open his eyes to watch the doctor leave.

Victoria was conscious of her hand in his now that he was awake, whether or not his eyes were open. Her cheeks heated. Had she really invoked Malachi's name? She wasn't a privileged loved one to sit by Adam's bed. She was his enemy. But his fingers tightened again when she tried to pull away.

"Has it always been this way? Have you always been a magnet for the damned?" Adam asked. Finally, a sliver of brilliant blue showed beneath his lush black lashes and a flush of color tinged his cheeks.

"Yes. Always. I've been a bloodhound for the Order of Samuel since before I could walk and talk. I'm drawn to the damned and they are drawn to me. We call it affinity. But you know exactly how it feels," Victoria said.

"Yes. I am intimately acquainted with how *you* feel,

but not nearly as intimately as my blood demands," Adam said. He voice was roughened by his pain. It's deep vibrations raised goose flesh on her skin.

"The music—my singing, my sister's cello playing—is an audio expression of the affinity. And it magnifies the effect," Victoria said.

"So when you hum for me…" Adam began.

"When you inspire me to sing, my affinity is magnified…strengthened," Victoria confessed.

"Together we increase your allure to others with Brimstone blood," Adam guessed.

"I'm almost certain. I can feel the amplification," Victoria said.

It was a cold and calculated way to talk about the song and the fire. Their passion physically manifested in sound and fury and they talked about it with textbook chill.

But her breath had quickened. His grip had tightened. Their bodies weren't fooled by calm discussion. Now his eyes were fully open and their vivid blue pierced her soul, delving into her and sensing her extreme attraction for him.

"I've regretted my deal with the devil many times, but not once since I met you. I'm thankful for every ember of Brimstone in my blood. I'm jealous of those who have more," Adam said.

"We can't be together," Victoria said, though their fingers had become fiercely entwined.

"No, Vic. That isn't true. There can never be an apart for us no matter the machinations of king or council," Adam said.

It seemed a vow. Her heart pounded with his promise. She recognized a tragedy in the making because she'd grown up creating tragedies for the stage.

Suddenly, before she could argue, he tugged the hand he held with surprising strength while he still reclined on the bed. Victoria fell against him and gasped as her silk-covered skin came into contact with his bare, muscular chest. He was hard and hot and no longer pale. A flush suffused his bared skin and she felt an answering rush of response when she recognized his rising color as a response to her…her nearness, her presence, her touch.

He still held the hand he'd pulled to bring her against him, but her other hand was free to splay against his chest. She gasped at his heat, at his lean, sculptured perfection. He was hard and toned beneath his sophisticated suits because he was a warrior.

She watched his eyes close in response to her on his skin.

"I asked you to stay for your safety, but I guarantee nothing if you touch me. You might be safer in the cottage after all," Adam warned. She could feel him holding himself very still as if he gave her the chance to flee.

"But you're weakened from your battle with the daemon. I'm not afraid," Victoria said. She caressed his superheated skin and spoke lightly, teasingly tracing his pectoral muscle with the pads of her fingers.

He released her other hand and quickly raised his palms to gently but firmly cup her flushed face. He held her steady and still so that their eyes would meet. She noted the varying shades of blue in his irises that gave them the vivid intensity she'd grown to crave.

"Stoicism is all I've had for decades. It's sustained me through loss and loneliness, but I burn beneath it all. I burn for you, Victoria. Be. Afraid. You're playing with Brimstone's fire and I can't promise to keep you safe from what you might kindle to life in me," Adam said.

"So you're saying I should run. That's what I do. It's

what I've always done. To survive. But running isn't living," Victoria whispered.

She leaned closer and closer to his face as she spoke and he allowed it. He gentled his hold. He relaxed his elbows. His hands cupped her face, but they didn't hold her away.

"The problem is I like it here. Right here with you. I don't want to run. I want to feel. I want to sing. I don't want to shut myself back in a cage," Victoria said.

Then she pressed her lips to his. He jerked and gasped in response, but there was nowhere for him to go. His head was cradled on his pillow, holding him in place for her soft explorations. She tasted his mouth from one corner to the other as his breath quickened, and he seemed to wait and watch to see what she would do next.

She pulled back to meet his blue gaze fully and then leaned forward again. She teased her tongue out to slip between his open lips. That's when his pause ended. His tongue met hers. He groaned and his hands slid from her face to her body, smoothing down her back to her waist then to her hips to urge her closer. He gathered her up against him and she went eagerly while their kiss deepened with gasps and dueling tongues.

She ended up straddled across his body, her silk dress rumpled and splayed until the most intimate heat of her was pressed to his bare abdomen. That sudden contact made her stop. Her entire body went rigid as every nerve ending was shocked by his superhot skin blazing against her core. Only the slightest hint of crimson lace between her legs kept them apart. She arched her back, pressing against him while he cupped her bottom. She rocked against his hard body. She could feel his erection beneath his singed trousers, rising up, proud and demanding against her heat.

"You're lucky I'm weak, *solovey*. I would have no patience to wait for your song. You would get no pleasure from how hard and fast I would claim you otherwise," Adam warned.

Victoria hummed as she moved against him, but before she could confess that hard and fast sounded very pleasurable his strong hands stilled her movements. Her dress was around her waist. Her body burned hotter than Brimstone. But he held her in place.

"Solovey?" she asked, her voice nearly as rough and low as his.

"Nightingale. My nightingale. I will make you sing. Only me. No one else. I want to hear you sing my name," Adam said.

He rolled her to the side and kissed her as she cried out in protest at the sudden separation. He whispered against her mouth and it was an erotic groan. "Let me open your cage. My *solovey*. Sing for me."

His hands pulled the folds of her silken dress from her body, carefully unwrapping the soft material from where it was wound until her lace-clad breasts and panties were revealed. She could see the appreciation for what he'd displayed in the glitter of his hooded eyes and still he didn't rush.

She hummed again and he twisted open the center clasp of her bra so the lace fell away.

"You are the song, *solovey*. You are the song," Adam murmured against her skin. He'd dipped his head and now he opened his hot mouth to suckle her bared breasts. First one and then the other. He bathed her with the heat of his mouth until her nipples were tender and distended, sending arcs of pleasure between her legs. She reached to bury her hands in the thick, damp waves of his hair, needing to hold on.

Her whole body was humming now—it was a secret heated song between them. One she should deny, but couldn't. She couldn't close the cage door against him. Not now. Maybe never again.

The heat between them flowed in a glowing aura between their bodies. She spread her legs to enjoy it, but his hand was even hotter as he brushed the last lace covering her away. Only then did she notice the steam rising from him where the doctor had moistened his skin and hair with wet towels. She watched the impossible white proof of their desire rise up into the air and dissipate around them, but then his finger found a slick entrance and her eyes closed as her hips rocked against the intimate penetration.

"Yes," he urged her humming response. "Sing for me. This is how I've longed to see you. Free with me."

With her eyes closed, she focused more fully on his mouth when he spoke against her breasts. When his lips then moved with whispery intent down, down to press beneath her navel and trail wet kisses to where his hand had claimed her, she sang out his name in higher notes than she'd hit since before the opera house fire.

He murmured his appreciation against the quivering folds of her most intimate flesh and then he pleasured her gently with a questing tongue. He lapped the bud of her clitoris as she cried out. And her song dissolved into delirious noises of release.

He hadn't claimed her with the erection she could still feel against her when he moved to hold her, but he had claimed her in ways she couldn't fully understand. He had denied himself to give to her. Even after he'd heard her claim Malachi's protection. She wrapped her arms around him and he allowed her to hold him with her palms against his "wings." The scarifications were deep ridges in his flesh, but they weren't ugly. He was wholly beautiful. In spite of his scars. In spite of his Brimstone blood. In spite of his loyalties, which worked against her.

He was already breathing the deep inhalations and exhalations of sleep. He'd slayed her with a heavenly orgasm after he killed a daemon to save her. He'd called her his nightingale. *Solovey.* Would she ever truly answer to another name? She traced his sleeping face in the darkened room. When his blue eyes were closed the whole world took on a darker hue. And that was bad.

The color had faded from his face again. His flush was gone. He looked paler than before. She should have made him rest, but it had been impossible to resist his persuasion when her affinity and his blood called to each other.

No. This wasn't safer than the cottage. Not at all. She should gather herself together and leave his rooms. She knew she still had to betray him, even though she thought she might be falling in love.

Her dress was a crumpled wreck, but she managed to put it on. Hopefully no one would see her slink from Turov's rooms back to the cottage clearing. She found her clutch with its precious contents thrown on the floor at the foot of the bed. She'd been more concerned with Adam's well-being than with her mission. She needed to go back to the cottage in order to see the dried cherry blossom reminder on her vanity. She needed to distance herself from the sleeping man on the bed.

He moaned in his sleep when she walked away. She paused, but only for a moment. Then she hardened her heart and climbed back into the cage the Order had made for her. No. More. Singing. Michael needed her to be stronger than she'd been before. She had to resist

Adam Turov for her son's sake. He might be hidden now, but she knew from personal experience that a D'Arcy couldn't hide from the Order of Samuel for long.

Chapter 11

Dawn lightened the horizon when Victoria slipped out of the main house and into the garden. Roses were heavy with dew, all their bright blooms darkened and drooping as they bowed their heads to pray for the sun.

She hurried to the cottage to change out of her conspicuous rumpled dress. The jar of dried cherry blossoms seemed to chastise her as she showered quickly and pulled on cropped pants, a T-shirt and sneakers. She twisted her damp hair up in a messy bun and grabbed a hooded sweater.

She had no idea how long Adam would sleep. She needed to take advantage of the early morning to explore and try the firebird keys in every lock she could find. The estate had been built during a time when barns, springhouses, cellars and sheds were staples. Those outbuildings still dotted the landscape of Nightingale Vineyards the way follies would have a less utilitarian property. Most of the buildings seemed abandoned now. Her instincts told her the more apparently abandoned, the better.

For instance, it wouldn't be possible to hide prisoners in the much-used utility shed where ATVs and tractors came and went with such frequency clandestine activity would be impossible.

The wine cave she'd discovered last night beckoned, but it was on the other side of the estate. The only way she could reach it quickly would be by ATV. It wouldn't be possible to borrow one of those during the day without notice. She would have to plan a trip to explore the cave later when she had more time and the added cloak of night to hide her intentions.

Victoria decided to try the pilfered keys at every building she could reach on foot while Adam was still sleeping, but she wanted to begin at the most likely. She'd already glimpsed a large gardening barn overgrown with ivy vines. The windows were completely covered and only indentions, not glass, showed where they had once been. She hurried there first, jogging down the path as if she'd gotten up before the sun to simply exercise. Once she was parallel with the building, she veered off the pebble path and sidled up to the vine-covered wall. She felt her way along the ivy until she found the entrance where an old iron handle protruded from the greenery. A rooster crowed in the distance and made her jump. She paused for only a second to calm her heart back down from her throat and then burrowed into the vines to find the keyhole beneath the iron handle.

Once she'd found where to try the keys, she dug them from her pocket. After several tries, she found a key that fit, but it took several more minutes of struggle and force to move the old tumblers that had frozen in place from lack of use.

Not promising.

If anyone was using the building, the door would have been easier to open.

She pushed the door inward anyway, forcing the tendrils of vine to stretch and break with the full weight of her body. The interior of the building was musty and obviously undisturbed. A long potting table was the only inhabitant along with the refuse from years of dead leaves and cobwebs. The webs fluttered gray and forgotten in the sudden fresh air.

Some broken pots and a few rusty tools were all that she found besides a scurrying mouse that caused her to jump as it ran away.

"My sleuthing skills need work," Victoria muttered to the mouse.

She wrenched the protesting door back into place and relocked it with additional minutes of effort. She couldn't do much about the torn vines, but she tried to arrange them so that her poking around wouldn't be discovered.

Victoria proceeded around the winding paths of the garden to a much smaller building. This one was a door set into a triangular protrusion from the ground. Nearby was a plot of earth reclaimed by grass, but she thought it had once been a vegetable garden. Slight depressions in the earth still ran in neat horizontal rows. A root cellar would have been a common feature at the turn of the century, even after refrigeration was beginning to take over.

It wasn't a great leap of logic to imagine that Adam's mother might have enjoyed growing more than grapes with her own two hands.

The tiny shed that covered the mouth of the cellar had its own curtain of vines, but not as heavy as the potting shed. There was some indication that the door had been opened. She could see where the door had scuffed the dirt beneath it somewhat recently.

The air around had begun to warm. The sun rose and the dew dried. She didn't have much time, but the disturbed earth at the base of the door and the sparse vines spurred her on.

She hurriedly tried key after key. Other birds had followed the rooster with wakefulness. Their tweets and twitters were tentative, but a full morning chorus would soon come. Finally she found the right key and the tumblers clicked, much easier to manipulate than the previous ones. She still had to jiggle the key, but though the lock was old and finicky it wasn't frozen in place.

She jerked when the latch gave way with a loud, echoing clank. The door opened outward and fell to the side when she pulled. The echo had told her she was right about the cellar before the open door revealed a stone stairway that led into a dark, dank hole in the ground. The stairs were framed by packed earthen walls.

It was only a root cellar. The kind of place gardeners stored vegetables before refrigeration made a cool hole in the ground obsolete. It would be nothing to use her cell phone's flashlight and pop down the stairs to look around. Still, Victoria's foot paused on the first green-tinged step. Not because the growth of green mold or algae tainted the air or made the stone slick, but because something inside her had sent a shiver of warning down her spine.

She couldn't blame the chill on the morning air or the cool darkness radiating up to kiss her face with damp.

In spite of her sweater, she had goose bumps on her

arms and when she forced herself forward, she could have sworn her first breath on the stairs showed in a slight, white puff from her lips.

But that was impossible. She was only anxious. Afraid of the dark and getting caught and what she might find. She was a singer, not a spy. A determined mother well out of her depth.

The light from her phone wavered in her cold fingers, but its unsteady beam revealed only more dirt as she descended deeper into the ground. The stairs were cut much deeper than she'd expected. It felt like she was on a journey to the center of the Earth, but finally she reached the polished earth floor and the large storage room that had been carved cavern-like into the ground. The room was shored up by oak beams.

How solid did oak stay after a hundred years?

Victoria shone her light on the beams, feeling like a she was in a mine shaft that might collapse at any moment. She clenched her teeth against the trembling caused as much by nerves as temperature.

She shone the beam of her light around. The cellar didn't seem to have another way out. It was a hole in the ground, lined with mostly empty bins and shelves where potatoes and onions and canned food might once have been. All that was left were a few glass jars with murky contents. She didn't explore those too closely.

The disturbed door hadn't led her to anything useful.

Victoria turned and made her way back to the stairs. She forced herself not to hurry even though the dank and dark felt threatening and spidery.

"Don't go. Not yet. We have much to discuss and I'd like to keep our meeting...discreet," a voice came from the darkness behind her, even though she'd seen the room empty seconds before. Victoria's foot froze on

the first step that would lead back up into the light. She
could see the square of daylight above her, far above
her, beckoning but out of reach.

She couldn't move. Motes of dust from decades of
moldering vegetables hung in the air suspended in front
of her face.

"I haven't agreed to any bargain with you, daemon.
Let me go," Victoria managed to say through nearly petrified lips. She recognized the pause of a daemon deal
forming in the air around her. The universe ground to a
halt when a promise was made that couldn't be broken.

"I am Ezekiel. The daemon your mother loved. I
know you'll agree to talk with me, daughter, thus the
deal is beginning to form," the daemon said.

Her affinity could detect him now. The burn of his
Brimstone blood was painful in the confined space beneath the insulating earth. She couldn't help the whim-
per of protest that escaped, but she did manage to bite
back against the others that rose in her throat. She shook
from the effort, burning and hurting and still frozen in
place.

"I'm sorry. I needed you to know I speak the truth
about who I am. But I'll spare you from the heat of my
blood now," the daemon said.

Suddenly, the pure fire of Brimstone was gone and
she was left frigid in its loss. Even though she couldn't
climb the stairs, her body could quake in the sudden
cold and it did. Her teeth chattered. Her breath came
from her lips in a fog.

"Will you speak with a daemon king, Victoria
D'Arcy?" the daemon asked, formally and loudly as if
he spoke for her and the universe to hear.

He didn't approach her. He stood with the whole
length of the storage room between them. But she was

still afraid. This daemon was so old and powerful that he could mask the burn of his Brimstone? Her sister had already met Ezekiel and had warned Victoria about his interest in their affairs. He had loved their mother. She had sacrificed herself to save him from the Order of Samuel. They had been fathered by a member of the Order who had performed his duty to provide the Order with more living, breathing daemon detectors. Their mother had been forced to marry him, but it was Ezekiel she had loved.

And he had loved her.

He had been kept very busy since with fighting against a revolution in hell, but he considered himself their stepfather.

He'd helped Katherine by giving her baby a hellhound puppy guardian when he was born. Katherine had named her son after this daemon king and Samuel who had saved their grandmother with his kiss. Her sister was happily married and reconciled with much of what they'd dealt with in their lives.

But Katherine still feared Ezekiel and she'd warned Victoria to be careful.

Daemons were not damned, but they were different, willing to face expulsion from heaven to rule themselves in the hell dimension.

But, really, what choice did she have and what harm could one conversation hold?

"Yes. I will speak with you," Victoria said. "I'll hear anything you have to say."

Her respiration stopped…for a frightening second. Life paused mocking her with what she had to lose. And then she was free to turn around and face the daemon responsible for the horrible pause that represented the sealing of the deal between them.

A conversation with the daemon king.

What could go wrong?

It was only in that second when her lungs expanded once more that she realized she'd agreed to listen without knowing what he offered in exchange.

When she turned, her cell phone light was unnecessary. The daemon king stood in an aura of ember light, his Brimstone glowing fiercely enough to light the darkness around him. Victoria lowered her phone, but she didn't tab off the flashlight app. She didn't trust Ezekiel's aura to be enough light for her too. She needed the glow in her own hands.

"You have grown into a lovely woman. And I know your beauty reaches deeper. To your heart. Like your mother's did. No wonder Michael fell in love with you," Ezekiel said.

He was a commanding presence in a plain atmosphere. The earth walls and cobwebs took nothing away from his royalty. He wouldn't have been more intimidating even if he'd been in a great castle hall on a throne.

Katherine had told her about Lucifer's wings that the Rogue Council had hacked from his body, bronzed and mounted on the wall above their council chamber. They had killed him during a rebellion fueled by the desire to claim the rule in hell, wage war on heaven and undo the choice Lucifer and his allies had made to leave heaven and rule autonomously in hell. Young Rogues who had never walked in heaven resented the loss of paradise and dreamed dark dreams of rising up to claim a higher realm.

Katherine had been instrumental in freeing Lucifer's Loyalist Army to fight the Rogues. Now Ezekiel wore Lucifer's wings as a royal mantle. They covered the scars on his shoulders where his own wings had been.

But there were other scars.

Reclaiming hell from the Council had been a bloody, ferocious conflict—a centuries-long battle, though only a few months had passed on Earth. Down Ezekiel's arms and across his hard torso were deep white slashes he'd wear forever. Another slash marked one of his lean cheeks.

Ezekiel was a king, but he was also a warrior. His claim on her and her sister felt more frightening than reassuring. Especially when her mission for the Order of Samuel was in direct opposition with his interests and desires. The Order of Samuel worked in league with the Rogue Council. They had hunted Lucifer's Loyalists almost to extinction before Katherine and her dark opera master had interfered.

"Michael sacrificed himself so that his baby could live. So that I could live. You didn't do the same for my mother. She died for you instead," Victoria said.

Ezekiel stilled. The aura around him deepened to a darker shade of red. An angry shade that shimmered with a heat she didn't feel.

"I didn't know your mother would risk her life to stand against the Order. I would have stopped her. I would have protected her," Ezekiel said.

"But you didn't and you didn't come for us either. We were left to fend for ourselves. Stalked for years by evil monks who only wanted us for our ability to help them hunt and kill. You wear your scars proudly, but we're scarred too. Deep. Where they don't show," Victoria said.

She didn't let the angry tears that stung her eyes flow. She cried only onstage when the part demanded it. She'd cried for Michael. Her beautiful fallen angel who'd still remained angelic even when he'd lost his wings. She hadn't cried since. She might never cry again.

"I was fighting for you. And to honor your mother's sacrifice. I was reclaiming a home to offer you and your sister," Ezekiel said. "And your sons."

"Hell? You're offering us a home in the hell dimension?" Victoria asked.

In spite of all she'd felt and learned about daemons, she still took a step back.

"You'll be safe from the Order of Samuel. Your son will be safe," Ezekiel said. He moved several steps closer to her and her heart pounded. He was even more different than her baby's father had been. He was obviously older and more hardened by the battles he'd fought. His eyes blazed, reddened by his aura's light. "Michael is half daemon. The hell dimension is his home. His rightful place. As Anne's grandchild—as my grandchild—to rule it one day will be his right," Ezekiel said.

It was a proclamation.

Victoria sank down onto the steps her daemon bargain wouldn't let her climb yet. Numb horror froze her even more irrevocably than her deal with the devil who offered her son a mantle made of Lucifer's wings.

"No," she whispered. She'd wanted freedom for her baby. Freedom from the Order of Samuel. Freedom from their stalking darkness. And now this. Darkness personified come to swallow them with Brimstone's fire. This was worse than affinity. Worse than evil monks. This was alien violence and awful responsibility. Blood, revolution and death.

"He's growing, and the Burn will soon be upon him. The Brimstone spark is already in his blood, but it will ignite before his third birthday. It could happen any day now. It would be better for him to be among daemons when the Burn occurs," Ezekiel warned. "We can help him contain the fire and learn to control it. His father might have helped him if he hadn't died, but a human will never be able to withstand the heat."

"Sybil is with him. She's very old. She can help him when this Burn takes place," Victoria said, but her body had turned to stone. A mother's love was no match for what challenges her half daemon son would have to face. More than she'd ever realized.

"Yes. I won't lie to you. Sybil is experienced in these matters. She probably stays with the child to watch and wait for the Burn. She would know that he shouldn't be without a daemon's support when it claims him. His blood will literally be flame in his veins," Ezekiel said. "But he would be safer in hell. From those that threaten him from without and from the blood that threatens him from within."

"His safety is my concern. My responsibility. I trust Sybil. She would have told me if we needed to ask you for help," Victoria said. But deep down, she wondered if the stoic Sybil would have voiced her concerns if she had them. "I'm done talking. I want you to leave now," Victoria said. She dragged herself to her feet, burdened with even greater purpose. Now she was working on an even tighter deadline. The full moon loomed ahead of them, but so did this mysterious Burn her son had to face.

Ezekiel's eyes had faded. They no longer glowed red. His aura was softened back to an ember glow. Like soothing firelight. She wasn't fooled. He could probably protect them from the Order if they went with him to hell, but she was determined to protect Michael herself. Here, on Earth.

"I would like you to leave us as well. This intrusion is not part of our bargain, daemon king," Adam came down the stairs as he spoke in a formal cadence she'd never heard him use before. He carried no flashlight. He boldly came down into the cellar's semidarkness as if he knew the way.

"The price of your freedom was service, Adam Turov. Do not stand between me and my grandson now," Ezekiel warned.

Victoria stood between the daemon king and the vineyard's master. She straightened her spine and squared her shoulders. Adam's presence was already warming away her former chill. Neither of them was her ally, but she knew who she would leap to aid if there was a fight.

Ezekiel noticed.

The daemon king's eyes narrowed at her sudden defensive positioning. A faint red glow began again in his flickering irises. He looked from her to the daemon-marked man behind her. The man he'd marked himself long ago.

"Our bargain has not ended, daughter. We will speak again. This conversation isn't over. You will listen as you've promised and I'll decide if our discussion should continue in hell," Ezekiel said.

Never trust a daemon. Their bargains can't be broken. Their wiles can't be bested.

She'd known this her entire life. Why had she allowed the daemon king to trick her into a bargain that might condemn her son to a childhood in an alien realm? The bargain she'd made was open-ended. She'd promised to listen to whatever he had to say even though daemons were preternaturally persuasive. She hadn't considered all the ramifications such as where the conversation would continue or for how long. She hadn't considered he might offer a throne in hell in exchange for her attention.

"There's no need for that drastic measure. I'm here. I serve you. I'll protect your grandson and your daughter," Adam said. He proclaimed it. He was trying to make a deal in her place. Victoria's breath froze in her lungs and she reached to grab Adam's arm.

But no pause came. The universe continued around them. Dust motes floated and fell. Ezekiel didn't accept Adam's offer.

The daemon king stepped forward. One pace. Then another. He was taller and harder than Adam, but the man who pulled from her hand to stand in front of her didn't flinch or cringe. He stood against a near immortal who was fully fueled by Brimstone. Not just a hint or a mark, but a furnace of hell's flame. Adam was tall and strong and honed by years of sacrifice and battle, but even with the daemon mark of Brimstone in his blood, he was only a man.

And yet he stood.

"I will talk with you again. But you of all beings must recognize the importance of autonomy. I won't be forced. I must decide for myself," Victoria said.

"And Michael?" Ezekiel asked. "Will he be allowed to choose?"

"He must have choices. Yes. When he's older he'll be free to choose. But, for now, I choose safety for him. And light. All the light I never had," Victoria said.

"I will give you time before we speak again," Ezekiel said. "But I will also give you a warning that I am king. Do not try my patience or my resolve to keep you both safe, in darkness and in light."

Adam reached for her without breaking eye contact with the daemon king. He pulled her up the stairs. They backed away from Ezekiel as if it wasn't a good idea to turn their backs. He watched them go, but he didn't follow. He did release the damper on his Brimstone burn and Victoria's affinity was seared by the passionate emotions he'd held in check. The care and concern of a daemon king stepgrandfather was another danger to Michael she hadn't known she'd have to face.

What would he do if she not only refused to follow him to hell, but aided and abetted the very Council who threatened to take his kingdom from him before he could bequeath it to her son?

Her focus was entirely on the daemon king behind her so she failed to read the burn coming off the man beside her. As Adam closed the cellar door, she continued to move away until they were several feet apart. Door closed. Feet planted. Face fully illuminated by the sun, and Victoria still stared at the cellar as if the giant Mephistopheles from Faust would burst out of it to devour them.

"Does he often just appear like that…without fanfare or warning?" she asked.

"He goes and comes as he pleases. He's a king. A daemon king. And you struck a bargain with him," Adam said.

His voice was very quiet. Too quiet. And crisp. His accent was as crisp and frigid as mountain snow. Yet she suddenly distinguished his fire from Ezekiel's as the daemon king's burn inexplicably faded away.

Adam Turov was furious. Around the edges of his vivid blue eyes a hint of red had begun to glow.

"You as well. He's the daemon that holds your soul. You serve the daemon king," Victoria said.

"Yes. I do. And I wouldn't have recommended it if you'd asked. If you'd listened to my warning and stayed with me this wouldn't have happened. I told you it wasn't safe for you to be alone," Adam said.

There was nothing safe about being forced to stay near him either. But she didn't want to bring up her hunger for his taste and touch.

"Our agreement is prisoners supplied once a month. He was here weeks early because of you," Adam said. "You can't hide from a daemon. You of all people. And once they find you they trick and trap. It's what they do. You, who have been ensnared your whole life, certainly know what that means," Adam continued.

He pressed both hands into his already mussed hair. That's when she really noticed how he'd come to find her. He'd thrown on his singed pants from last night and a stray oxford he hadn't bothered to button. His movements revealed his lean muscled chest and taut abdomen.

He was also barefoot. Better to focus on his feet rather than how badly she wanted to nuzzle his stomach the way he'd nuzzled hers.

"You know who I am," Victoria said.

"I basically work for your stepfather," Adam said. "I've served the daemon king for a hundred years, give or take. At some point, you and I were bound to run into each other."

Victoria looked hard at the rumpled and raw man whose anger over her agreement with Ezekiel could only be rooted in his concern for her. And still she tried to hold on to whatever was left of her disguise. She was a horrible spy, but the stolen keys were still in her possession.

"I came for a vacation. I had no idea it would lead to my son being offered the throne to hell," she said.

"Only a vacation," Adam said. His eyes had gone back to pure blue. He approached her and she didn't back away. The firebird keys were crammed into her back pocket and covered by the tail of her sweater.

Adam hadn't seen her unlock the door. He might think Ezekiel had opened it to lure her inside. She could still fulfill her mission. In fact, Ezekiel's threat might give her cover by distracting Adam from her intentions.

He stopped just inches from her. The heat of his body was close enough to make hers hum. She held her breath. He raised his hand to touch her face, and she met his gaze, even though it was a mistake. Suddenly, he was neither warrior, sophisticated business owner nor vintner but an inseparable blend of all three.

She couldn't see the winglike scars on his back, but she knew they were there. It changed her perception of him. She saw the memory of that pain in his eyes.

"I don't think you've vacationed a day in your life, Ms. D'Arcy. You don't have a restful bone in your body. You are emotion and movement and always poised on the verge of flight. I find myself needing to touch you just to confirm that you're here with me on the ground. And when my touch causes you to forget about flying away? That's when I taste heaven," Adam said.

He caressed her cheek, lightly, barely touching her skin with the pads of his fingers. The heat flared in her cheek and elsewhere at his allusion to the night before. A wicked smile tilted one corner of his sculpted mouth as he noticed her reaction with an intensity that had her expecting him to take up where they'd left off. Right here in the garden. Her knees turned to liquid and her breath caught in her throat. She couldn't exhale. They stood without moving except for his fingers, which traced from her cheek down to her parted lips. When he lightly teased across her bottom lip with his thumb, she finally exhaled in a quivering rush. He watched her reaction.

"We both need a vacation. A reprieve. Can you imagine the sabbatical we would make together?" he whispered.

She thought he'd replace his thumb with a kiss, but he stepped back instead. The sudden chill was torturous. Lonely and cold. Reality settled back onto her skin.

"A Rogue daemon. A daemon king. The Order of Samuel. And that's only the first weeks of your getaway. It isn't safe for you to be alone. The cottage has several rooms. I'll move in to one of them for the remainder of your stay," Adam said.

She couldn't argue. It made perfect sense. He was a warrior. She was a singer. She would be happy to have his protection if she wasn't trying to discover and sabotage his secret prison and outmaneuver an overbearing daemon king.

She was doomed.

Chapter 12

Sybil sat in front of the computer screen in a beach cottage all the way across the country in Connecticut. Victoria had already spoken to Michael as long as his toddler interest would allow and she could now hear him playing with his cars in the background. Every now and then a "Move, Gim!" could be heard as the hellhound apparently got in the way. With his massive body materialized, there would be little space for him in the cottage's living room.

"Of course I know about the Burn. As the daemon king well knows. I have handled many babies as they dealt with the moment when their spark becomes a flame. You have nothing to fear," Sybil said. "I may be a seamstress, not a nanny, but I have lived many centuries. Such a life doesn't come without basic knowledge."

"This isn't comparable to teething," Victoria said. She leaned closer to the screen to try to read Sybil's smooth face. "You're downplaying the danger. Michael isn't a daemon baby. He's a half daemon. My blood also flows in his veins. Will that affect his ability to handle the ignition?"

Sybil glanced over her shoulder and a hint of a smile tilted her lips at something that Michael had done. Victoria felt a pang when she realized she was missing a month of her young son's life.

"It's possible that the Burn will be harder for him to endure. It's also possible that it will be lessened by your blood. That the Burn will not be as strong. I'm with him every moment of every day. Grim is an even stricter nanny than I am. We watch. We wait. In all likelihood, if you were present when it occurred you wouldn't be able to help him without risking immolation," Sybil said. "I didn't want to worry you. Do what you've gone there to do. Find your voice."

"The daemon king wants Michael to join him in hell. He sees Michael as his grandson and his heir," Victoria whispered. She could hear her son laughing now. Apparently he'd decided the hellhound was more fun than the tiny toy cars.

"I have no advice for you on that score. I, myself, have chosen to stay on Earth. L'Opera Severne is my home. It's a new building, but it was built on the foundations of the old. I belong there. Perhaps Michael will have to decide where he belongs one day when he's older, when the time is right," Sybil said. "For now, you choose for him. Your intuition will guide you. You are his mother whether you are in the same room with him or a thousand miles away."

"Thank you, Sybil," Victoria said. She ignored the sting of tears in her eyes and the squeeze around her heart. The daemon seamstress who was moonlighting as a nanny turned and reached down to pick Michael up for goodbyes. The squirming toddler placed the smear of a wet kiss on the screen and when Sybil chided him he calmed and placed his hand on the screen. Victoria placed her palm against his.

"I love you," she said.

"Wuv you," he replied.

He didn't look like he had a ticking time bomb of nuclear proportions flowing in his tiny veins, but Victoria was suddenly terrified that there were too many dangers for them to face. Without his father, she could rely only on herself to make the right decisions, to do what was necessary to save him from the Order and help him transition from a baby to a child.

Long after the screen went dark, Victoria sat with her hand on the cooling glass.

The rest of the month passed in a blur. As the moon waxed so did her courage. It had to. Necessity propelled her beyond her fear. Days after her arrival, when she'd learned about the Firebird Gala, Victoria had called her sister. Katherine had sent the crimson ball gown, no questions asked. It had arrived by courier in a glossy white box and mounds of crisp tissue paper to protect the tulle and satin. Years ago, when Victoria had purchased it from a charity sale hosted by an Italian opera company, she'd not known when she'd ever wear it but she hadn't been able to resist.

Victoria lifted the dress from its bed of snowy paper. It was more vividly colored than she remembered, multihued with various shades of tulle panels in the voluminous skirt, which softened the brighter crimson, creating an ombré effect.

The brightest shade of crimson was in the satin bodice and the formfitting underskirt that flowed straight to her heels. The underskirt showed through the lighter translucent tulle as a brilliant flash when the wearer moved. Victoria held the dress up to her body. She'd known. She'd remembered the glittering gold beading on the bodice that flared over each breast like flames. She wasn't going to be a nightingale for Adam's gala. She was going to be a firebird that no prince, no matter how dark, could keep in a cage.

Adam had freed her in many ways. She'd felt passion again with his touch and his kisses. She'd even sung once more, very nearly destroying her entire mission with her song. But he wanted to keep her safe and the only way she could truly be free was to give Malachi what he wanted. To free his men and then she and Michael could be free of the Order forever.

Out of the cage.

She refused to believe that hiding in hell was the answer.

She told herself all this as she dressed even though she wasn't sure she believed it. When had she ever known the Order to be satisfied by what she gave them? They always wanted more. It might be that hiding in hell would be Michael's only refuge.

The ball gown fit a little more snuggly than it once had, but she couldn't find fault with the nipped waist and full bust she saw in the mirror when she styled her hair. She smoothed her auburn tresses into a tight chignon so that the gold feather-shaped pins she placed on either side flared like a bird's crest. Gilded feathers.

Her one concession to the clandestine activities she planned later in the night was gold satin ballet slippers, flat and practical. Her skirts swept the ground and mostly hid her shoes anyway. She could deal with the reduced height and the choice, if it was noticed, might be seen as a choice made for dancing.

In the mirror she seemed the opposite of a treacherous ninja in every way. Bold, bright, impractical. But beneath the tulle the crimson skirt had a high-cut slit for ease of movement. Her flat slippers should help her run quickly and silently when necessary. And once again the firebird keys were concealed in a small clutch, a glimmering gold one with red glass beads sewed in the shape of roses.

Not exactly girded for battle though. She didn't own a weapon. Victoria painted her lips her boldest shade of stain and then she turned away. She didn't need to look closely at the expression in her eyes. They were wide, dark, and she'd had to use concealer for the shadows. Yes. She was afraid. Tonight, she would betray a man she thought she could have loved under different circumstances. There was nothing more terrifying than that… except Malachi and Brimstone threatening her child.

That was the ice in her veins and the spur to her step as she made her way outside.

The quiet, ordinary, day-to-day operations of the winery didn't prepare her for the crowd of guests that amassed for the birthday gala. The front doors of the main house were thrown wide and a line of vehicles delivering guests to the walkway at the end of the drive stretched far into the night, all the way to the highway.

But the monthly event was well-organized so that this special yearly event only necessitated extra staff. The caterers brought in additional waiters and waitresses who flowed seamlessly from room to room with trays of sparkling champagne and pinot noir from a vintage that was only opened on Elena Turov's birthday.

In spite of the inconvenience her dress might cause later in the evening, Victoria was glad she'd worn it to honor the woman whose keys she carried in her clutch. This was the Firebird Gala. Nods to Elena's favorite fairy tale were everywhere. Crimson, gold and green blazed in all the floral arrangements and twined with fairy lights over and in all the birdcages that had been moved and artfully arranged. Victoria stopped and stared in amazement at the translucent muslin screens that had also been arranged in each room, where they hung floor to ceiling as hidden projectors beamed the illustrations from Elena's Russian fairy tale book like beautiful, ghostly memories. The firebird art was breathtaking among the flowers and cages.

And then she saw Adam Turov. Of course he would be wearing a vintage-style tuxedo complete with a pristine white vest and tie beneath a sharply cut black jacket with tails. Against the crimson and gold, his black and white shone. His hair gleamed like his coat and his narrow-tapered trousers, but it was his blue eyes in the glow of the fairy lights that stunned when his gaze fell on her.

She stopped. She breathed deeply. She continued. All in the space of seconds, but it seemed to take an eternity to reach him. She'd stood up to the daemon king, but facing Adam was harder.

"You'll dance with me?" he asked.

It could have been an order. He was royalty here. But instead he gave the words a slight lilt of an accented question on the end. It slayed her. That he would ask when dancing with him was all she ever wanted to do 'til death do them part…even if she was the cause of his death.

"Yes," she answered. Burying a forever pledge where

it belonged. Deep and unexpressed because they didn't have forever. They had a few hours before she betrayed him. Only that. It would have to be enough to last her a lifetime and him an eternity in flames.

A chamber orchestra played for the crush of dancers in the largest room in the house. Furniture had been removed and the French doors to the terrace were opened. Several couples danced out in the dark where garden lanterns were dwarfed by the full moon's light. She wasn't surprised when Adam pulled her into his arms and swept her gracefully and easily onto the terrace where they could become anonymous shadows.

She could no longer see his eyes, but she could feel his Brimstone heat. She couldn't help it. She leaned into the warmth, enjoying every degree, her own body heat rising in response.

The song the orchestra played was a familiar one. A love song from a time before she was born. No surprise that Adam's taste in music would be as long-lived as himself. But this song had stood the test of time and even she had heard it often enough to know the lyrics.

The words came easily to her lips and she sang them softly into his broad, lean shoulder for him, only for him, lyrics full of longing.

"You're torturing me on purpose. Why? Do you want me to carry you off like a barbarian? I'm a man not of this time. Don't tempt me to throw modern, civilized behavior away," Adam warned.

He was the warrior talking to her in a tuxedo disguise. She shivered in response, thrilled and also afraid. She did test his control. They couldn't be together but his desire for her was an irresistible mystery. How much did he want her? How powerful was their connection?

She whispered the lyrics against his neck, then across

his lean jaw, his cheek and into his questing mouth. His lips found hers in the dark. His tongue shushed her song, but not the deep-throated hum of pleasure their dueling tongues inspired.

He urged her deeper into the shadows with his body. She didn't resist. She also wanted the privacy of the rose-covered corner of the house. He pressed her against the wall and she welcomed the weight and pressure of his muscular form by wrapping her bare arms around his neck. His hands moved from dancing positions to grasp her waist as he deepened the kiss.

His mouth devoured her hum and the Brimstone aura only she could see with her affinity suffused them in its glow. She'd tempted him to this with her song. She'd tested his control. Now she rode the loss of it in waves of heat and pleasure. She tasted the sweet salt from Adam's upper lip on her tongue. She suckled his lower lip between her teeth.

But they weren't alone.

The music stopped and dancers came and went from the terrace. Shadows and roses weren't enough to hide them. Night air chilled and dew fell on her skin. Brimstone heat created the slightest steam as the dew evaporated away.

Adam broke away and moved his face until his lips pressed into her hair above her ear. His breath tickled the lobe and down onto her neck. Hot. Heated from their kiss and his Brimstone curse.

"You know what I must do tonight. I can't be distracted from it. The daemon king will have his due. But… Victoria…stay away. I won't let him have you too, even if it means standing against his Loyalist army. You don't belong in hell. We can't be together, but I won't allow him to urge you into darkness. You have a right to choose the light," Adam said.

His deep voice was accented by an innocent boyhood he'd left behind long ago. No one had saved him. Poor Elena. How she must have tried. Just as Victoria would try to save Michael.

"Ezekiel means only to save me. He doesn't realize I intend to save myself," Victoria said.

She gripped Adam's arms as she said it, not intending to hint at her intentions, but willing him to somehow understand.

"You don't have to fight Malachi alone. You don't have to hide from him in a hell dimension either," Adam said. "Once I fulfill my duty to the daemon king tonight, I'll help you protect Michael. I swear it on my life."

Another door had opened and suddenly they were bathed in lamplight. Adam raised a hand to cup her cheek and, self-control be damned, she leaned into the warmth. His gaze tracked over her face, but she closed her eyes before he could read the secrets that dwelled in their depths.

"Stay away. Don't make it easy for him to take you. Let me do my job. Then I can help you," Adam said.

She didn't nod. She didn't agree. She didn't lie. Someone staggered near them, probably tipsy from too much wine, and Adam stepped away. He offered the crook of his arm and she accepted. They walked back into the crowded party and he left her by a table filled with pretty desserts. She accepted a glass from a passing tray and sipped.

Adam moved away to be swallowed by the crush and the crowd, but she saw him, head and shoulders taller than the rest when he turned and looked back at her.

She was a traitor. She met his gaze. She lifted her

glass in a wordless toast. For Michael. Adam turned away and she swallowed the bitter taste of treachery that tainted her sip of wine.

A waiter passed and she placed her glass on his tray. She wouldn't pollute the rest of the lush liquid with her intentions.

Not when she had no course but to proceed.

Heart pounding, nerves not even slightly eased by the one sip of wine, Victoria followed Adam into the moonlit night.

Chapter 13

It was the first time she'd seen the garden in the full moon's light. She couldn't decide if it was a wonderland or a shadowy mazelike nightmare. All of the hedges and bushes seemed to have morphed. They danced grotesquely as bluish strings of clouds moved across the giant glowing orb in the sky—blocking, filtering and revealing the moonlight in strange ways over a nightscape of greenery that seemed to cavort as midnight approached.

Okay. So her nerves jittered beneath her skin and she was projecting that mood onto the world around her.

Victoria paused. She took a deep breath and pressed her hands into her abdomen to find the strength she always counted on at her core to carry her through a performance. She could do this. She would do this. For Michael. Her nerves settled as her hands met firm flesh. Maybe not as firm as she once was, but definitely there and solid and ready to go.

Shadows still danced caused by moonlight and clouds as she continued on, but her own jitters had eased. She lifted her skirts to aid her movement and was sure she looked like Cinderella searching for a lost glass slipper, but her heart was feeling as ninja-warrior-spy as necessary to get this job done. The firebird keys were ready in the clutch that hung from a delicate chain looped around her wrist.

Her plan was to hurry to the utility shed and hijack an ATV, then drive herself to the abandoned wine cave she'd found the night she'd had dinner with Adam. The night he'd killed a Rogue daemon to protect her. She hadn't been able to fully explore the cave that she had found to be wired for interior light, but she was certain the well-maintained doorway and the electricity weren't a coincidence.

As she traversed the garden with her skirts lifted off the dewy ground, her attention was drawn away from the utility shed in the distance. There. Off to her right toward the potting shed a soft flash of white moved in her peripheral vision. Could she have mistaken Adam's destination? When he'd left the party, she'd been certain he was on the way to the utility shed and the wine cave she'd found.

She strained her eyes to see where the flash of white had gone, but there was no other movement and the wash of moonbeams on the garden made a clear evaluation of what she might have seen impossible.

Instincts prickled where jitters had given way and Victoria decided to follow the slight tingle of affinity, urging her toward where she thought the white had been. Nothing else moved in the garden. The terrace was on the other side of the house. Here no lanterns beckoned strollers or dancers. There were no softly illuminated benches where assignations could take place. None of the vine-covered arbors were bright enough to serve as backdrops for photographs.

All was quiet when she reached the pottery shed. No light trickled between the leaves from inside. She stood indecisive for a few moments while her heartbeat calmed after her rush down the path to this spot. If she wasted more time chasing a will-o'-the-wisp in the garden, Adam may very well deliver his prisoners before she was able to set them free. But her affinity was urging her down the path in the opposite direction she'd need to go to borrow an ATV.

She'd been a spy for less than a month, but she'd known her affinity to be reliably persistent her entire life, even when she tried to ignore it.

At its urging, she hurried down the path toward the grassy former vegetable garden and the cellar she'd avoided since the daemon king had made his offer in its dusty depths. There. Again. She saw the glimmer of white. She stopped. There were ornamental bushes and trees between her and the flash of light-colored fabric. She supposed it could have been a glimpse of Adam's white shirt, but the flash had been whiter than she thought he'd been wearing.

She didn't want to run into Ezekiel in the garden as midnight approached. Her affinity worried her—she didn't feel a song bubbling up in her throat the way she did when Adam was nearby. But neither did she feel the scorch of the daemon king's fire. She made the decision to hurry forward. By the time she made it to the utility shed, impeded by her skirts, it would be too late to follow Adam to the wine caves.

When she came around the corner of the path to face the root cellar doors, she stumbled to a halt.

Elena Turov stood in the moonlight.

Daemons were real. They spoke of heaven and hell as dimensions that physically existed, not amorphous religious concepts. But encountering a long-dead woman in the eerily glowing garden as moonbeams came and went with the clouds was more than Victoria's mind could accept. For long moments they stood across from each other—both paused, both gaped, both stared. Victoria shivered because the gaze she met was empty and dark and obviously not that of a living person.

And then Elena Turov moved to the side. She didn't speak. She simply pointed at the cellar door. Her arms and hands were porcelain in the moonlight as was her face. She wore a very similar dress to the one Victoria had seen in the picture. It was as gray as if she'd stepped from the black-and-white photograph itself to take a stroll in the garden and point Victoria toward…what? The dead-end cellar where a daemon king who fancied himself her father might drag her to hell?

Victoria wasn't sure if she would have been brave or stupid enough to approach the dead woman whether time was running out or not. In the end, she didn't have to make that decision. Elena slowly faded away. Clouds passed. Light and shadow ruled in quickly alternate moments. And she was gone as if she'd never been standing there in the first place.

Victoria rushed forward. As much to check for footprints as to follow the dead woman's gesture, but when she arrived near the cellar door she found something else instead. In the dirt smoothed by the door's movement, she saw a glint in the pale light. She swept her skirts back out of the way and knelt to pick up a metal object halfway buried in the dust.

She could feel the shape of it in her palm before the

full moon bathed her in its light. A bare patch of sky had finally allowed the moon to shine unimpeded. Victoria opened her clenched fist and a brooch was revealed in the palm of her hand. It glittered darkly, but its form told Vic what colors the gems would be in the daylight—red, gold and green—because it was a firebird she held in her hand.

Victoria looked around. There was no other evidence that Elena Turov had been here. Maybe her nerves were worse than she had thought. Maybe the brooch had been dropped long ago and only uncovered now after the door had been recently disturbed. Or maybe the ghost of Adam's mother had left her a gift?

She'd also pointed Victoria toward the cellar door.

Victoria placed the brooch in the clutch and took out the keys. In the dark, she fumbled to find the one that would unlock the door, but she finally slid the right one home. Her heartbeat thumped in her ears and she admitted to herself that part of her fumbling was caused by fear that Elena Turov would return. Between her shoulder blades a cold warning seemed to skitter. She imagined Elena's porcelain fingers, icy and dead, trailing down her spine. Why would she help Victoria to betray her son? Adam Turov was bound to make this delivery of prisoners to the daemon king.

If Victoria interfered, she broke his promise to the daemon king and endangered his soul, not to mention his life, if the monks banded together to fight him.

"I'm sorry, Elena. But you understand, don't you? You understand what it's like to have the Order of Samuel take your son. You want to help me because you remember that horror," Victoria said.

But she was very glad when she was able to open the door and step out of the garden where dancing shadows now all seemed to take the shape of a woman in an old-fashioned dress—pointing with her dead arms.

Victoria paused long enough to exchange the keys for her cell phone in the clutch and then she continued down the stairs lit by its wavering beam.

"And here I am again in a dead-end hole in the ground," she said.

The time on her phone was less than an hour from midnight. Far too late to rush for the utility shed and drive to the wine caves before midnight. Her affinity had frozen during her encounter with Elena Turov, but now it tingled once more. Surely it was only a residual reaction to the former presence of the daemon king. Yet it urged her toward the back of the cellar where darkness reigned.

But it wasn't only darkness she found when she followed the urging of her affinity to the furthest corner of the root cellar. There, behind a floor-to-ceiling shelf surprisingly free of the dust that covered every other surface, she found a stirring of air. She stood in the smudged ball gown illuminated only by her flashlight app glow and felt the tendrils of hair that had escaped around her face move—ever so slightly—as an almost indistinguishable breeze touched the strands. The movement tickled and she shivered. It was a cobweb feeling. A ghostly feeling, as if someone touched her face. But she didn't cower because almost immediately she understood what the breeze meant.

Why hadn't the daemon king followed them out of the cellar that day? He was a solid being. At first she'd thought he might have powers she didn't fully understand. Maybe he could travel between dimensions without a portal or a gate. She'd thought it possible that he waited for them to leave before he'd climbed the stairs himself. But now the truth dawned on her.

The cellar had another entrance.

It didn't take her long to find the curve in the wall that led to an opening. Nothing but darkness had kept her from seeing it before. She had to feel the air moving and then position herself just right, her light shining at the right angle to reveal an opening. And not just an opening, but a tunnel that stretched into the distance.

Spelunking was not a hobby she would ever enjoy. The weight of the earth all around her and the musty scent of dirt and roots and crawling things was something to endure, not something to seek out for fun. She should be in coveralls with a miner's hat on her head. She should probably also have a sword or a gun. Or a tank. Instead she had a vintage ball gown, a ring of keys, a firebird pin and a dark path to take.

Victoria ran. The floor was packed and smooth, her flat slippers slapping against it. Her skirts billowed back from her legs. The slit in her underskirt allowed her to pump her knees high, and her clutch thumped against her hip.

As she ran, the tunnel narrowed. She didn't slow down. Soon she realized she was running through tendrils that grew out from the walls. The earth around her was no longer polished. It was alive with roots so close to her sides that they brushed her arms as she passed.

A thousand acres of roots and she ran through them to save her child.

He didn't need roots. He needed her.

She burst from the tunnel into the wine cave just before midnight. Her phone glowed with numbers that gave her hope. She had time to release the prisoners. If her luck held. Unlike the dining room cave, this cave wasn't clean and polished. The floor was littered with broken barrels and leaves. The air was as musty and dank as the root cellar she'd left behind.

But it was illuminated with electric fixtures. Naked bulbs hung from wires in the ceiling and they allowed her to see the prison cells. In long rows, cage-like cells held monks in preparation for the daemon king's arrival. Many were on their knees with their heads bowed in prayer. *Forgive me, Father, for I have sinned and I liked it?* Victoria thought. Others were holding the bars of their cell with their faces in various stages of anger and denial.

These were the warrior monks. The ones who hunted. The men who had stalked her all her life so that they could be led to the Loyalist daemons they would condemn to death and worse—eternal imprisonment by the Rogue daemons who wanted a battle with heaven. She'd seen their prison. On the walls of l'Opera Severne, a frieze seemingly carved from solid cherry had held every banished daemon in a horrible sentient stasis. They had been bound and helpless. She'd seen the father of her child on that wall. Forever separated from their love. The Loyalists had been freed from the walls by a fire that burned the opera house to the ground, but it had been too late for Michael's father. He'd used all his energy to manifest as an icy shadow to try to fight the Rogues and the Order.

After the fire, he'd been gone.

But most of the Loyalist army had survived their imprisonment. They had been freed to follow their new king, Ezekiel, and their sudden great numbers and the surprise attack had given them the advantage to finally defeat the Rogue Council and reclaim rule over the hell dimension.

She didn't want to free these evil monks.

She didn't want to help Malachi. She didn't want to betray Adam or help the Rogue daemons. And Ezekiel? Although she felt as if the daemon king had abandoned her and Katherine when they needed him most, she didn't want to work against all he'd accomplished. Michael's father would have fought for Ezekiel. He was a Loyalist through and through. He didn't want a war with heaven.

She thought of all this as she approached the cells. The monks were too disciplined to call out to her. Perhaps they could see indecisiveness in her movements. But it didn't stop her from reaching out for the first lock with the firebird keys in her hand.

"How did you know about the tunnel in the root cellar?" Adam asked.

Victoria paused with her hand on the lock. She'd yet to insert the first key. The monk looked up from his place on the floor, glancing from her to Adam and back again as he slowly rose to his feet.

"It's a long story. You wouldn't believe it. And it seems cruel to tell," she whispered. Her voice was throaty and full of emotion. She couldn't tell him about seeing his mother in the moonlight. Not on her birthday. Not when she had helped Victoria prepare to betray her son.

"Back away, Victoria. It isn't safe to get too close. They don't say much, but they're like snakes, always coiled to strike," Adam warned.

Victoria didn't need to be told. But she also wasn't sure she was finished here. Adam may be prepared to stop her, but she was pretty sure she could unlock this cage before he reached her side. The monk would attack Adam, enabling her to open other cages. There would quickly be too many monks for him to fight.

She would fulfill her mission. Adam would be badly hurt and possibly killed. The trade-off seemed impossible to make. After all, Michael was still safe. He was protected by Sybil and Grim.

"Stay back," she repeated Adam's advice back to him and inserted a key in the lock. The monk came forward another step. "That goes for both of you," she continued, glaring at the man in the cell.

"Malachi has sent you," the monk said.

Murmurs echoed the dreadful name all around the room.

Adam visibly paled. Then, in the dimly lit cave, his eyes glinted as his jaw hardened. His vivid eyes went silvery blue and then the irises gleamed with embers of red.

"You do not want to serve Malachi. He's the worst devil that ever lived outside hell. Helping him will not help your son," Adam said. "He asks this of you. Then he'll ask for more and more and more. Nothing but your blood and your son's blood will satisfy him and even then not for long," Adam warned. "Trust me. I know."

Her affinity was choking her with song while she stood in the worst moment of her life. When Michael's father had fought Father Reynard to save her, she'd been holding Michael against her chest. When the opera house burned to the ground, she'd also been holding her baby close, protecting him from the flames while she choked on the acrid smoke. Now again she had to determine the best way to protect Michael, but now there was no obvious route. She couldn't hold him close. She couldn't shield him from death and destruction with her own body and soul.

"Let the daemon king take these men to their just reward. My bargain with him is a dark one, but it serves what's right. They need to be kept from hunting. You know that. You've tried to avoid them for as long as you can remember. They have been stopped and now they must answer for what they've done and who they have served," Adam said.

He was right. He was only echoing what her own heart felt. The truth of his words thumped loudly in her chest. The monk in the cage saw her expression change. He leaped for the keys, but she was already stepping back from his frantic hands, taking Elena Turov's keys with her. She put them back in the clutch when she was far enough away from the cell to maneuver without danger.

Adam had also leaped forward, but the monk now cringed against the back of his cage. The righteous rage on Adam's face was impressive for a damned man. Victoria didn't blame the monk for cringing. Not at all. She squared her shoulders and faced Adam's anger, but just like that it faded. It wasn't for her. It had all been for the monk who had threatened her.

"I'll protect you. I don't need a bargain with Ezekiel to pledge my skills to you and to your son. And you don't need to fear this promise. There are no strings attached," Adam said.

Victoria wasn't so sure. She could feel the strings between them. Binding and twining and twisting and drawing them closer and closer together. Like tendrils of grapevine roots growing in ways she couldn't predict or understand.

How could a man with Brimstone in his blood make

a promise so pure? There was no pause. The universe didn't stop around them. The oxygen didn't freeze in her lungs. And yet it somehow did in the most mortal of ways. He took her breath, standing there beside all the evil monks he'd defeated with violence and blood. She knew it wasn't the hope of more violence that caused him to want to protect her and Michael.

He wanted to spare her son.

She didn't fall to her knees. She refused to be that weak in front of the Order's men. She stood tall and squared her shoulders in her dirty and torn firebird gown. There didn't have to be a daemon bargain between them, but she wanted to acknowledge what he'd offered.

"I accept," she said.

Lucifer's Army didn't arrive from the tunnel or from the wine cave's door. They stepped from the stacked stone walls as if the walls didn't exist. Suddenly, en masse, they came from the walls like a frieze come to life, like the one that had haunted l'Opera Severne.

"At midnight on the night of the full moon the line between our world and the hell dimension softens because of my agreement with Ezekiel. My bargain invites them in. I give them passage to come to this cave," Adam explained. "Though, as you've seen, Ezekiel is capable of abusing the parameters of our agreement."

"He used the tunnel to come and see me," Victoria said.

Adam had moved closer and she didn't mind when he stood tall and strong beside her. When the daemon king stepped from the wall, surrounded by an army of his Loyalist followers, Adam placed his hand on the bare skin above the small of her back where her dress dipped low. Her affinity burned for him and him alone.

But she suspected the daemon king buffered the lure of his Brimstone to be polite.

"I have arrived to accept your offering, Adam Turov," Ezekiel proclaimed.

"Just as promised, daemon king," Adam replied.

The daemon king walked as if the weight of the bronzed wings on his back were nothing to him. Yet she could see their weight in the carriage of his broad shoulders and in the ember of light glinting in his eyes. To the last monk, the men in the cells fell to their knees when Ezekiel passed. He did not give them a glance. There was no mercy evident in the line of his clenched jaw.

He stopped in front of Adam and Victoria.

His burning gaze followed the movement of her hand when she reached to hold Adam's arm. Adam's hand pressed into her back in response. Reassurance. Or fear?

"Am I correct in supposing that you aren't ready to return with me, daughter?" Ezekiel asked.

"We can speak another time," Victoria responded.

The army around them was unlocking the cells and claiming the condemned men. Iron manacles and chains rattled.

"I will have my hands full for some time," Ezekiel said, looking around at the silent prisoners. "But our conversation won't be put off forever. Go and collect your son. He should be here when I come again."

Her body tensed, but Adam's hand rose up to press around her waist, gathering her closer against him. She bit her tongue. Better to not directly challenge a daemon king feeling paternal.

"Continue to serve me well and you shall earn back your soul one day," Ezekiel said.

"I will," Adam replied.

It was a ceremonial exchange that must have been going on for a hundred years.

This time when the army stepped back through the walls they hauled their prisoners with them, but the transition to the hell dimension must not have been smooth for the evil monks. They had been mostly silent since she came to the cave, but when they passed through the wall, they screamed.

Dozens of screams echoed and filled the expanse of the wine cellar. And then they were cut short.

Victoria pressed her face into Adam's chest. Would the transition to hell make her baby scream?

Chapter 14

Adam had driven her back to the main house in an ATV. The warmth from his Brimstone contrasted with the numbness of her rebellion. What would Malachi do now? She was certain she'd made the right decision. Complying with Malachi's demands would have only emboldened him to demand more and more. But her open defiance might cause him to act right away to prove his dominance over her family.

She'd already texted Katherine and Sybil to warn them. Neither had responded. Sybil and Grim would have to be enough. She could think of no better nanny than the ferocious hellhound who had protected John Severne for two hundred years.

Except perhaps the silent man at her side.

"I won't bring him here," Victoria said.

"You shouldn't. Ezekiel isn't your master. You don't have to obey his commands. Leave your son in hiding. I'll take care of Malachi and the daemon king," Adam said.

The heat radiating off him had increased. Victoria tasted perspiration when she moistened her lips. Her body hummed to his Brimstone call, but his anger had an edge of scorch to it very similar to the daemon king's. In the tiny confines of the ATV, her nerves returned. This time she wasn't afraid of the unknown darkness in the garden. Her fear was clearly defined. Adam Turov's darkness was bubbling closer to the surface than she'd ever seen.

And she'd seen him behead an evil monk in his garden. She'd seen him bathed in daemon's blood. She'd seen the scars from violence he'd endured that had given him dark angel's wings.

"I was a poor Russian peasant boy. I worried about food in my belly and chores that had to be done. I wanted a better horse than the swaybacked mare we used behind the plow. I slept beneath a sweet thatched roof that still smelled of grass when it rained," Adam said. His hands were clenched on the wheel. She could always sense his emotions by his heat, but if it wasn't for the Brimstone in his blood, she could have read him by the set of his hard jaw and his hands. He always held on to something when he was beset by strong emotion. Tonight she could see white knuckles plainly even in the dim light of the dashboard.

"The Order stole my innocence. They've paid for it in blood, but they haven't paid for all the other innocent lives they interrupted without permission. They lie. They steal. They hurt, maim and kill. Your son is in good company. So many children that deserved a better life."

Victoria fingered a piece of shredded crimson tulle

in her lap. She twisted it around her finger and unwound it again and again. She ached for Adam Turov. For the boy he'd been. For the man he was now.

She also wanted to make love to him until he forgot every lash he'd ever received. It was a sudden desperate desire that had to be ignored.

"The only way Michael and my nephew, Sam, and others will be spared is to defeat the Order once and for all. They can't be held off with deals and favors. There'll always be another request. And they'll always be lurking in the shadows to take what we don't give willingly," Victoria said.

"A hundred years of experience with them tells me this is true," Adam said.

He pulled the ATV to a sudden stop in the drive near her cottage, pebbles crunching beneath its wheels. Clouds now filled the sky so that the moonlight was mostly kept from the garden. They both exited the vehicle and walked the lantern-lit path. It wasn't companionable. She couldn't deny the logic of his staying with her. She had no means to fight if monks or Rogue daemons decided to strike. And what if Loyalists came to call? There was some concern that Ezekiel would decide that he wanted to continue their chat, in hell, before dawn.

But needing protection and feeling safe in close quarters with a man who emitted waves of Brimstone heat so that her affinity throbbed with need that couldn't be indulged were two very different things.

Adam was angry. If Malachi had showed his face in the dark garden, the warrior at her side would have done more than behead him. She thought he might tear him limb from limb with his bare hands. Tuxedo or not. And it made her want to soothe him, to take away his anger and pain.

She wasn't sure where his jacket had gone. He now wore his white shirt open and tieless down to the top of his vest. His cuff links had been removed and his cuffs rolled back to reveal his muscled arms. When they arrived at the cottage, he allowed her to dig out her key and unlock the door even though she knew he must have a key on his iron ring that would undo the latch as well. She lifted her heavy skirts over the threshold and stepped into the living room, illuminated by a lamp she'd left glowing in the corner.

Adam followed her inside and she heard him close and lock the door behind them.

She hadn't expected company. She'd left a cup of cold tea on the table beside her favorite chair. There was a sweater on the floor, discarded shoes wherever she'd kicked them off and crumbs on the kitchen counter. It was his cottage, but he stood in the French country-style living room looking like a warrior in a lady's parlor.

For some reason, the effect made her heart rate increase.

His hair was mussed. His perfectly tailored clothes were in disarray. His color was heightened by his emotions and that blush of Brimstone made the rest of his skin look pale. He'd stopped several feet from the door. He closed his eyes. He took a deep breath. And then another. Victoria watched, captivated by his battle for control. Was it Malachi or Ezekiel that had stirred him so greatly? Which one infuriated him the most?

When he opened his eyes and looked at her, his chest now rising and falling at a more regular pace, she edged away toward the teacup on its pretty saucer. Tidying up seemed pointless in the face of his fury, but it gave her something to do. Maybe it wasn't Malachi or the daemon king who had him so riled. The intensity of his eyes as he looked at her said that it might just be a former opera singer with an affinity for Brimstone that drove him wild.

The teacup rattled against the saucer in her hands.

"I'm here to protect you. Not to threaten you in any way. I can't change the fact that I'm a damned man, but I'm not here to corrupt or despoil," Adam said.

"You are aware that this is the twenty-first century, right?" Victoria said. The cup and saucer in her hands were now silent and still. Her earlier thoughts of making love to him returned. "And that you're in as much danger of 'despoilment' from me as I am from you?"

"You're drawn to me because of the Brimstone and I'm captivated by your song even when you aren't singing. It's as if I hear the potential for song every time you speak. I see it in the way you move," Adam said. "But the Brimstone doesn't rule my actions. I don't allow it to."

"Protect me from Malachi and Ezekiel, by all means. But don't try to protect me from myself. I'm a big girl. I've lived with the affinity for a long time. It draws me toward beings with Brimstone blood, but I'm fairly certain I'd be drawn to you if you didn't have one speck of an ember in your heart," Victoria confessed.

If she'd taken one of his swords and stabbed it through his chest, he couldn't have looked more gutted standing there in the lamplight. He bled because of her words, but she couldn't unsay them. He'd been alone for a long time. He saw himself as damaged and damned.

Now he knew she wanted him anyway.

If he'd never sold his soul for freedom and the chance to bring his evil captors to their knees, if her grandmother D'Arcy had never experienced Samuel's Kiss… she would still want Adam Turov. His magnetism burned with natural chemistry that even Brimstone couldn't enhance.

Victoria carefully carried the cup to the kitchen and poured the old tea down the drain. Then she washed the teacup and saucer and put them on the drain board to dry. All the while she tried to ignore what Adam might be up to. He didn't stay standing in the living room. He moved around. She thought maybe he was checking all the rooms in the tiny house to be sure they had no unwanted guests. Or maybe he checked all the windows to be sure they were latched. As if you could latch a glass window against a warrior monk or a daemon.

She was fairly certain he was avoiding her.

She was also fairly certain he wouldn't refuse her if she decided to ignore damnation and affinity to come to him as a woman hungry to taste and touch.

Victoria made her way to the main bedroom. The poor firebird ball gown was ruined. She peeled it from her body and let it fall to the ground. She stepped out of what now seemed a pool of tulle flames on the floor. The bathroom became a heaven of soap and steam and water hot enough to soothe her bruises and sore muscles as she washed the dirt of the tunnel and the wine cave away.

Not once did she put Adam from her mind. In fact, she luxuriated in thoughts of what she would do to him if her conscience allowed. He had pleasured her with his mouth. She dwelled on that memory too. The heat and roughness of his tongue had taken her to an edge she'd never been to before then pushed her over into a free fall that made her forget everything else for long, lava flow moments.

He had taken nothing for himself. He'd remained on the cold, hard earth unsatisfied and alone. They weren't free to be lovers, but Adam needed to be touched and she wanted to touch him.

There might be no future for them. She was tangled in a political mess of biblical proportions and he had bartered his soul to a daemon king. Her top priority was protecting her son and ensuring his happiness without thought to her own. Adam's top priority was defeating the Order of Samuel and paying his debt to Ezekiel to free his soul. Those goals clashed at shadowy intersections Malachi controlled.

But the night had eased into a Neverland of possibilities because they were alone together. The cottage was a refuge they shared.

Victoria draped herself in a robe after her bath. She didn't bother with anything else. She'd heard the old water pipes in the walls protest as another bathroom was utilized. The sound called to her like a siren's song.

She padded out of her room and down the hall to the second bedroom. The door had been left open. She stepped over the threshold. Adam's clothes had been stripped off and lay in a path like breadcrumbs showing her the way. She followed. Past vest and shirt and pants. Past boxers and socks to the bathroom door. It, too, wasn't closed against her. He'd left it open. In invitation? Or just to be sure he heard if there was any danger?

Victoria stepped into the second bathroom cloaked in roiling steam. She walked over to the shower and leaned against the wall. The glass door of the shower stall in this smaller second bathroom wasn't opaque. It was clear and easily allowed him to see her approach. It also allowed her to see when the hot water from the tap began to bubble and evaporate off his skin.

"I couldn't knock. The door wasn't closed," Victoria said.

Adam Turov had the hard, toned muscles of a man who used his body like a war machine. Veins popped on his arms as he smoothed soap from his chest and down his stomach. Steam swirled, but she could see the evidence that he didn't mind her intrusion. Still, she needed the words. She hadn't been this bold in a long time. She'd almost forgotten how to follow where her passions led her when she was offstage.

The man in the shower reached for the glass door and slid it slowly open. She closed her eyes in response. Only for a second. Only because the glass had slightly shielded the effect he had on her. Not his Brimstone. That was throbbing and burning and making her feel faint on the spot. But *him*. He might be damned, but he was also beautiful. Tragically beautiful. Every scar. Every hot flushed inch of him. But especially the way he held himself back even though she could see he was fully aroused.

"I would never close a door against you, *solovey*. I have no soul, but my heart is yours," Adam said.

He stepped from the shower with rivulets of water running over his skin before they turned to steam and rose into the air to envelop her. She wasn't afraid to touch him. Her affinity would protect her. Still, she hissed when she did reach her hand to slide her open palm and spread fingers up and over his muscled chest to the side of his neck. She pulled him down to her mouth and he didn't resist. He tasted of minty toothpaste and wood smoke. She delved deeply with her tongue, showing him how hungry she was for him. For the rough and slick textures of his tongue and mouth.

He groaned. She hummed. His hands came up to pull her—hard—against his even harder body. She was crushed. She didn't care. Her robe slipped and Adam helped it along. She felt him tug on the belt. She heard the soft thump as it fell to the ground. And then his hands were burrowing beneath the soft material to find the even softer skin beneath.

His hands gentled. He kneaded her bottom and used the movement to press her against him. She gasped in response to the urgency of his erection against her bare stomach.

But she hadn't forgotten why she'd come to find him in the first place. He'd pleasured her while asking for nothing in return. She was inspired to do the same.

"Victoria," he said, in protest or surprise when she knelt in front of him. A plush wine-colored rug cushioned her knees.

She tilted her chin to look up at him while she took the length of him in her hands.

"There's no bargain between us. No deal. No devil. I'm a woman who wants to taste and touch you. Because you're beautiful," Victoria said. She opened her mouth and bathed the head of his penis with her tongue as she lightly suckled just the tip between her lips. "Because you're delicious."

"Solovey," Adam breathed out. He reached to thread his fingers in her hair, but he didn't direct her movements. He only touched her as if he couldn't believe she was real.

"You are my song tonight," she responded.

She took him in her mouth again and he made no coherent words for a while.

Adam had lifted her into his arms when he was finally able to move again. He lifted her and carried her into the bedroom and placed her on the bed he'd turned back in preparation for sleeping alone. He had been determined not to obey the Brimstone urging him to take her. But she'd thwarted his control. She might regret it in the morning. Although it was already morning and she didn't regret anything she'd done. She'd discovered another Adam in those moments. One very like the warrior, but he'd surrendered to her mouth. Shouting out the conquest of his control like a man willing to enjoy defeat, but only if it was a sweet one with her kneeling at his feet.

She tingled with pleasure at the memory, but Adam joined her on the bed and suckled her breast and she was suddenly swept up in the here and now. She buried her hands in his wet black hair and he rose up to meet her gaze, the intensity of his blue irises almost enough to steal her breath.

"You have unleashed me. Tell me to stop now or you will get no sleep this night," he warned.

"I would never close a door against you," Victoria teased.

Adam continued to gaze at her face as his warm hand slid up to the juncture of her thighs. She opened for him and he leaned down to lick her lips in approval while sliding his hand between her legs. She jerked. She couldn't help it. Pleasuring him had already made her more than wet and ready for his touch. He chuckled against her mouth and kissed her deeper just as he claimed her gently and firmly with his finger.

She cried out. She rocked against his thrusting hand. The pad of his thumb teased her clitoris. And once again he brought her to an edge she hadn't known she'd craved before she'd met him.

"Victoria," he urged and she opened her eyes to meet his gaze.

She reached to hold on to his broad shoulders while

she thrust her hips to meet his stroking finger. This time his vivid blue irises held her as she fell and helped her float back to Earth in his arms.

But there was something besides Adam Turov waiting when she caught her breath and her heartbeat slowed down. The naked man beside her tensed because he heard it too. A loud whine came from the living room and then the *tick-tick-tick* of hard hellhound nails pacing to and fro.

"No," Victoria said. "Please no."

She rose with a blanket draped around her and ran into the next room before Adam could stop her or urge caution.

She collapsed to her knees when she saw Grim. The hellhound was a shadow in the form of a giant dog. The tips of his fur blurred as if he'd brought smoke with him from wherever he'd been as he traveled in between. Hellhounds weren't limited to earthly pathways. They were amorphous beasts, only flesh and bone when they had reason to be.

Grim bared his teeth at the man behind her as Adam hurried into the room, fastening his pants.

"Not now, Grim. He's…it's complicated," Victoria ordered.

The hellhound was fully materialized now and as solid as he would need to be to pounce on the stranger if the situation went in that direction. His teeth were larger than she remembered, but they'd never been displayed against a man she'd been in bed with seconds before.

"If he's here, then Michael is in danger," Victoria said. Tears she'd fought for weeks filled her eyes so that she could hardly see. She kept them from falling. Barely. She rose and went for her phone that she'd left in the charger beside her laptop.

Neither flashed messages or voice mails.

"Where's Sybil, Grim? Where is Michael?" Victoria asked.

The hellhound growled and whined at the same time. The sound sent shivers of revulsion down her spine. Such an ugly sound couldn't indicate anything good at all.

When the phone rang in her hand, she tabbed the answer icon beside her sister's photograph, but she was almost afraid to put it up to her ear. Grim came to her. He pressed his hulking German shepherd–like body against her legs. His head came up to her chin. She'd seen him cushion her baby's head on his furry side.

"Sybil called us, but we got here too late. The Order has Michael. We were traveling with Cinder in response to Sybil's call and didn't get your text. They'd already taken Michael hours before you warned us that they might," Kat said.

Cinder was Sam's hellhound puppy. Much too young to safely ferry himself and his humans through the in between. It had been a dangerous and desperate action to try to save her son. *Too late. Too late. Too late.* Katherine's words echoed in her ears.

"I thought he'd be safe with Sybil and Grim," Victoria said.

A single hot tear had escaped her control. It trickled hotly down her cheek, scorching as it went.

"Malachi must have lied. He intended to take Michael all along. Whether I freed his men or not," Victoria said.

"There's a lot you haven't told us, but Cinder is going to need too much recovery time for us to come to you and I'm guessing you have no time for a long telephone conversation," Katherine said. It was unthinkable to consider sending Grim for them. He would need to return to

Michael's side as soon as possible. It was miraculous that he'd managed to come to her to seek help so far from his master. The strain on the poor hellhound was obvious in the smoking fur that swirled around him as he paced.

"I'm sorry, Kat. I'll explain everything when I can," Victoria said.

"Tell her that Malachi has sealed his fate," Adam said.

"Who is that?" Katherine asked.

"Adam Turov," Victoria replied.

"The wine guy?" Katherine guessed.

"I'll explain everything when I can," Victoria repeated. "More than a wine guy. Much more."

She tabbed the end icon and pushed Grim away. The hellhound padded away with stiff legs and haunches high. He still didn't trust the man whose Brimstone blood he could definitely detect. Nothing got past Grim. Least of all a whiff of damnation.

"I might have let the monks go. It was fifty-fifty. I almost did," Victoria said. "I would have released them and Malachi had already taken Michael."

Adam walked to her and stood behind her, as if he knew she needed her quivering spine propped up by his hard body. He placed his hands on her shoulders and held her tight until her shaking eased.

"But you didn't. You knew he couldn't be trusted. There's only one thing left to do," Adam said.

He let go of her shoulders and backed away toward the cottage door. She turned with a question on her lips, but he answered before she could express it.

"There's a journey I should have made long ago. One that might have prevented this from happening. I never wanted to return to those mountains. I never wanted to see that compound again. But if you hunt a wolf, you have to expect to follow it all the way to its lair," Adam said.

He turned to unlock and open the door and she saw his scars in the lamplight. Grim rumbled deep and low in his chest as if he reacted to the sight of them as well. She'd caressed them tonight. He was beautiful because of them, not in spite of them. He'd survived. And now he was willing to go back to that horrible place to help her son escape it.

"This time you'll have a nightingale with you," she said. She was no warrior, but nothing would keep her from going to Michael. She would fight for him in the only ways she knew how.

"It isn't a place for songs," Adam said. He sounded stark and empty, as if the decision to go back to the monk's compound had drained him of emotion. Or maybe he needed to be cold to face his darkest memory. "There's no singing there."

He spoke to the door without turning around. It was a warning, but he seemed to fear that he would succeed in scaring her away. He needed her. Her son needed her.

"I could sing for my son anywhere, even with this new, damaged voice that I've found," Victoria promised.

"I can still smell the dungeons…and the blood. You've never been surrounded by the Order of Samuel. The very air is polluted with Malachi's madness. He follows in Father Reynard's footsteps," Adam said.

He turned to look at her. His fear was gone. He stood alone, as if he always had and always would. The very name of Reynard sent a shiver of revulsion down her spine and Grim growled again, as if the dead man who had founded the Order of Samuel could come back from annihilation. He'd killed Samuel. He'd killed Michael.

But Katherine had killed him. She'd stabbed him

through his putrid heart rather than let him burn in the opera house fire. It had been more mercy than he deserved and certainly more than he'd ever showed others.

She shouldn't be surprised that his horrible legacy lived on. Not when he had brooked nothing but blind devotion and frenzied belief from his followers.

To think they'd hoped his death would finally mean freedom from the Order of Samuel. They should have known another zealot would rise to take his place.

Victoria walked to Grim's side and placed her hand on his smoky fur. She grabbed a handful of his ruff as much to root herself in the moment as to hold him. He was troubled. She could see him phasing in and out of solid existence. She could feel the trembling strength of him against her, but it came and went, as if he was having trouble staying with them when Michael was so far away. He'd come to alert her, but he was desperate to get back to his tiny master.

"Take us to him, Grim," she said. But the hellhound only whined. His body flickered between transparency and solidity. Her fingers held fur and then they held smoke. Again and again. Something was wrong. She realized the poor hellhound couldn't obey her command.

"It's okay, Grim. Go. Go find him. We'll follow as fast as we can," Victoria promised.

The hellhound disappeared in a sudden vacuum that sucked air from the room and from Victoria's lungs. She stumbled backward gasping for air.

"I have to arrange transportation. It will be a long journey. Wait here while I make preparations," Adam said. He turned back to the door, but paused with his hand on the doorknob. "I'll retrieve Michael. I swear it."

"I've fought the Order of Samuel my whole life. It's

time for me to fight them at the source," Victoria insisted.

Adam didn't reply. He twisted the knob and pulled the door open with more force than necessary, but closed it quietly behind him. The snick of its closing seemed more final than it should have.

Chapter 15

Victoria had no idea what to pack to storm a castle. She pulled her laptop from her backpack and refilled the interior with a change of clothes and a few necessities. She didn't own a battering ram or a Trojan horse. She had to hope Adam was handling that type of luggage. She probably was completely out of her depth when it came to a physical battle, but she couldn't stay away. She had to go to Michael. She had to go with Adam. He needed her. Her affinity thrummed that truth in her heart with its every beat.

She changed into dark jeans and a black T-shirt. She dug a belted leather blazer with utility pockets from the bottom of a suitcase Kat had filled with extraneous things she'd never need. She found a pair of boots and swapped them for her sneakers. She knotted her hair up tight in a thick bun.

And then she paced.

Her bulging little backpack mocked her from the chair where it waited.

When she stepped onto a stage—well-rehearsed and gifted with the natural tool of voice she needed for whatever part she played—she was never afraid. This was so different she didn't know how to handle the hyperventilation and fear except to move toward what she was most afraid of.

She waited far longer than she should have. She should have known Adam Turov believed in sacrifice more than he believed in her.

Once Adam made the decision to go after Michael all the way to the Order's compound in the mountains, his other decision was also made. Victoria D'Arcy could never be allowed to go there. The idea of her in that most corrupt of places was more than he could accept.

Hell was a better alternative.

In his rooms was a cold brazier he'd used sparingly in the past hundred years. He used it now. He inscribed the necessary words on parchment and held it over the brazier. He cut his palm deeply with a small ritual knife. When his blood dripped onto the page, smoke rose in acrid curls to creep around the room. The parchment didn't burn, but the words blazed ember bright. Adam spoke the summoning aloud while his wrist cauterized itself.

He called the daemon king.

He called him by name.

To protect Victoria D'Arcy and to lose her forever.

Victoria stopped in the middle of the cottage's living room and gasped. She pressed her hands to her stomach, but the muscles there didn't ground her. Her diaphragm didn't tighten and respond. The hum that had hovered near her lips since her first kiss with Adam was gone.

A more scorching burn had returned.

"No," Victoria protested. Sweat broke out on her forehead and trickled down her face. She tasted perspiration on her lips. "You don't get to decide how best to save me," she told Adam as if he could hear her.

She stumbled to the chair and picked up her backpack. She slung it over her shoulder and went for the door. She was not going to hide in hell while her child suffered in the hands of the Order of Samuel. And it was time to let two arrogant men know exactly what she thought of their making such a decision for her.

Adam Turov might be damned, but he had no idea what hell he'd just unleashed.

Chapter 16

She'd felt the burn of the daemon king. She wasn't surprised to find him in the great hall of the main house, but she was surprised to find him alone. She'd expected an army come to take her away.

"Adam Turov called me," Ezekiel said.

"That was not his call to make," Victoria said. "Malachi has taken Michael and I intend to go and get him back."

Ezekiel looked at her with ancient eyes.

"I regret not doing the same. I allowed myself to be too distracted by war. I should have fought for you and your sister. I never should have abandoned you," the daemon king said.

"You were fighting for us. We just didn't know. We felt more alone than we actually were," Victoria said. She couldn't help a glance at the grand staircase behind Ezekiel. Adam had to be on his way. She didn't have much time to convince her daemon stepfather that she could take care of herself.

"You are stronger than I ever imagined you would be. The song of your affinity is more powerful than you know. I am ancient. I am always. Yet it nearly brings me to my knees in your presence. Your lover doesn't understand. He wants to protect you. As I want to protect you. But, I think, you need warriors by your side. Not as your keepers," Ezekiel said.

"I've been kept since I was born. The Order has owned me. I don't want to be a possession," Victoria said.

The daemon king walked toward her and she braced herself. She had only her strength of will. She had no weapon other than her song and she didn't know how to use it against him.

But Ezekiel didn't touch her or take her. He simply stopped a foot away and reached beneath the bronzed wings on his back. Lucifer's wings gleamed in the lamplight. The knife he pulled from beneath them didn't gleam. It was dull and black and its short blade had been forged in a graceful, but deadly curve. She could see its thin, sharp edge. Its hilt was black too, but beneath the iron-like metal from which it was made glowed a fluid that flowed like molten lava.

"This is my blade. This is my blood. By rights, my blood should flow in your veins. I loved your mother. I couldn't have her. I couldn't save her. But I can give a part of myself to you in reparation for her sacrifice. This blade and my blood in exchange for my life. She gave a gift and nothing was returned. I would give this to you to seal the bargain that has remained open-ended for too long," Ezekiel said.

His words were formal. Victoria recognized the tone.

This was a daemon deal. She should turn and run far away. The daemon king's blood was a gift she should never, ever take. Yet when Adam came to the top of the stairs and started to descend, she reached for the dagger. When her fingers closed over the glowing handle, Adam paused. The whole universe paused. Her lungs stilled and dust motes hung suspended in the air. Adam was dressed in the same black tactical clothing she'd seen him in when she'd first arrived at Nightingale Vineyards. Like a dark ninja in a modern military-style uniform, his pause only allowed her to appreciate just what a threat he could be with a hundred years of experience in his muscles and his mind. Even a blade from the daemon king himself might not give her the leverage she needed to decide for herself how she would save her son if Adam decided to stand in her way. He wouldn't hold her. She wouldn't cut him. An impasse was possible.

But the power of the daemon king's knife certainly couldn't fail to tip the scales slightly in her favor.

"It is done. I am with you. Wherever you go, whatever threat you face, I am by your side. You'll never be abandoned again," Ezekiel proclaimed.

Adam heard him. The pause was over and he made his way toward them with a storm-cloud brow and Brimstone eyes.

"So you won't take her to hell where she'll be safe while I go to retrieve her son?" Adam asked.

Ezekiel's positioning changed in the blink of an eye. One second he was facing her, and the next he stood in front of the man who had summoned him. He began to circle as he spoke. Walking around Adam as Adam stood stiff and still.

"My kingdom is hers whenever she wishes it. It will be her son's when he comes of age. But it will be a gift, not a prison cell. You of all people should understand how I feel about prison cells, Adam Turov," the daemon king said. "Of course, I shall be very persuasive when the time comes for my grandson to take his place on the throne."

Victoria carefully brought the wicked blade closer and tucked it into the outer pocket of her backpack as if she was pocketing a viper. Never trust a daemon. Especially a daemon bearing gifts. The blade was going to prove more trouble than it was worth, but she would worry about that when the trouble revealed itself. For now, she had a weapon and she had foiled Adam's attempt to shelter her from the battle at hand.

It didn't matter that her heartbeat thumped in her ears when the hardened daemon king seemed to threaten Adam with his posture, with his harsh tone.

"I'm ready to go. We're wasting time," Victoria said.

She suddenly wanted Adam away from his daemon master. Ezekiel might claim to be her stepfather, but he was a being from a different realm. Daemons couldn't be trusted. The daemon king wasn't an exception to that rule. He proved it every time he drew breath. He ruled a whole hell dimension of beings who couldn't be trusted. As their king, he could be trusted least of all.

"You and I have an agreement, Adam Turov. It does not include standing in the way of Malachi's demise. The opposite, in fact. I agreed to help you bring the Order of Samuel to justice. Victoria must go. This is what her affinity sings to me. And I listen," Ezekiel said. "If you value your soul, you will help her. Not hinder her."

"Once you're there, you'll wish you had let me save you from it," Adam said. He didn't even acknowledge the powerful daemon who surveyed him so closely and carefully. He ignored Ezekiel. His focus was entirely on her.

"I sang my baby a lullaby through the flames of a collapsing portal to hell," Victoria said. "I've got this."

Adam tilted his head. It wasn't a nod of agreement or acquiescence. It was only acknowledgment that he'd been outmaneuvered by a hundred-year-old daemon deal and a mother who refused to be kept from her son. If he'd compared the power of the two, the latter would have come out on top.

He turned on his heel, never more removed from his peasant beginnings than now when he refused to bow before a daemon king in order to walk away with his shoulders squared and his head held high.

"I have been his master for a hundred years and I give you this warning…he will put your safety above his soul. It is entirely up to you if you let him," Ezekiel said.

Things would never be easy between them. It wasn't how to deal with Malachi or Ezekiel that came between them. It was the best and worst of Adam Turov himself. He wanted to protect and save. He wanted justice. But his desire to shield her threatened her worse than the Order of Samuel ever had because it warred with her desire for him to regain his soul from the daemon king's clutches.

"If it's up to me, he'll find himself in paradise one day. He's certainly earned his wings," Victoria said.

"Heaven doesn't require wings. Only complete subjugation," Ezekiel said. His smile curved up slowly on one side. "I prefer to stand."

She blinked and he was back beside her. She tensed, but he only leaned over to place a kiss on her cheek. She swore she heard her skin sizzle, but there was no pain.

"Take care, my love. You're strong, but I fear your

feelings for Adam Turov might be stronger. Don't let them sway you from your path," Ezekiel said.

He turned and walked away, gradually disintegrating from the top of his dark hair to his chest to his waist… until nothing was left but his booted feet and then they, too, disappeared.

She imagined Adam Turov had done something in his rooms to undo his summoning of the daemon king, but leave it to Ezekiel to make it look casual and voluntary. She walked over to the hall mirror and looked beneath the hand she'd placed over her cheek. Only the slightest redness remained where the daemon king's lips had brushed her skin.

Why did she feel like she was marked for eternity as his?

Chapter 17

Adam upended the brazier into the sink. He turned the water on and washed the ashes from the burned incantation down the drain. The sooner he sent the daemon king back to hell, the better. Victoria needed no more encouragement to be reckless with her life. Her son was all the inspiration necessary.

Could he blame her?

He'd never had a child. He'd only been a child, but he knew firsthand that his mother would move heaven and Earth to help him. Why else would her spirit still linger at Nightingale Vineyards except to watch over him? It must be proving a long, lonely vigil indeed.

"She's determined to go. And now the only way I can stop her is by losing any chance of redeeming my soul," Adam said to the empty room. He'd never seen his mother's spirit here. She was strongest in her beloved sitting room where he'd gathered all her earthly treasures to try to help her find some measure of peace. He hated the idea of her wandering restlessly for eternity because of him.

There was no reply. Of course. She never spoke. She rarely showed herself. He'd only seen glimpses since the one clear manifestation on the day of her death. She had appeared to him that day almost as solid as a living woman. As maternal as ever. As accepting of his damnation as ever. But also as full of hope as she'd ever been that, one day, he would see heaven.

But now he must return to hell on Earth.

"I'm going back. For her. For her son. It's time. Long past time," he said.

The room was quiet except for the drip, drip, drip of the faucet in the sink.

Adam moved across the room to retrieve his bags. One held his sword. They would take a private jet to Targu-Mures in Romania, refueling as necessary. His work required that he keep transportation on standby. It was only now, when his efficient transportation network threatened Victoria's safety, that he wished he didn't have the world at his fingertips.

She could die.

She could live with the images of that compound engraved on her heart forever.

Either was unacceptable.

His hands tightened on his bags as he left his room to meet Victoria downstairs. He'd never hated his servitude to the daemon king more than he hated it at that moment. For a hundred years all he'd cared about was bringing an end to the Order of Samuel and freeing his soul. That had changed. He now cared about something—someone—more.

* * *

They rode silently in the vintage limousine to a small airport where a private jet waited. It was already whirring loudly in the dead of night. Though by the time Victoria was gestured to board, there was a pink tinge on the horizon. Turov wealth and influence was obviously a means of speedy transport. It had only been hours since they'd learned of Michael's abduction. When they raced down the tarmac and the plane lifted into the air, the physical exhilaration of liftoff was dampened only by fear.

She wasn't afraid for herself.

Adam moved from the cockpit back to the plush seat reserved for him near hers. His seat had been modified to accommodate a larger table that had a built-in computer monitor that flipped up automatically as he sat down. Pressure sensors? Or was it cued by movement? Either way, it was a graceful display of organization and well-practiced procedure.

He knew about storming castles. Or at least he knew about hunting monks and Rogue daemons.

"Shaken martini, not stirred," Victoria mumbled. But no automated tray appeared with a calming drink for a wannabe spy with a daemon blade in her backpack.

"Could you please prepare Ms. D'Arcy a midflight cocktail?" Adam asked.

Whether he addressed the air or pressed a button she wasn't sure, but in a short while a man in a crisp uniform carried her a drink that was citrusy but not too sweet, and she sipped it gratefully while her companion focused on his monitor and keyboard.

He was still dressed in his tactical gear and she saw why when he flipped open a cuff and seemed to download maps and satellite data onto a curved monitor that was molded to his lower arm.

"Enjoy the amenities while you can. We'll only be able to go so far by plane. Once we land in Romania, we'll switch to train. Then we'll have to hike to the compound in the mountains. It's steep. And we'll have to keep up a fast pace. We can't give them time to send out a welcoming committee," Adam said.

He didn't look at her. His gaze was on the data streaming across his arm. The glow of the screen reflected on his face. But it didn't matter where he was looking—she could feel his focus on her. He'd heard her mumble about a martini. He'd noticed she was sitting on the edge of her seat instead of relaxing into it.

His attention caused her to feel even more on edge. The cabin of the plane was roomy, but confined enough to cause Adam's Brimstone blood to heat the space between them. She was worried and anxious to get to Michael as soon as possible. That heightened emotion jangling her nerve endings made her want to lean into Adam's warmth. She wanted to soak up his heat and strength to recharge her failing reserves of hope. She hadn't wanted to sing since Grim had appeared in the cottage's living room.

He didn't offer. She didn't ask. But he noticed every time she shifted in her seat or every time she sipped her drink. When it was empty, he asked the man in uniform to bring her juice and a silver tray of cheese and crackers.

He didn't try to talk her out of going to the mountain compound again.

It was a long flight. She finally allowed the soft seat to claim her whole body. She couldn't touch Adam, but she didn't try to resist the buildup of Brimstone in the cabin. His warmth lulled her to sleep. She woke briefly during a refueling stop to find a blanket had been tucked around her. From behind drooped lids, she caught Adam staring at her across the aisle. Before he realized she was awake, his face was as raw and honest as she'd ever seen it.

And he was neither warrior nor sophisticate in that moment.

Fear for her shone in his eyes. The set to his jaw was pure marble sculpted by time and desolation and determination.

She stirred, pulled the blanket closer and pretended to sleep.

The train was something out of a time that civilization had forgotten. There was car after car of worn seats that had absorbed a century's miasma of different government policies. But there were also private sleeper cars—also worn—for wealthy riders who could afford to bribe their way into a little luxury. Adam bribed. Victoria was happy to be shut away from the crowd.

But only until she realized that they were going to be on the train for hours in a much smaller space than they'd shared on the plane.

Adam left the car so that she could freshen up in private. There was a tiny sink with running water, although to call the meager trickle "running" was an overstatement. Still, she was happy to brush her teeth and wash up and have a short reprieve from Adam's magnetism— Brimstone and otherwise.

When he returned, she did the same for him. She hiked to the dining car for a very strong coffee. Unfortunately, she couldn't stop herself from mistaking every other passenger for an evil monk. In half an hour she had jumped at twenty false attacks and she retreated back the way she had come, hoping that Adam would be clothed and cooled.

He was clothed. He would never be cool. And the car seemed smaller than it had seemed before when she rejoined him.

There were two benches that faced each other near a window that looked out on the darkness of night as they passed hill and dale and all the towns and villages in between. The benches folded down into two bunk beds that came within a few inches of forming one bed. If it hadn't been for their desperate mission, she would have thought she'd found herself in a romantic comedy.

She didn't feel like laughing.

Victoria tried to breathe lightly, but her senses were filled with the sensual aroma of wood smoke and male. Even thousands of miles from his vineyard, Adam carried the scent of spice and berry from his pinot noir ever so subtly on his skin. He was sweet, smoky and salty. Total recall of the taste of his skin claimed her. She stood in the doorway, swaying with the movement of the train. And Adam looked up.

"I'd promise not to accost you, but I remember what happened last time I promised that and I'm afraid you'd think I was asking for more," Adam said.

"I'm not sure how I'd react. If you asked for more," Victoria confessed. He had called Ezekiel to try to stop her. It hadn't been Adam's decision to make even if it showed how much he cared about her safety.

"I won't ask," Adam said.

He stood and manipulated his bench into its bunk form and sank down on a travel pillow with a scratchy red blanket that had seen better decades.

It probably would have seemed a final rejection if her affinity didn't feel the burn of his Brimstone grow brighter as she took the steps necessary to fold down her own bunk and settle onto it.

"I'll die before I let them have him," Adam said.

"I know," Victoria replied.

The burn was unbearable. But her song was stuck. Wedged tight and impossible in her gut, all the notes he inspired atrophied in a hard, hot knot of impossibility. She could accept him dying to save Michael. But she couldn't accept him sacrificing his soul for her and she was afraid that was where they were headed.

Adam reached up to flick the switch, plunging them into a dark that was only slightly less black than the view outside their window.

"What if I ask, Adam? Would you hold me? Would you warm me and help me forget what might happen tomorrow?" Victoria whispered.

There were only a few inches between their bunks. Seconds after she spoke it seemed like a chasm, but then the muscular male body she craved rolled over the separation as if it was nothing.

"I serve a dark master, but he is not why I'm here with you," Adam said. "Your song is a light I can't quite touch. One that calls me away from the daemon king. I want to give you all the heat I possess. I may never regain my soul, but I sense the possibility of finding redemption in giving you all that I have left."

His kiss silenced her objections over his offer of sacrifice. She couldn't pull away from the lips she craved, and in the dark she hungrily devoured them more fiercely than she'd allowed herself to before. She sighed between deep plunges of his tongue. She reached to hold on to his shoulders and then to thread her fingers through his soft hair. When he rolled to press her under him and settle between her parted legs, she wrapped herself around him and held fistfuls of hair as their tongues twined.

The song in her chest was painfully constricted. She couldn't express it. But his kiss nibbled away at her inability. He eased her ferocity. He reached back to take her desperate hands from his hair and he pressed them down onto the bunk. He held her immobile while he gentled the kiss. She gasped and begged, but he teased her tender lips. He licked. He nipped. He suckled her lower lip. Until she followed him into a long, slow, gentle exploration of the depths of his mouth and hers. It was rough and smooth and sweet. Their mouths tasted of mint and rich coffee and smoke and all the flavors mingled together into a sensual blend that melded perfectly with intimate textures and sighs.

She panted when he broke from her lips only a few millimeters to catch his own breath. She tried to move her hands, but he held her still.

"Shh," Adam said. "Relax, *solovey*. This? I've got."

He moved against her and she moaned. She'd already removed her jacket when they entered the sleep car, but she still wore pants, a T-shirt and boots. He rocked back and away from her to reach for one of her feet in the dark. It seemed an eternity before she could exhale along with the rasp on the zipper being released down to her ankle. He pulled and tossed the boot to the floor. Then he reached for the other. All the while, she lay still and ached while his Brimstone blood grew hotter. The other zipper rasped and that boot was also pulled free and dropped on the floor. Her socks followed.

"This can only get more and more interesting if you allow it," Adam said.

"Oh, I allow. I definitely allow," Victoria said.

His hands smoothed across her stomach, under her T-shirt, and she gasped again instinctively sucking in her tummy because the air was so chilled compared to his fingers. He found the zipper of her pants more quickly, but he pulled it down centimeter by centimeter until she was breathing shallow and quick when he finally came to the zipper's end.

"I dream of your sweetness. Every night. I listen to you sing as I fall asleep and I dream of you rocking your release against my face," Adam said.

Victoria grabbed handfuls of scratchy red blanket to keep from reaching for his hair again. But she couldn't stop her hips from undulating with the memory of his tongue and he chuckled deep and low. The knot that had formed around her song in her chest loosened at the sound.

"So, so sweet. And your hum? Even sweeter. I want you to hum for me again," Adam said.

"Adam," Victoria said.

It was a breath, a sigh, but it was also a claiming. One she shouldn't allow. He wasn't hers. He would never be hers. He was a servant of the daemon king. He was a damned man and a hardened warrior through and through, but for now…she could be with him. Her song knew it. She felt it rise up to her throat.

"Yes. I'm here with you. Just you and me. The Brimstone burn and your sweet song," Adam promised.

He pulled her pants off quicker than she'd expected him to. Maybe his teasing with the zipper had frustrated him too. She was left in her T-shirt and underwear, but not for long. He hooked his fingers under her shirt and lifted it from her body. She moved with his effort to allow the material to slide easily away.

And then a cell phone light came on.

Brighter than a candle but more intimate than the overhead lamp, Adam's cell phone illuminated their bodies. He placed it on a nearby shelf beside the bunk and turned back to gaze on what he'd revealed. She didn't mind. She liked to look at him too. His hair was disheveled. His tactical outfit, which he'd covered with jacket and jeans earlier when boarding and moving around the train, was now back in play. But that meant she had no idea how to undress him. He must have seen her confusion because he rose to stand beside the bunk and with several fluid moves he had undone hidden fasteners at his neck and wrists, hips and lower legs.

But when his clothes loosened she rose up on her knees to stop him from sliding the one-piece suit down. Instead, she worked the material down and off his body following its descent with her lips and teeth and tongue. It was her turn to enjoy his gasp, his hiss, his shuddering exhale as she came to the vulnerable and sensitive dips beside his hip bones.

His penis was fully aroused when she pushed the uniform lower to reveal it. He cupped the side of her face with both hands when she leaned down to reacquaint herself with its girth and length. She measured him with her mouth and tongue. She suckled and he jerked, but he was careful. Too careful. Between her thighs a throbbing heat nearly equal to Brimstone urged less caution. *Please, please, please.*

Adam seemed to sense her need. Or maybe it mirrored his own. They had pleasured each other before, but tonight they needed more. He stepped out of the uniform and left it crumpled and forgotten on the floor. He didn't need armor with her tonight.

He stood naked in front of her, perfect for her because of his terrible scars. She wasn't an ordinary woman, so an ordinary man with an ordinary past would have been too easily consumed by the fire her affinity called.

Adam could take the heat. He was the heat. And when he reached to pull the bra from her body, the lace gave way against his strength as if it was paper. Her freed breasts drew his attention and he pressed her back on the bed by taking them in his hands. He suckled one and then the other as she fell back. Her song burst forth in humming moans and he kissed her lips as she sang his name.

Her underwear was the last impediment and Adam tore them from her legs with a snap that stung, but he soothed the sting by distracting her with the hot length of his erection. He worked himself against her moist heat and she opened for him. She reached for his back and he didn't pull away when she caressed over the ridges of his "wings." He sighed into her mouth.

"I've dreamed of this too."

He reached to help his penis find entrance, but she was so slick very little help was necessary. They joined as if their bodies had made the decision that they were meant to be together long before they allowed it. He buried himself in her and she rose to meet his thrust. Heat and song mingled so deep that it was impossible to tell where one ended and the other began.

He cried out as he plunged, shaking and quaking with the furious rise of his climax and release. She held on tight but then tumbled over the edge of her orgasm. She gasped, suddenly scared of the fall, but Adam grabbed her. He pulled her close, crushing her to his sweat-dampened chest.

He was damned. She was cursed by Samuel's Kiss. They had created a temporary heaven in each other's arms, but it couldn't last. In the end, they were just a man and a woman on a train bound for hell.

Chapter 18

Their cabin had a sink, but no bathroom. The restroom was located off the exterior hallway and was shared by all the cabins in their car and the sleep cars directly fore and aft. Glamorous. But after midnight while Adam lay sleeping, Victoria was forced by necessity to brave the amenities.

She took her backpack with her.

The daemon king's blade was warm beneath her hand even through the thick layer of the backpack's sturdy waxed canvas. It was both soothing and frightening to think of his words when he'd given the blade to her.

This is my blade. This is my blood. By rights, my blood should flow in your veins.

Her mother had loved Ezekiel. It was hard to imagine. She'd been a tiny woman. Even more petite than Victoria was herself. Her rich contralto voice had always startled the audience when it flowed richly from her breast. She'd been small but ferocious with anyone other than Father Reynard. She had feared him. She'd told them it had always been like that, but Victoria had always wondered if she had been less easy to control before they were born. Father Reynard had known exactly what he was doing when he'd forced her to become pregnant. Anne D'Arcy worried over her daughters and how they might be used by the Order. It had eaten away at her until she was a shadow of her former self by the time she'd left them. Victoria had remembered a time when her mother was curvy, with rosy cheeks and a ready smile. In the end, she'd been frail and frazzled.

But her love of the daemon king had been as strong and as passionate as ever.

It is done. I am with you. Wherever you go, whatever threat you face, I am by your side. You'll never be abandoned again.

She held the backpack close because the daemon king's blade was dangerous to others.

Never trust a daemon.

It was advice her mother had always lived by even when she loved one.

And, yet, she didn't keep the daemon blade close only because it was a dangerous object that might harm anyone who stumbled upon it. She kept it close because she'd been alone for far too long. The warmth of Brimstone came from a stepfather she'd never been allowed to know, but his strangeness didn't negate his offer of paternal affection.

He was a creature from the hell dimension. But he had loved her mother and he now offered that love to her and her sister. They'd never had family. They'd never been allowed to grow roots. Their lives had been about running. The daemon king offered his home and his Brimstone heart. It was a dark gift. One she was pretty sure they should never accept. But it was a gift all the same.

She kept the backpack close because she treasured and feared the offer at the same time.

The narrow hallway was lit by dim lights in the ceiling and skylights that showed the starry night sky far above the train. The openings were spaced far enough apart to cause swaying shadows with the movement of the train as they passed cities and towns. The doorways to all the cabins were closed, but Victoria was conscious of them as she passed, one after another. Behind any of them might lurk a monk or a Rogue daemon waiting to strike. She had never been safe from her stalkers, but this wasn't about using her affinity to hunt daemons. They hunted her now to keep her from removing her son from their clutches.

She walked down the center of the aisle directly beneath the ceiling lights, glancing from the blur of stars above to the doors on either side. Any movement above her head had to be caused by exterior lights. Even a Rogue daemon wouldn't be comfortable on the top of a speeding train. There would be no pale angry face glaring down at her. Yet she checked and checked and kept the daemon king's blade pressed close against her.

The bathroom was empty when she reached its door. She engaged the lock that would show a red occupied disk to anyone walking down the hallway. It took her only moments to use the facilities and wash her hands, but when she turned the latch and opened the door, the hallway was completely dark. All the lights had been extinguished.

She wasn't alone. Lit only by starlight and lights from the town they passed, Victoria reached inside her backpack and provided a warmer, redder glow to the ambiance. She'd drawn the daemon blade just in time as a hulking dark form rushed toward her from only a few feet away.

Victoria wasn't a warrior. But she had a warrior's heart and a warrior had given her his blood. Her affinity hadn't warned her about her attacker's presence, but it sang a cry to battle when the large man threw her against the wall.

"You defy Malachi. You work against him with one of his greatest enemies, but I've watched and waited until Turov slipped up. You're alone now. You're mine," the hooded man hissed against her ear. Relief flooded her when she realized she wouldn't have to fight a Rogue daemon. The Order of Samuel was her lifelong enemy. And one monk alone would never take her. In the garden at Nightingale Vineyards, Adam had beheaded her stalker to save her. But she didn't require his sword this time. She had her own blade.

The monk had begun to violently fumble with the fastenings to the pants she'd pulled on when she'd come in search of the bathroom. He obviously intended to rape her against the swaying wall of the train's dark corridor. The Order had always seen the D'Arcy women as vessels for their seed. No. More. She was finished being anything to them, but most of all manipulated and abused. The daemon king's blade pressed easily into the monk's black heart. He croaked in surprise and reared back, bathed in the glow of the nearest skylight full of distant stars. She must have pierced a lung as well because blood trickled from his lips as he moved them to try to speak.

"Your mistake… I'm not alone anymore," Victoria said.

She wasn't talking about Ezekiel or Adam. She

wasn't alone because she had a child to protect and care for. He wasn't physically with her, but he was always on her mind and in her heart. She would never be alone again.

Adam helped her dispose of the body once she woke him and explained what had happened. The monk had fallen faceup with his back slumped against the wall. The faded scarlet carpet with its black paisley design hid any sign of blood. She wasn't strong enough to lift and carry the monk to the connecting doors at either end of the car, but Adam easily wrapped the monk in his own robes and carried him while Victoria handled his feet. Adam kicked open the maintenance access door between cars. Air and noise buffeted against them, but they managed to drop the monk from the speeding train. Darkness ate his body. A fitting funeral for a rapist.

"You should have woken me. I would have watched the hallway while you—" Adam began.

"You could have killed him deader than I did?" Victoria interrupted. "Severed heads roll. They get blood everywhere. A small daemon blade is very discreet."

"I'm sorry I slept while you killed a man," Adam said.

Victoria took a deep breath. He understood the weight taking a life left behind.

"You're beautiful when you're sleeping. I watched you for the longest time. I wonder that the monk didn't expire from impatience waiting for me to leave our cabin," Victoria said.

"I'm going to finish the night in the hallway outside our door. Go back to the bunk and get some sleep," Adam said.

He was all business. Gone was the lover who had unzipped her pants so slowly she'd thought she'd die. The

monk had done something to put the lights out in the corridor and she was glad. She didn't want to see Adam's eyes
gone distant and cold. The fire from his Brimstone had
been banked against it. His flames burned low, merely a
flicker at the edges of her perception.

She moved to him anyway. She lifted herself on her
tiptoes and pressed her lips to his. He jerked in response,
uncrossing his arms as if he would hold her, but only
for a second before he crossed them back tighter than
before. He held himself back. His body was stiff beneath the hands she pressed to his broad chest to leverage her move.

But his Brimstone sizzled.

"I'm only a few steps away," she said.

"Close the door behind you," he said.

"You told me you'd never close a door against me,"
she reminded the muscular Russian who frowned at her
in the darkness. Starlight and ambient light from the city
outside bathed his face in alternate patches of glow and
shadow, glow and shadow. She didn't close the door. She
walked into the cabin and left it hanging wide.

Adam was the one who reached to slowly and firmly
push the door closed behind her.

A rosy glow woke Victoria. She was alone in the car.
The sun was only beginning to rise, and a very green
scene greeted her outside the window when she rose and
washed. The water was lukewarm, but it trickled in a
steadier stream than the night before. No doubt fewer
passengers were using water at the crack of dawn. She
saw evidence of Adam's ablutions. A damp towel and
water droplets on the side of the small sink. Whatever
toiletries he'd used were already packed back in his bags
that sat at the ready by the small outer door.

The mountains were majestic in the distance. As she brushed her hair before twisting it up and clipping it practically out of her face, the train brought them closer and closer to Budapest, Hungary.

Their destination was Poprad-Tatry, a city in Northern Slovakia at the base of the High Tatras Mountains. Adam had avoided the airport there, opting for a roundabout approach in order to arrive undetected. The extra time necessary for caution caused Victoria's gut to ache, but she also knew Adam was right. Their train had debarked from Romania nearly seventeen hours ago. Every minute of the long trip wasted precious time, but hopefully bought them the element of surprise.

Landing in the Poprad-Tatry Airport in the Turov private jet would have been an invitation to every monk and Rogue daemon in the region. The trains were probably routinely patrolled, but there were far more trains and passengers to oversee. They had been unlucky to run into one hunting monk. To meet an expectant army would be much harder to handle.

Adam planned to take a car to Poprad from the Budapest train station. Those three hours would be the worst. Confined in a small space with the damned man who had taken her to paradise multiple times in the night while she ached for all that might happen and all that could never be.

Years of stepping onto the stage in front of demanding audiences helped her to exit the sleeping car like a casual traveler and go in search of food and coffee. And Adam. Part of her worried that he might have somehow exited the train while she lay sleeping. That he'd decided to forfeit his soul to keep her safe in spite of Ezekiel's warning.

When she saw him seated at a small booth with a

steaming cup and a plate of scrambled eggs and sausage
in front of him, she breathed a sigh of relief. Though
her stomach ached, her chest was no longer constricted.
Adam's lovemaking had released her song. It fluttered
in her throat as she approached him. He glanced up and
then back down at the newspaper he held in his hands.

"Good morning," he said as she took the seat opposite
him in the booth. "The coffee is good. The eggs aren't."

"You didn't jump off the train," Victoria said.

A waiter in an old-fashioned white uniform brought
her a cup and poured from the stainless steel pot already
at the table. It sat on a raised edge coaster that was fas-
tened to the table so that the rocking of the train didn't
budge the hot beverage server.

"Thank you," she said to the waiter. But she looked
at Adam when she said it. He lowered the newspaper
to meet her gaze.

"I have no intention of abandoning you in Eastern
Europe, Victoria," he said.

This morning he was dressed in clothes that might
pass for relaxed traveling attire, if a person didn't notice the extra pockets and rugged material of the pants
that made his khakis more like fatigues and the rough
wool of his sweater that made it more survival gear than
fashionable.

"But you do want to protect me," she noted. She was
going to ask the waiter for a menu, but another server
was already approaching with a plate of toast points and
jam in a single-serving glass jar.

The plate was presented for her approval and she
nodded to indicate it could be placed in front of her on
the table.

"I asked them to bring you something besides eggs,"
Adam explained.

She wanted to sing to him but, instead, she spread some sort of black jam on her toast. A battle was coming. One with the Order of Samuel and one with a hundred-year-old man who thought he knew best how to protect her even if it meant sacrificing his soul. If he hadn't looked so normal and civilized, she might have climbed onto his lap and kissed him until he admitted he had every intention of keeping her out of the fight.

But she needed to mimic his calm because they were trying to travel discreetly beneath the Order's radar. Bad enough that they'd allowed the affinity and Brimstone to bubble up and boil over…repeatedly…the night before. For now, she had to bide her time and wait to counteract whatever measures he took to protect her and go for her son alone.

His concern for Michael caused her stomach to ache in unexpected ways. Michael's father had been killed before he'd ever known his son. Before she'd ever experienced what it was like to have a partner in caring for her child. Adam's determination to help Michael interfered with her equilibrium. She needed to be on guard. Instead, she just wanted to kiss him.

He reached for his cup and drank the dark, thick liquid as if it was ambrosia. For several seconds, she watched him close his eyes, lick his lips and swallow. She blinked and looked away when he opened his eyes and caught her staring. She picked up her own cup and sipped, but the brew wasn't as delicious as Adam seemed to think it was. She coughed against the strong flavor of the beans that had been ground to make it.

"This is the taste of home. My mother's coffee was just like this. We would use half a cup of sugar to make it palatable, my father and me," Adam said.

Victoria accepted the heavy porcelain container full

of sugar packets that Adam slid toward her once he set his cup down. She added one after another as he watched until she was certain that he wanted to knock her out with a blood sugar crash in order to go to the mountains alone.

"You haven't mentioned the firebird keys," she said. "I'm sorry I stole them. I never would have disturbed your mother's things if it wasn't for Michael. I thought she'd understand. Especially after...well, there was an unusual incident in the garden. Night before last when I found the tunnel to the wine cave in the root cellar. The tunnel isn't the only thing I found," Victoria continued.

Adam had placed his newspaper to the side as he drank his coffee. He cupped the white porcelain mug in his palms now. His vivid blue gaze was as bright as the cloudless sky that showed in the rectangular windows around them. More people were joining them now and her nerves bombarded her with unnecessary warnings just as they had the night before. Her gaze constantly flickered to the people entering the dining car. Were any of them dangerous? She detected no Brimstone, but in all honesty she had to admit that Adam filled her affinity and her senses. She wasn't sure anyone but the daemon king himself would have enough Brimstone power to show up on her radar with Adam so close and burning so bright after last night.

Because his casual appearance was a lie.

He was as torn and tangled beneath the surface as she was.

His Brimstone burn caused his cup to steam even though he hadn't freshened it from the pot. Her coffee had already cooled. The steam from his cup worried her, but she needed to talk to him about what she had seen.

She needed to return the firebird brooch she'd found. It had been his mother's. She was sure of it.

Victoria shifted and reached into a small pocket of her backpack. When she pulled the firebird brooch free, Adam sat straighter. His jaw hardened. His eyes glittered in the morning sunlight streaming through the window's glass. She had brought the brooch with her because it seemed disrespectful to leave it behind.

"I found this after seeing…a figure…near the entrance to the cellar that night. Almost as if someone was leaving me breadcrumbs in the way I should go," Victoria said.

Adam reached to take the brooch she offered in the outstretched palm of her hand. The ruby-and-emerald jewels of its body and tail sparkled. Its sapphire eye twinkled.

"You've seen the photograph of my mother in the hallway outside her sitting room? She wore this always. My father gave it to her shortly after we came to America. She's wearing it in that photograph," Adam said. "What you don't know is that she was buried wearing it."

Victoria's stomach dropped. Tears gathered in her eyes. She knew better than to think anyone would disturb Elena Turov's grave. Except, perhaps, the ghost of Elena herself.

"She has showed herself to me a few times. Only when there is great danger or pain. Most often she'll leave clipped roses in unexpected places. I think she's also the one who always makes sure every single birdcage is kept open. I used to close this one or that one. Just to test her presence. But that was long ago. I've accepted it now. She's tied to Nightingale Vineyards because of my damnation. I don't think she'll be free until I have regained my soul," Adam said.

Victoria watched the man across from her place his mother's colorful brooch on the table beside his coffee. His internal control had strengthened. She could feel his Brimstone burn cool. His cup no longer steamed.

"She helped me find the monks. She led me to you that night," Victoria said.

Adam looked from the brooch to the passing scenery outside. They were nearing Budapest. Bucolic scenes of pastures and hillsides had been replaced by urban sprawl.

"She would want me to save your son. I have no doubt. No matter if it meant she would be kept from peace in heaven. She understands the loss of a child. She knows the evil I've seen. She tended to my back when the wounds were fresh," Adam said.

"She lingers to watch over you. To save you. She understands my maternal feelings, but she doesn't want you to burn forever. She gives up her peace to watch and wait for you to reclaim your soul. Not for you to accept eternal damnation," Victoria said.

Adam rose. He left the brooch on the table.

"We'll be arriving at the station soon. Be ready to disembark quickly. I've already messaged ahead. There'll be a car waiting for us," he said.

Victoria rose as well. Her stomach hurt and toast points weren't going to change that. Adam was leaving the brooch because he intended to damn himself to save them. It was a final goodbye to the mother he'd never join in heaven.

"I'll stay close to you. I wouldn't want to get separated in the chaos of a busy train station," she said.

Adam turned to walk away, but Victoria took the brooch from the table and placed it in her pocket before she followed him out of the dining car.

* * *

His preparations fell into place as they always did. He had a hundred years of practice with international travel and it was common for him to travel circumspect routes to avoid being followed. Though he wasn't at his best. He was distracted. His companion's song was seductive even when she didn't utter a note out loud. It was almost like his blood could hear her sing on a subliminal level and the Brimstone responded by boiling him alive.

He led Victoria to an alley several blocks from the train station where one of his people had left a car that couldn't be traced. It was an older model white compact with no distinguishing features. His effort was divided between practiced movements and tamping down on the urge to carry the woman who followed him away from monks and daemons until they were alone as they'd been last night.

Once Victoria had settled into the passenger seat and he had smoothly inserted the car into the honking chaos of Budapest rush hour traffic, he saw dozens of similar cars winding their way between beaten-up taxis and bikes. He managed to avoid the traffic jams that were common this time of day as parents drove children to school and commuters avoided the notoriously overcrowded public transportation system.

She was silent, but constantly on alert. She seemed to watch every person in the city, including him, to judge whether they were a threat. The daemon blade was in her backpack. She clutched it close, as if she could shield the world from corrupt forces with the palms of her hand on the bag.

He wanted to take the burden of the bag from her. Instead, he ran through possible scenarios of how he could keep her from climbing the mountain as they drove out of the city. It didn't matter that it was tantamount to planning his own destruction. He pushed thoughts of his mother's spirit from his mind. She would wander. He would fall. But Victoria and her child would be safe and free. That was now his most important goal. It had surmounted his lifelong goal of destroying the Order. It trumped the importance of his very soul.

He would protect Victoria. He would save Michael.

He would accept the loss of his soul with no hope of reclaiming it.

Only that dead, hollow man could walk back into the Order's compound and survive.

Chapter 19

Poprad-Tatry was a ski resort and major holiday destination. It was a small city with under sixty thousand full-time residents. Some parts looked like a picture postcard. Some parts were less than pristine. There were landmark churches and historic houses. There were also stray dogs on the streets and obscenities shouted by lost tourists from one car to another.

Adam managed to find another quiet alley—did he have them all memorized in every city and town?—and they left the car there. He said one of his people would pick the car up before it could be found and traced back to them by the Order. Were there monks out searching for abandoned cars? Victoria suspected that Poprad was the most dangerous place they'd been. Adam said they were only an electric tram and forty-five-minute hike from the monastery and castle-like compound the monks had claimed once it was deserted by Orthodox Catholics after the revolution.

She still waited for him to betray her. She expected him to try to ditch her at every turn. But they walked several blocks to the tram station without incident. He was wearing a hoodie and loose khakis over his tactical gear. She had pulled on her jeans, boots and leather jacket with a fresh T-shirt and underwear that morning.

Though she was sure they were nondescript, she felt as if every eye in the city was on them when they bought their tickets for the electric train that would take them as far as Štrbské Pleso. She carried only a backpack. Adam left one bag in the car, but carried with him a large soft-sided case. He was casual with it even though she knew the contents were deadly. She'd seen him use his sword the first night they'd met. She'd pretended ignorance, but he'd decapitated the monk who had stalked her without compunction.

Most of the other passengers were headed for the health resort that called the last stop on the tramline home. During other, colder seasons, the tram would have been packed with tourists and skiers. Maybe the others thought she and Adam were hikers without boots or poles. Inexperienced hikers. One of whom had a face that didn't look inexperienced in the least.

"The compound is on the dark side of the mountain where it's craggy and almost impossible to climb. There are switchbacks and rock slides only the initiates and monks know how to traverse. They exist in plain sight as a religious order too small and insignificant to be visited. Monks often avoid the tram altogether. Children are brought in at night and they're often secreted away in shipments of supplies that are carried up the mountain by strings of mules," Adam said. "I remember that long, cold journey."

Victoria touched his arm. It was the first time she'd

touched him since they'd made love on the train. He looked down at her as if startled from a memory that weighed heavily on him in spite of all the time that had passed.

"You can wait at the resort for me to return," Adam said.

"I'm coming with you," Victoria replied.

They exited the tram and moved with the flow of foot traffic until Adam took her arm and pulled her to the side where a narrow path allowed maintenance personnel to access the electrical workings that powered the trams up and down the mountain. He could have easily slipped away without her, but he probably knew she would try to follow.

He didn't release her. Instead, he allowed his hand to slide down her arm and take her hand. They walked for a half an hour in the opposite direction of the resort. The mountain was green and pink where grass and wildflowers converged in a brilliant, lush landscape dotted by patches of boulders, which made footing rough and dangerous. In the distance, she could see the glacier lake and groups of hikers and tourists. Surreal to think her young son was in such desperate danger on the other side of the mountain from this lovely, peaceful setting.

They came to a small building that leaned from decades of breezes and snowfalls on its steeply pitched roof.

"We'll stay here tonight. It won't be safe to challenge the mountain pass in the dark," Adam explained.

Victoria followed him into the tiny cabin. The romance of the train was lost. They were too close to the compound to escape in each other's arms. But that didn't negate the Brimstone and the affinity that drew them closer and closer together, even when evil tried to keep them apart.

* * *

The cabin was clean and neat inside and furnished with sturdy wooden furniture that seemed as old as the walls themselves. On a plain oak table in the middle of the room, someone had left a box of supplies.

"Your people?" Victoria asked. The anonymous, invisible people Adam employed around the world were really no laughing matter. He'd had decades to build a network of loyal employees who were obviously ready at a moment's notice to aid him.

"My most loyal person. He's seventy-five and he was once a novitiate. I helped him. So now he helps me and he agrees to stay this close to that accursed place that almost devoured him," Adam said.

He had placed his bag near the bed in the corner. Set into the front wall was a small fireplace already laid with materials for a fire to keep the chill of the night away.

Victoria had stopped mid-rummage through the box hoping for chocolate and wine. She turned slowly to look at Adam although he had busied himself with removing his jacket after he had spoken.

"Your people are all the children you've saved from the Order through the years. Esther, Gideon…your chauffeur, the person who provided us with the car, the pilot of the plane. Gideon told me you'd given him the sun. They've grown up free and they help you because you helped them. Nothing to do with daemons and hell's politics. You saved them. Again and again," Victoria said.

He was uncomfortable with her realization and busied himself by lifting his bag onto the bed and opening it. He pulled a sword sheath from it and turned to lay it on the table beside the supplies.

"How many have you saved? How many people…

all over the world…are alive and well and living mostly normal lives because of you?" Victoria asked. She came to his side to ask it. She placed herself in front of him so he couldn't ignore her question.

Adam looked down at her. Stoic as ever but burning brightly inside. So brightly that he lit the universe—but with a dark, dark flame.

"I haven't kept count, Victoria. There are many. Men and women who were boys and girls who didn't have to sell their soul to escape the Order's clutches," he said. "I help them to disappear so that the Order can't hunt them down once they've escaped."

His vivid eyes gleamed in the light of the one small gas lantern he'd lit when they'd first come in the door.

"This time you'll free Michael. And one day he'll get a call from you for a car or a box of supplies or whatever you might need. He'll provide it. But I'll be the one who is eternally grateful," Victoria said. "And you probably won't call on me at all."

She turned away from the emotion that created blue diamonds in his eyes. Her own burned. The knot of song in her chest had hardened again. Unsung.

"I'm not staying behind. I don't care if you're the expert. I'm the mom. And I go too," she said without facing him again. She focused on the box of supplies and forced her tears back to the unshed place they belonged.

Adam came to her. He stood close behind her as she unpacked a large insulated thermos, a container of fruit slices, and another of cheese and crackers. There was also a carafe, cups, spoons and bowls. Adam's person in Štrbské Pleso had packed them a hardy picnic.

"I haven't managed to save them all, Victoria. You should know that. I've failed before. The first was a boy named Thomas. We were novitiates together. I tried to help him, but he grew weak and sick. I waited too late to try to get him out of the compound. There had been so much snow that winter. It took too long to melt. My only consolation is that he died free beneath a blue sky in a patch of wildflowers," Adam confessed.

He reached for the thermos and opened its lid. Aromatic potato soup filled the air with the scent of pepper, onions and cream. Victoria breathed deeply of the comforting smell to try to fortify herself against the lingering loss and despair her companion suffered.

"You must have been very young yourself," she said as she set the table with bowls and spoons. There had also been linen napkins in the box and she placed those beside each setting. She placed the containers with fruit, cheese and crackers in between and Adam poured steaming soup into the bowls.

"By that time I was a young teen. I'd been a prisoner for seven years. I'd seen others weaken and die. I'd seen some die from beatings or from training battles intentionally brutal to weed out the frail and promote the strong. Only the ruthless survive. I was as ruthless as I had to be. You understand? I was not able to abstain or refuse. I maimed. I killed. I was bathed daily in blood. My own. And that of others," Adam said.

He sat on one of the sturdy plain chairs. He picked up his spoon and bowed his head over his soup as if he prayed, but his white knuckles led her to believe that if he did pray it was not over the meal, but for the ability to punish and stop the monks who had tortured him and others for so many years.

"Father Reynard never took no for an answer. My mother, my sister and I led him to many Loyalist daemons over the years. We tried to resist. We tried to drown out their call with music. We didn't realize that the music was actually part of our affinity. A means of expressing the magnetism we experienced with Brimstone blood, especially when we tried not to answer its call," Victoria said quietly. They both dipped their spoons, blew on the thick soup to cool it and then swallowed. Bite after bite. It was soothing as well as necessary to fuel their hike the next day. The meal had been provided by a man Adam Turov had saved from the Order of Samuel. His gratitude made the soup even more delicious and eating it a profound experience. Now a thousand gestures and words from the cook at Nightingale Vineyards made sense. The lovely scarred woman served Adam as if it was a sacred responsibility to care for him because he had freed her from hell.

Victoria remembered her glimpse of Esther's scars and she suddenly vowed to hug the woman when she saw her again. To survive such an experience with twinkling eyes and rosy cheeks and joy in tea and cookies… Victoria poured hot tea from the carafe into their cups. It was dark and strong when she sipped, a rich blend to steady her nerves and her heart.

"You were a boy. The blood on your hands is on their conscience. Not your own. You survived so that others might live. Hundreds of others," Victoria said. She glanced from her cup to Adam. He'd poured tea for himself as well. He had gulped a cup of the hot brew as if it was already cold.

"After Thomas died, I dropped his body in a deep crevice in the mountain before the monks found me. They didn't search hard. They'd already known he was dying. They took me back for punishment. I met Ezekiel that day. He was in the dungeon beneath the monastery keep. They had him bound with sanctified chains. I think that's what made up my mind. They had no right to inscribe prayers in iron. I knew by then that they were no servants of heaven. Although I didn't know that they served Rogue daemons who would war with heaven," Adam said. "I learned that later so it doesn't absolve me. I freed one of Lucifer's Army because I wanted freedom and revenge."

"It might be freedom and revenge that you sought as a teen, but you've brought salvation and justice to so many who suffered because of the Order," Victoria said.

Adam had placed his cup back on the table and left his fist lying near it. She reached to place her hand over his, cupping her palm over his fist. It was simple commiseration until their skin touched. Then it became so much more. Her song fluttered in her chest as if it was an actual nightingale fighting to spring free from the cage of her ribs. She gasped.

Adam's body stiffened and his chin jerked up. His eyes blazed as they met hers. Not with anger. It was the first time she'd seen the Brimstone flame in his eyes in response to her affinity alone. Her touch. Her song. He was ripped from his painful memories to a present that was more pleasure than pain. Although the arc of connection between them wasn't easy. It roared through all of her nerve endings and brought them to sensitized attention and she thought from his body's sudden tension that it had done the same to him.

"I'm no better than the daemons I serve. Their Brimstone burns in my veins. Ezekiel is my master and he wears Lucifer's wings on his back. My mother's soul doesn't rest because she frets over mine. I have taken more lives than I've saved. You should know that before you waste your affinity to reach out to me. I am lost. I was lost long ago," Adam said. He sat stiffly. His fist was hard beneath her hand. His angular jaw was clenched in a razor-sharp line and his shoulders were made of stone.

"You've been an angel of mercy to many. Esther worships the ground you walk on. That sweet woman would be dead if it wasn't for you. I caught a glimpse of her scars," Victoria said. She stood without releasing his fist and took the two steps necessary to bring her body against his side. When she pressed her softness against him, she could feel the shudder that quaked him and she marveled at his control. Her breasts were pebbled. Her heart pounded. She had gone to pulsing liquid from her heart to her knees.

"I'm more devil than angel," Adam warned.

"So tonight I'll share refuge with a seductive devil who has an angel's heart. Do you hear me complain?" Victoria teased.

"Will your affinity protect you from the taint of my Brimstone?" Adam asked.

He finally looked up at her. He reached to cup her bottom and pull her even closer than she had pressed. His face brushed the side of her breast and she drew in a shuddering breath. She threaded her fingers into his wavy hair. It was one of the only soft things about him. His hair and the sensual curve of his lips. She gloried in the idea that they were hers, if only for tonight.

Victoria leaned to press her lips against his forehead.

"If Brimstone taints, I have been tainted since I was born. Stepdaughter to the daemon king. Hunter of daemons. Mother of a half daemon prince. And now, drawn to a man who burns so bright," she said against Adam's warm skin and soft hair. "But I don't think it taints. Greed is what corrupts. Hurting others for power and gain. The Order of Samuel tries to taint everyone it touches, but it's up to us to stay true to ourselves no matter what flows through our veins."

"I'm damned," Adam said. He kept stiff and still, but his respiration had quickened at her nearness. When she swiveled to lift her leg and settle onto his lap, he gasped and his hands lifted to hold her waist as if of their own volition.

"Your mother isn't worried about your soul. And neither am I. You won't be damned forever. You'll have your redemption. I know it," Victoria said. She trailed her lips down the side of his face to kiss along his stiff, clenched jaw. She stopped when she came to his lips, allowing a hair's breadth of distance between their mouths so she could speak a mother's truth she felt all the way to the marrow of her bones. "Elena's soul isn't at rest because she doesn't want you to be alone. You're surrounded by people, your devoted people, but you keep them all at a distance because you're ashamed of your Brimstone blood." Adam closed his eyes. From the truth she uttered or the heat of her breath on his lips, she couldn't be sure. "I know your Brimstone. I feel it. My affinity craves your heat. You don't have to hide it from me."

Suddenly, Adam erupted. He moved one hand up to the back of her head to crush her mouth to his. She'd teased and tempted him. Now he took what she freely offered. The heat of his mouth melted her entire body. She met his questing tongue with her own, but she couldn't keep up with the hungry, devouring plunges as he delved deeply to find the velvet heat of her mouth. Her every cell sang. But her song hummed in soft sounds of need and pleasure she uttered into his mouth.

He pulled her T-shirt up and over her head to reveal the practical sports bra she'd donned for this leg of their journey. He didn't seem to mind the lack of lace. In fact, he pulled the bra from her to uncover her breasts so quickly that he might not have noticed the plain black cotton. She'd never seen a sexier sight than his dark waves of hair as they tickled against the pale pink skin of her areolas. Her nipples were already sensitive and distended, as if they perked to meet his tongue. He gave them what they seemed to beg for. Taking each one for long, torturous moments of suckling in his mouth as he laved them with his rough tongue.

"I will call you a devil if you don't help me with these pants right now," Victoria growled. He threw his head back and the grace of his full smile caused her breath to still in her lungs, her whole body pausing in response. She reached to place the pads of her thumbs on either side of his smile. She caressed the swell of his lower lip, so pink and flushed from their fierce kisses. "Your smile is more powerful than Brimstone to me," she confessed.

He arched to kiss her again. But this time his kiss was gentle. He held the back of her head and slowly tasted and explored the tenderness she'd expressed.

Between her legs, she could feel the swollen length of his erection pressing insistently against her even though it was still restrained by his tactical pants. She moved her hips and reached for the buckle and button and zipper, but it wasn't until he helped her with all the fastenings and the shifting of his hips necessary to pull his pants down that she was finally rewarded with the revelation she sought.

The lantern's glow illuminated his flushed shaft and she took his heat in her hand. His head fell back and he groaned her name. She teased him with stroking movements while she tried to undo her own pants with only one hand. He noticed her struggle. He opened his eyes and through heavy-lidded slits he helped her unbutton the waist of her denim. She released him long enough to stand and unzip her boots. Then she shimmied out of jeans and boots both, leaving them abandoned on the ground while she reclaimed the warmth of his lap.

He'd pulled his sweater off so they came together skin to skin. A mere touch of their hands had scorched them. When Victoria settled herself onto Adam's erection, taking him inch by inch to the heart of her womb, she was claimed by the fire of her affinity fully melding with his Brimstone. Her body stiffened. Her back arched. She cried out as tremors of release racked her body.

Adam held her. He supported her as her orgasm took her to edges she'd never seen. He caught her against him as she fell, even as his release flooded her. He cried out and she sang his name.

The tiny cabin didn't have a kitchen, but it did have a serviceable bathroom. The pipes were bare, the fixtures seemed decades old, but the room was clean. Only a small web in one corner with an eight-legged denizen and its carefully silken-wrapped midnight snack it was saving for later gave indication that the bathroom wasn't as civilized as it could be.

Victoria even found the water hot when she undressed to shower. Hot, but cool compared to Adam. She shivered beneath the steamy flow and tried to prepare for the morning. She could already feel the warning tingle of unfriendly Brimstone blood over the horizon. Just like Father Reynard, there would be monks who had sold their soul for longevity, strength and the power that came with it.

Adam had murmured his plan against her ear when they'd moved from the hardback chair to the bed. He'd cradled her in his arms, spooning against her back as if they were a regular couple, while he talked of sneaking in the monastery keep through tunnels that had been painstakingly dug, decade after decade, one spoonful of dirt at a time. She had experienced a thrill when she'd thought of rescuing Michael through tunnels that Esther, Gideon and countless other rebellious novitiates had created. The Order corrupted those it devoured, but there were people who resisted. There were novitiates who escaped.

Adam had escaped a hundred years ago, but he'd never left his ordeal behind. He'd worked to build a network of people to help him infiltrate and influence. He had suggested the tunnels be dug. He had saved all he could while still focusing on an endgame many of his people wouldn't live to see.

They knew they wouldn't see it. And they worked for Adam anyway.

Because he was a good man.

He'd sold his soul for freedom and revenge, he'd said. But the truth was that he'd sold his soul for the freedom of all he'd saved and to work for the downfall of the Order so that they would face the justice they deserved.

Victoria rinsed away the last of the soap that she'd found on a shelf wrapped in a design that screamed 1952. She toweled dry, marveling how she'd just made love to a time traveler, basically. How many of his people had he watched grow old and die before they lived to see the Order stopped once and for all?

She dressed and braced herself for whatever she would find tomorrow when they infiltrated the compound. Adam was sleeping when she rejoined him on the bed. As her eyes closed and she tried to join Adam in sleep, she felt the scars on his back against her palm.

She remembered Esther's scars. She thought of Gideon's formal coveralls with their long sleeves.

Michael was not quite three years old.

Her heart thudded in her chest when she imagined him scarred by evil hands. Adam stirred and shifted in his sleep and he gathered her close to him as if he'd been disturbed by her thoughts. Even his Brimstone heat couldn't soothe her fears away. Adam would sacrifice himself to save her and Michael. He would never be satisfied until he had saved everyone but himself.

Chapter 20

They left the cabin as weak sunlight barely filtered through the clouds with the rising sun. The resort was asleep. There were no other hikers silhouetted in the distance. Only trees, the glacier lake and wildflowers greeted them as they wound behind the cabin and began to climb a steep trail that was mostly overgrown with grasses. Soon they left even that sign of direction, but Adam seemed to know. He confidently placed one foot in front of the other and Victoria followed.

She was glad of her coat. The morning temperature on the mountain was chilly. Summer in the Carpathians was short. Morning and evening were more likely to resemble early spring in Louisiana. Her breath didn't fog, but her nose was cold as they followed a route that meandered, but steadily carried them higher and higher.

The resort was out of sight now and the ground was far too craggy to encourage casual hikers to brave this area on the mountain. They encountered larger and larger patches of gray, sharp-edged boulders, but they barely slowed Adam down. Soon she realized he knew the way over and around even in situations that seemed impassable. There were switchbacks and tricks to the passage that could only have been man-made.

"The Order discourages casual visitors to the compound. The old monastery did as well, which is why it was ultimately abandoned as civilization encroached. But the Order actively maintains this part of the mountain. They block passes and create ravines and rockfalls. Trusted novitiates are taught the route by the time they become monks. I figured it out on my own," Adam said. He reached back to pull her up over a particularly jagged blockade of boulders that seemed to have fallen naturally from an outcropping above them. "It only took about fifty years."

In several places they encountered official-looking signs. Adam translated for her as they passed. "Danger, rock slides, steep crevasse."

With every step her anxiety heightened, but the knot in her chest loosened because she was climbing closer and closer to Michael. Her sides ached by the time they paused just below the final ascent. The ground was all rock now. Only sparse areas of wildflowers broke up the look of desolation. Wind whipped this side of the mountain. The sun had risen, but the wind chilled her to the bone.

Adam told her to sit and catch her breath on a sheltered boulder and she complied without argument. She dug a water bottle from her backpack and drank while Adam walked toward a jumble of large rocks that seemed to shelter around the dark slit of a crevice in the ground. He crouched beside the crevice and sat back on his heels. She thought she saw his lips moving, but the wind whistling in and around the boulders carried the words he spoke away.

After Thomas died, I dropped his body in a deep crevice in the mountain.

She lowered the bottle from her lips as she realized Adam was visiting Thomas's grave.

They didn't pause long. Adam rose and came to her. He gestured for her to follow him again. She didn't mention Thomas or try to soothe him. She could feel her son nearby, and her drive to go to him superseded all else. She did murmur a prayer that none of them would end up in an unmarked mountain grave before the day was over.

Her first sight of the crumbling castle monastery Reynard had called home caused her to stop in her tracks. The giant keep rose high above them and leaned into the mountain itself, as if its walls had grown naturally from the gray stone. It seemed like a poisonous mushroom that had pushed out of the mountain, rending its peaceful crags, but continuing to suck life from its soil and rock. If it had ever been a holy place the vibe around it was no longer peaceful and holy. The stone block used to build the wall and the monastery itself was striped with calcified streaks from rain and melted snow, as if the stone wept dirty white tears. The dark shadows of ravens circled the high towers of the castle-like keep and, though she couldn't hear their cries, she could imagine what grim feasts had drawn them to this place. Whether it was her imagination or not, a whiff of decay seemed to reach them on the wind.

"The entrance is small. Have you ever been spelunking? We'll have to crawl before we can walk," Adam warned.

Like ants they scurried across a clearing from the rock cliff to the base of the wall, but their fast movements didn't feel fast enough. Victoria's back was stiff with the feeling of being watched. There were raised places on the wall that would have been perfect for sentries to be shielded from view while still being able to see everything that went on below. There were glinting narrow windows in the keep itself. Hundreds of them. Where monks could look out at the world and possibly see two interlopers come to take one of the most important novitiates they'd ever kidnapped. A half daemon prince who might grow up to rule hell itself. A toddler boy who held the power of Brimstone and Samuel's Kiss hidden in his heart.

But he was only Michael to her. The baby she loved. And she had come to simply take him home.

The entrance was worse than she'd expected. She was petite in spite of the slight maternal curves she'd acquired in the last few years, but she had to wonder how Adam had managed to fit his broad shoulders into the tunnel when she dropped to her knees to crawl in behind him. She had to take off her backpack and push it ahead of her. Adam's body blocked the dim light of the flashlight he'd pulled from one of his tactical suit's pockets. She was left in the dark, following blind through a dirt-and-rock tunnel that scraped against her sides.

She didn't consciously decide to hum, but a soft sound of reassurance crooned from her throat nonetheless. Adam paused, but only for a second before he began to crawl again. Her heartbeat sang, "Michael. Michael. Michael," with every beat. Her hum was something else. A bayou lullaby she'd often sung to him when the lonely nights were long and he was teething and restless. His restlessness had echoed her own.

They'd been a pair standing against a dangerous world for a long time. Although they had Grim and Sybil as well as Kat and Severne, it was the bond between mother and child that had seen them through the loss of Michael's father.

Yet it felt so right to follow Adam Turov into the dark.

They crawled for an eternity. Victoria focused on movement, song and the memory of Turov's smile. She thought of Michael's hot little hugs and his laughter when he played with the ferocious, ugly hellhound she'd slowly learned to trust with her greatest treasure.

She breathed as shallowly as she could as the air grew dank and decayed. Far beneath the Order of Samuel's compound, the earth seemed to be tainted by all that went on above it. The tunnel didn't smell of soil and natural crawling things. It smelled of desperate sweat and blood, of death and mold and stale tears. Just as she thought she couldn't bear another second of being buried alive in such a grave, the tunnel opened up. Millimeter by millimeter the space around her expanded to allow a foot of space above her head and a glimmer of light to reach her from Adam's flashlight.

"The dead can't hurt you. That's a hard lesson to learn. Keep moving. Don't look at the tunnel walls too closely," Adam ordered.

Victoria tried to obey, but in the wavering light she couldn't help seeing what he'd warned her to ignore. Bones. The dirt walls of the tunnel weren't only dirt. Bits of filthy fabric stuck out from the earth as did other, more gruesome things. She stopped. She closed her eyes against the sight. But Adam kept crawling. Soon he was several feet away and the idea that he might turn a corner to leave her in the dark with human remains was enough motivation to spur her on in spite of the hideousness of the path she must crawl.

She hurried after Adam, but it didn't save her from the clear shape of a skeletal hand protruding from the wall as if in supplication, nor did she manage not to see the dirt-filled eye sockets and gaping mouth of a skull.

Her hum had stopped. Her crawl had turned into a scramble. The tunnel no longer squeezed against her, but she could remember where it had. She could remember bumps and pokes that she had assumed were rocks and roots. Her whole body began to quake with a shuddering she couldn't shut down and bile rose to her throat.

And still she hurried toward Michael. He had to be saved from this horrible place. Even if she had to crawl through purgatory to reach him.

Finally, the tunnel opened even wider and before she knew she'd made it through, Adam's feet disappeared in front of her and were replaced suddenly by strong arms pulling her from the nightmare shaft. He continued pulling until she stood against him, surrounded by his muscular arms.

"They are beyond our help and are hopefully at peace now. The real monks must have entombed their dead here before the Order arrived. My people didn't realize they were tunneling into catacombs before it was too late. Decades of work would have had to be abandoned," Adam said. "I've never crawled through the tunnels myself. I didn't know how bad it would be or I would have warned you."

Victoria had lived a dark life. This was the first time she truly understood that Adam's had been much, much darker. His scars had warned her. His longevity was certainly an indication that he had seen more than a normal man had seen. "Bad" didn't come close to what the tunnel had been. Yet if it helped her save her son and if it had provided a means to save others, then she would force herself beyond her reaction to the skeleton-lined pathway.

"I told you I was coming with you. I didn't expect a cake walk," Victoria said. But she said it into his chest as the shivers died down.

"I have no way of knowing where they'll be holding him. We might have a long, dangerous hunt ahead of us," Adam warned. "There'll be other things no one should ever have to see."

"For Michael," Victoria reminded herself. She pushed away from Adam and stood on her own two feet. His light revealed that they'd exited the tunnel into a damp, forgotten room that must once have been a cell. There was rotten bedding in one corner and rusted bars fallen to the side across an opening that led into a passage. The flashlight illuminated only so far and then the view was swallowed by shadows.

"For us all," Adam corrected.

She looked up into his face. Backlit, his features were as swallowed by shadows as the mysterious passage beyond. He'd promised he would retrieve Michael from the Order, but now she wondered what else Adam might have planned. He'd held her to soothe her, but the outline of his face was as hard and stark as stone. She couldn't see his bright eyes and his Brimstone burn was banked. It simmered so low she could barely detect it. Was he beginning to learn how to shield his heat from her the same way Ezekiel did?

Or had crawling into this place of nightmares chilled him to the bone?

Chapter 21

What she'd assumed was rotten bedding was actually a pile of discarded robes. Adam pulled one from the middle of the stack and it turned out to be in better shape than the ones on top. Victoria shrugged into it when he offered its grimy brown folds to her. She wore it over her backpack, utilizing the bulk of it as part of her disguise. She ignored the robe's musty smell. She pretended not to notice the stiff darker stains that she feared were dried blood. It took Adam several tries to find a robe long enough to accommodate his height. He finally found one that worked if he stooped. She copied him when he pulled a voluminous hood over his head. The cowls of both robes drooped over their faces.

"If we meet anyone, let me do the talking. There are expected words and phrases, but a novitiate is often under an order of silence so that will be assumed if I speak for you," Adam advised.

"I can feel him. I can feel Michael," Victoria said. She placed her hand on Adam's arm and he paused on his way out the door.

"There are a lot of people in this compound. And many of them have bartered their souls to Rogue daemons. Are you sure it's your son you feel?" Adam asked.

"How did you know it was your mother who left the roses? Love knows," Victoria replied.

They stood in the doorway. She still held his arm, but he didn't pull away.

"You take the lead. We'll follow your affinity unless I need to divert you away from danger," Adam said.

Victoria nodded and let go of Adam's arm. She was immediately colder. His heat had buoyed her for a moment in this place that froze her soul. She didn't tell him that it wasn't purely her affinity that pulled her toward Michael. She was afraid a hardened warrior may not trust the instinctive thread between mother and child. She hadn't understood it herself until Michael was born.

They walked carefully but quickly through the passage that took them to a flight of stone stairs. As they passed some doors, the smell of decay was stronger than others, but when she would have paused to look inside Adam placed a restraining hand on her arm.

"They are beyond help. Nearly dead before they're left here to rot. We can help them most by continuing on," Adam said.

She'd always known the Order was evil. Her mother had taught her from birth to fear them. But in this place she tasted their corruption in the very air around her. So much suffering. So much torture and death.

"Ezekiel explained it to me once. Long ago. Some who barter with daemons seek redemption. They work to regain the soul they've lost. Others give in to the corruption. They feed the connection with their daemon in despicable ways. Loyalists condemn the practice, but Rogues have encouraged it," Adam said. "They want to win at all costs."

His soft whisper held the darkness at bay as they traversed passages and climbed stairway after stairway.

"Good versus evil," Victoria said.

"Nothing is ever so simple as that. I, for instance, fall somewhere in between. I have killed. Often. That blood has fueled Ezekiel and my cause. I'm no angel. I never will be," Adam said.

"But you are also no Malachi. Or Reynard," Victoria said.

They had paused at the top of a particularly tall flight of stairs that opened up into a room instead of a passageway. Adam edged around her and walked across the empty room to open the door just enough to scout ahead of their path.

"Are we close?" he asked.

"Yes. I think so," Victoria answered. "I think he's very near."

"There are men at the end of the next hallway," Adam said when he'd come back to her side. "They seem to be guarding a door."

"Michael," Victoria said. She stepped forward automatically, but Adam reached to grip her arm and stop her.

"Better if you call them here," he said.

Victoria's gaze lifted quickly to meet his. Beneath the cowl, the light from the narrow slit of window in the room seemed to settle on his eyes. They were blue diamonds in a shadowed face, hard and brilliant but faceted, as if he was afraid she would agree.

"Brace yourself," she warned.

Her hum was low and scratchy, but she put her whole being into its expression. Unlike the hum she'd used in the tunnel to calm her nerves and get her to the other side, this was intentionally a siren's call. She forced her attention beyond her companion—nearly impossible— to the monks in the hall outside. She could feel them. She took a step toward the door as she opened herself to the magnetism of the strange Brimstone blood, but when she took another step a warm hand closed on her wrist. Her concentration was broken. She looked back at Adam, surprised to see his hood thrown back and beads of sweat on his upper lip.

"Brace myself? As if I could possibly prepare…" Adam said.

She wasn't prepared for the fierce tug that brought her up against him. Or the hard kiss he pressed against her lips. But she didn't reject it either. She enjoyed the heat of his tongue against hers and the taste of salt until he stepped back. He retreated several paces toward the door and stood to the side in preparation of the monks who would enter in moments.

"Again," he urged.

She could see Adam plant his feet and firm his shoulders before she hummed again.

They both stiffened when they heard the steps outside the door.

Adam's sword came out of its sheath with a stealthy hiss. He cut off the cries of both men before they could make a sound. They slumped to the floor with gaping wounds across their throats. She'd expected a Brimstone flare, but their blood ran black as charcoal instead. He motioned for her to come forward and she did. She stepped over the two dead monks and followed Adam into the hallway. At the end of the long passageway, there was only one door.

"It's a tower room," Adam said. "They thought one entrance and exit would protect their prize."

"Have they treated him like a prize or a prisoner?" Victoria wondered. Tears burned the backs of her eyes. Adam didn't stop her when she hurried forward to find out if Michael was well enough to save, or if Malachi had fed his Rogue daemon master with her child's blood.

Chapter 22

The last barrier between her and her son was a heavy oak door that was worn with age and bound by iron strap hinges that reached from edge to edge. The hinges were inscribed with layers upon layers of letters. Victoria couldn't make out the jumble until they were within a couple of feet. She peered closer and noted several Latin words and phrases, but most of the inscriptions were indecipherable.

"Prayers to bind," Adam said. "Scratched deeply into the iron for decades by the unholiest of men."

He touched the door, but drew back his hand quickly when the Brimstone in his blood protested contact with the inscriptions. Victoria reached her own hand out to touch the iron, but it was cool to her touch.

"They interfere in a conflict they don't understand. They invoke these prayers without having a right to do so. But the conflict between daemon and heaven is there.

The powers that be weren't happy with Lucifer when he chose to fall and rule a kingdom of his own. These inscriptions will have been painful to Michael if he's on the other side of this door, Victoria," Adam warned.

"I'm ready to face whatever we find," Victoria said.

She stepped back with Adam and bolstered her nerve, but she wasn't prepared for the sudden burst of violence that erupted from him. His body leaped forward, his leg lashed up and out, and the door burst inward with a splintering render of wood from iron. The door was left hanging loose to the side. The seal the corrupt prayers had created was broken.

And Victoria fell to her knees. Because as intense as Michael's Brimstone cry of distress had become, the binding of the Latin phrases had shielded her from the magnitude of his Burn.

She struggled back to her feet and rushed forward. Her son was alone in the room. He stood crying in an iron crib fashioned fully enclosed like a cage. The bars he held glowed with heat. The crib was also inscribed with layer upon layer of words, but they hadn't stopped Michael's Burn from coming upon him.

Ezekiel had warned her that the Burn would come no matter the circumstances. He'd also warned her that without help, a half daemon child might not be able to stop himself from immolation.

"Michael… Michael, I'm here. I'm here," she said. His eyes were scrunched to swollen slits. His face flamed red. Though he cried and cried, his tears evaporated before they could roll down his chubby cheeks.

"One of those guards might have the key," Adam said.

She vaguely registered his words. She'd placed her hands over Michael's, even though touching his hands was like touching a hot iron. She felt her skin burn. She didn't let go.

"I'm here. I'm here," she repeated again and again.

Adam disappeared and returned seconds later with a key. The pain in his face as he touched the sanctified object to free her son mirrored her own as her hands continued to burn. He inserted the key into the crib cage lock and opened the hinged side so she could reach for Michael. Adam grimaced as he released the inscribed iron, dropping the key on the bedding and backing away.

Victoria ignored the heat. She moved to pick up her baby. At first he resisted when she tried to lift him from the crib, but she continued to murmur his name and re-assurances. Finally, he let go of the glowing iron and allowed her to bring him up into her arms.

She cried out in pain from his heat and his condition. Her rough robes smoked from the contact with Michael's skin. He was dressed only in a rough gown made of the same material as her robes. Curls of smoke rose from the material as it scorched against his skin. He was dirty, but she couldn't see any blood or bruises.

"Hurry. We have to get you two out of here before Malachi tries to stop us," Adam said.

Victoria held Michael close even though he was still stiff and crying. He seemed completely unaware that his mother held him. He was lost to fear and the pain of his Burn.

"He has to be stopped," Victoria spoke over Michael's crying. "The Order has to be destroyed from the inside out. You can't get us out until you've dealt with Mala-chi."

Adam stepped toward her. She could see his inten-tion on his face. His jaw was set in stone. His blue eyes blazed with a Brimstone glow. She could think of only one thing to do. She jumped into the cage with Michael and reached to jerk the hinged side closed. The sanctified lock clanked fast against Adam before he realized what she intended to do.

The key was beneath her on the bedding. Adam was locked outside. She was in a cage and as Michael screamed she thought of all the birdcages at Nightingale Vineyards that were open. Always open. Because the ghost of Elena Turov dreamed of a day when her son, her firebird captured in the service of a dark prince, would be free.

"No. Damn it. No," Adam shouted. He reached for the inscribed iron bars of the cage and gripped them with white-knuckled hands, even though she could hear the sizzle above Michael's screams as his Brimstone reacted to the prayers.

"I won't let you sacrifice your soul for me. Or for Michael. You have a daemon bargain to fulfill. You've avoided this compound for a hundred years, but it's only a place. Your loathing of it is remembered pain, but it's the men that dwell here who are evil. They will continue to create tortured souls like Esther and Gideon. Like you. It isn't just the daemon king their destruction will slake and serve. You've saved as many as you could for as long as you could, but now you have the chance to save them all," Victoria said.

Adam looked from her to the toddler in her arms who just might burn her alive if she couldn't calm him.

"But it won't save you. The Burn is claiming him, Victoria. He's going to combust and take you with him," Adam said.

"I wouldn't survive if he went to ash without me, Adam." Victoria leaned down to kiss her crying child's round cheek. Her lips parched instantly against his flaming skin. "I came for him. I'm here to hold him. There's salvation in that even if we both burn."

"I won't leave you," Adam insisted.

"Of course you won't. You'll go for Malachi. Your blade has been tempered with a hundred years of blood for this moment. We'll be here when you come back for us. I promise. We've been through the fire before. My little one and me. We can do it again." Victoria was grateful that her tears evaporated before they had a chance to fall. The heat was unbearable. She was in terrible pain. But she bit back the whimpers that rose against it.

Adam came to her. She braced herself to argue if he continued to try to free them, but he only leaned to kiss her. He felt cool. She marveled at the coolness of his lips. He moved from her mouth to the top of Michael's head. She allowed the move through the bars of the cage. She didn't scoot away. He kissed the dirty blond curls. Then he backed away. He backed all the way to the door, as if he would memorize the way they looked, mother holding child, smoke rising from their robes to fill the room.

"My soul is worth nothing without you," he said. "I do this for them. For all of them. And for you and your family too. The Order has haunted too many lives for too long."

"Save your soul for me, Adam Turov. And I will survive to claim it and you for the next fifty years or so," Victoria said. Her voice was hoarser than ever. Michael's cries continued.

She was no daemon. She had no power to make a deal bound by universal laws. But the moment still seemed to pause for them. Smoke seemed to slow its swirl. Michael hiccuped and his cries stopped for a split second.

When they resumed, Adam turned and ran out the door. His blue diamond eyes hidden from her sight.

She was in a cage. Her son was burning on the inside. He had no resources at his toddler disposal to deal with the gift his father had given him. Victoria had only one gift. It had been stolen from her in the first fire she'd walked through, shielding Michael with her body from the flame.

But Adam had helped her find it again.

Her hum began scratchy and low. But she didn't let that silence her. Not this time. She grew louder instead. Claiming the new sound that came from her, older and wiser. Gone was the ingénue soprano she'd been. A new woman lifted her chin and opened her throat. Her diaphragm tightened and her lungs expanded. The smoke didn't bother her. This voice had risen from smoke and ashes.

Victoria sang.

And the entire castle keep beneath her shuddered.

Michael took a deep breath as if he prepared to fuel another cry, but he released the air in a great sigh instead. His stiff little body collapsed against her. She gathered him closer while continuing to sing. She sang a lullaby she'd always crooned to him under her breath. This time she gave it full volume and expression. She looked down at the quieted toddler in her lap. His face was still swollen, but his eyes glinted up at her from within his reddened lids.

The cage was shaking now. Its legs jittered on the stone floor.

Victoria continued to sing.

"Mom," Michael croaked. His voice had been made as raw as hers by his crying.

His temperature had cooled. Smoke no longer rose from their scorched robes.

She wasn't sure the danger had passed, so she continued to sing as she fished under her for the key. She held Michael close with one arm while she unlocked the cage. She carefully kept his chubby bare legs from the inscribed iron as she climbed out and stepped down onto the floor. Her song was a purer prayer. *Please. Please. Let me save him.* Beneath her feet, the stone trembled. She wasn't sure what was happening, but she knew that the structural integrity of the keep she'd seen through tunnels and passageways and crumbling rooms wasn't as strong as it needed to be to withstand an inexplicable earthquake on top of a Carpathian peak.

Michael wrapped his arms around her neck and his legs around her middle. He hummed now along with her. He remembered the lullaby although she'd always whispered it before. He was the son of a daemon. But he was also the son of a former opera singer with an affinity that was only beginning to be tapped and understood.

Victoria walked across the room toward the open door. It was hard to keep her balance against the shimmying stone. When she reached the passageway, it wasn't only the movement that frightened her. There was a rumbling growl rising from far down below where the keep met the mountain. She couldn't possibly take Michael back down to the narrow tunnel lined with moldering bones. The keep continued to jerk and lurch beneath her feet as she made her way to the stairs. Even if she thought he would recover from the gruesome experience of crawling through the tunnel, she now feared that they would be crushed beneath tons of stone.

And still she sang as Michael hummed along with her. She stumbled many times as they went down stairway after stairway. Her jeans were torn. Her knees bloody. Her back screamed against the weight of her child. Her out-of-practice throat hurt and her voice became even scratchier. She continued on. She didn't know where Adam had gone. She didn't know why the earthquake went on and on. She only knew she couldn't stop until she and Michael had made it outside.

Several stories down, she began to run into monks who were fleeing the crumbling structure. They didn't accost her and Michael. The walls had begun to fall. At first in sprinkles of stone dust, then in trickles of disintegrated pieces and finally in crashing blocks that threatened to crush and maim. She pressed Michael's face into her neck and hoped his humming would distract him from the cries of monks who didn't successfully avoid the crashing stones.

A young child's snuffling cries stopped her. She looked back the way she'd come. A chorus of childish voices had joined the crying. Before she saw the children, a familiar dog-shaped shadow came into sight. His eyes blazed more distinct than the rest of him. His fur billowed like smoke around his massive body. Grim. He'd found his way to the castle. He'd come to help. But the prayers inscribed on Michael's door must have kept him away from his master. The children he had found shuffled behind the hellhound as if he was a ferocious Pied Piper come to lead them. Victoria gasped when she saw them—from the tall to the small—the boys and the girls were grimy, bruised and malnourished. The bigger children carried those that were too weak or tiny to keep up with the necessary speed of the evacuation.

None of the adult monks even paused to help. She shouldn't be surprised. They had treated the children horribly. Their deplorable condition gave testimony to how little they were valued and cared for.

Grim saw Michael in her arms and he leaped to her, blinking out of existence as he left the ground and reappearing back at her side. The group of children came to a stop, confused by the abandonment. She felt the familiar press of the hellhound's heat against her legs. Michael was too drained from his Burn to notice his faithful companion's return.

"I've got him, Grim. Lead the children out of the keep. We'll follow," Victoria said.

Grim touched a fully materialized muzzle full of large white teeth gently against Michael's hip. Then he returned to the children. The oldest boy carried a girl who snuffled and cried. He gestured for the others to follow as Grim continued his role of guide down the stairs.

Victoria followed Grim and the children toward the front of the keep where a safer exit might be found. The steady stream of evacuees made her feel like she was headed in the right direction.

But then she smelled the smoke.

She stopped on a landing just above a large courtyard at the center of the compound. They had exited the castle keep. High walls surrounded the courtyard in a large semicircle. Grim continued to lead the children down the stairs, away from the courtyard toward the gates where other evacuees fled.

It wasn't until she looked down on a battle that she saw the smoke coming from a large fissure that had opened in the earth. The courtyard dirt was smooth and polished from years of training, but the sides of the fissure were jagged gray stone. Men climbed up the stone as if it was an unnatural staircase the earthquake had provided. They leaped through the rolling smoke to engage the monks in combat.

Victoria had continued to sing, unsure if Michael's danger was past. When she stepped out onto the landing and stopped, all the men from the fissure looked toward her. They stood as if in salute for a long moment before turning back to the monks they fought.

They were daemons. Lucifer's Army had risen up beneath the catacombs of the Order of Samuel.

Grim and the children had disappeared out of sight. They would be clear of the compound soon.

Michael stopped humming. He wiggled to turn his head beneath her hand. She hoped the smoke disguised the blood and destruction.

"Go?" he asked.

"As quick as we can," Victoria answered.

And that's when she saw Adam at the edge of the fissure. Smoke swirled around his tall form as if it framed his strength and purpose. He had also turned to look at her and, even though she'd paused in her singing, he of all the men in the courtyard had still not looked away.

But their connection had never been safe or easy.

As their gazes locked across the battlefield of the courtyard, Malachi ran toward Adam from behind. She gestured. Too far away to do anything more. It was enough. Adam turned with the sudden burst of speed she'd seen him use before. He raised his own sword to stop the blade that Malachi had raised against him.

The two were locked in a standoff of blade against blade. Adam was taller. Malachi was broader. Both had been trained to kill. The balance shifted. Malachi pushed Adam to the edge of the fissure. After all, Malachi enjoyed killing. The crack in the earth had been widening with every rumbling shudder. Adam's feet slid on loosened earth and rocks. Victoria cried out. Michael squeezed her tighter and buried his face back in her neck. Did she detect a slight rise in his temperature? She closed her lips against her distress. She began to hum again, patting her son's back to soothe him.

But she also moved toward the stairs.

She wasn't a warrior, but she did have the daemon king's blade in her bag. She also had to make her way down before the stairs deteriorated to the point that they weren't passable, pushing into the flow of monks as they fled from the upper stories. She tried to shelter Michael against her body. Lucifer's Army was coming for the Order in spite of the crumbling castle. Fights occurred all around. Several times daemons interceded with monks who threatened her passage. Halfway down the stairs she realized that the flow of monks had been parted by Lucifer's Army like the Red Sea to allow her to pass. She continued to sing even though her throat was raw. Michael hummed again. Quietly. His body was limp. His skin was cool. She thought his hum was slow and a little off-key. At the bottom of the stairs, she looked down to see his eyes closed and his breathing deep and regular.

Her half daemon prince had fallen asleep as the walls came down, as the Order of Samuel fell, as Adam…

Through the clash of violent bodies and the smoke, she could see Adam and Malachi fighting at the edge of the fissure. Adam wasn't giving his full concentration to the evil monk. He searched for her even as he fought. She stepped into the courtyard, hoping the swirling smoke would allow him to see she was okay so he could shift his attention back to defeating Malachi and regaining his soul.

But Adam froze when he saw her.

And Malachi slammed into him.

It took a thousand years for the monk and the damned man to fall over the edge of the fissure. Victoria received flash burns from Michael as she screamed and he woke with his Brimstone flaring in an instinctive response to a threat he couldn't understand.

She ran onto the battlefield. She dodged dead bodies on the ground and daemons and monks alike as they continued to fight each other. The daemons were winning. She could see that. There were more monks on the ground than there were daemons. Ezekiel would be triumphant. But that hardly mattered as her heart continued to scream. Outside, she had calmed herself for Michael. He was awake now, but he was so young. Surely he wouldn't be able to process all he saw around them. Thankfully, the smoke was thick. Much of the battlefield was cloaked.

When she came to the edge of the fissure, the ground was shaking hard enough to cause her to carefully place her feet. Finally, she was close enough to peer into the earth. She'd expected an empty black hole. Instead, she saw Adam stretched out on his stomach across one of the craggy boulders that protruded from the earth, several yards down from the fissure's edge. He held Malachi's arm. The monk's body dangled over a black abyss that stretched down, down, down as far as she could see. Deeper than the tunnel she'd crawled through in the catacombs. If hell had been a place at the center of the molten earth, that's where it seemed the crater reached.

Of course, she knew that wasn't where Lucifer's Army had come from. Hell was a different dimension. The fissure had opened a portal that allowed them to invade the monastery. At the height of his Burn, Michael must have shrieked an invitation to his grandfather, or an order to Grim.

"Gim!" Michael shouted in her ear.

Victoria looked in the direction that her son strained and saw the great guardian hellhound springing from rock to rock to reach their position. He was solid as he landed. When he leaped, he turned to amorphous shadow in the air. Wisps of smoke curled around him, darker than the smoke that rose from the fissure.

The hellhound landed near them and pressed against her legs, as if to keep her from falling into the crater at her feet.

"Grim, did you do this? Did you show Lucifer's Army the way so that they would save your master?" Victoria asked.

The hellhound's eyes glowed and he pressed even harder against her, as if to say, *it will all be for nothing if you don't leave. Now.*

"You have to take Michael to safety. Do you understand? You have to get him out of here," Victoria told the hell-spawned hound.

Michael eagerly held on to his ferocious best friend when Victoria placed him on Grim's back. The daemon dog immediately moved to distance his rider from the quaking fissure. If Malachi hadn't kidnapped Michael, Victoria was suddenly sure that his bond with the ugly hellhound would have helped him through the Burn. He was completely cool to the touch when she felt his forehead and placed a kiss on his temple.

"The way is blocked. I can't get him out on my own. You have to do it, Grim. Take him home through the paths only you can find," Victoria said. Her throat closed as she said it. Her eyes burned. Without Michael's Brimstone burn evaporating them, her tears threatened to fall.

Grim whined. He stepped toward her as if to urge her to come along too. But she stepped back toward the fissure.

"Go. Now. Before it's too late," she said.

The hellhound turned away. His stiff-legged walk turned into a lope that turned into a run before he and his rider faded into the smoke and shadows. Michael's laugh floated back to her as he disappeared.

The separation tore something inside her. Michael and Grim were traveling in between this world and countless others. He was gone. She pressed her hands against her stomach and closed her eyes. Her body swayed, but then she firmed her spine.

Adam.

He was forfeiting his soul.

Ezekiel wouldn't accept that the Order had fallen if Malachi survived. It wasn't the compound that was evil. It was the man in charge of corrupting everything he touched. Reynard's man. His protégé risen to power now that his master was gone.

Victoria stepped to the edge again and looked down to see Adam still holding Malachi in his viselike grip. He wouldn't let the monk fall into the abyss. The tumble down to the rock ledge that now supported him had shredded Adam's tactical fatigues. She could see a glimpse of the scars on his back. The horrible deep ridges had somehow become beautiful wings on him. Fitting wings for a damned man. Adam was trying to save Malachi even though the monk had kidnapped him and tortured him.

Ezekiel might hold his soul ransom, but Adam Turov was already redeemed. With every Esther and Gideon he saved, he had built a new soul with his own actions.

He was no angel. He would never be. He would carry the darkness he'd survived in his heart forever.

But that's why he made her sing. No Brimstone necessary at all. Because he still believed in saving others.

With superhuman effort, Adam lifted the big-boned monk with one arm. His muscles bulged and his own body slid toward the edge of the ledge he lay across, but he didn't let go. He pulled. He strained. Inch by inch, he brought the evil monk up to the ledge.

Victoria felt the presence of Brimstone around her even though her affinity was fried from Michael's Burn. She looked away from Adam long enough to see that the edge of the fissure was ringed on either side of her with daemons. Lucifer's Army had come to watch their greatest enemy fall. They stood motionless as Adam saved him.

But as Adam dragged Malachi onto the ledge, a movement from deep in the crater caught her eye. The constant movement of the earthquake crumbling the castle stilled as the daemons around her came to life with mutters and murmurings she couldn't translate. Then, as one, they all fell to their left knees and hundreds of heads bowed. The noise of the movement was audible. Adam looked up. Malachi rolled to his back and placed his arm over his eyes.

Ezekiel rose from the pit. Lucifer's bronzed wings were stiff on his back. They could no longer be used for flight in any discernible way and yet the daemon king rose from the fissure as if he flew. He also glowed brighter with Brimstone anger than she'd ever seen. His eyes. His ears. His nose. His mouth. All allowed the glow to beam out from his body. Malachi protected his eyes from the glare. She didn't have to. Even in anger, Ezekiel thought of her and shifted his body to shield her.

Adam wasn't so lucky. He rose to his feet and turned his face away to avoid the glare as Ezekiel floated to the ledge. Victoria started to protest. She feared that her stepfather would punish Adam for not killing Malachi. But she discovered that the daemon king knew better how to manipulate bargains than that.

"Thank you for delivering my enemy to my feet, Adam Turov. You have served me well," Ezekiel said.

In a blur of movement, the daemon king's arm shot out and he grasped Malachi by the neck, but as he sprang up, Ezekiel's speed decreased. He moved as if in slow motion. The Loyalists around her raised their heads to watch Malachi lifted up and over their ranks, but they continued to kneel in the presence of their king.

Victoria didn't kneel. She watched as Adam made his way across the rocky ledge to the fissure's wall. The muscles in his arms bunched and strained as he climbed up to her. When he'd leveraged himself up on the edge to stand beside her, she turned to face Ezekiel.

"This man has been a faithful servant of the enemy we have fought for millennia, though only a short time has passed for him on Earth," the daemon king said. "The Order of Samuel has fed the Rogue daemon army with blood and the corruption of countless innocent human souls."

The Loyalist daemons still knelt on one knee, ringing the abyss. Smoke still rolled. The mountain had begun to shake again and loosened stone continued to fall. Ezekiel spoke over it all as if it was inconsequential. Behind him and the evil monk he seemed to hold easily with one ancient hand, the polished dirt field of the courtyard ran with bright rivers of crimson blood and black streams of charcoal-tainted corruption. Hundreds of monks lay dead or dying. Only the young had been allowed to flee.

"Rise and witness as judgment opens its gaping maw to swallow this tainted human whole," Ezekiel said. His voice wasn't a bellow, but it rang out all the same. It carried over the sound of grumbling earth and crumbling castle keep.

Lucifer's Army rose to their feet around her and Adam. As one, they turned to stand at stiff attention at the bidding of their king. Ezekiel lowered Malachi to the ground near Victoria, but instead of crumpling in a heap, the evil monk also stood straight and tall. He endured the righteous gazes, but it was as if he walked across glowing coals. Sweat trickled down his brow and he looked no one directly in the eye.

"Victoria D'Arcy. It is your right to cleanse the earth of this stain. He took your son without bargain and without permission. He almost allowed the Burn to immolate the grandson of Anne D'Arcy, who would have been my queen. Her blood runs in your veins. It is fitting that you plunge the daemon blade I've given you into his black heart," Ezekiel said. His hand was still gripped on the nape of Malachi's neck. With this hold, he presented the evil monk to his stepdaughter.

Adam stiffened beside her.

"No. She shouldn't carry the burden of his death on her shoulders the rest of her life," Adam protested. He stepped forward toward the daemon king and his prisoner. His fists were clenched. Blood from scrapes and cuts ran freely down his face and hands. His shredded clothes stuck to his body where more serious wounds bled. But he stood between her and the daemon king as if he would shield her from the pain she'd carried with her since she'd been born.

She'd been born different. Her affinity had seemed a curse for most of her life. But it had turned out to be a blessing. She might never have braved the connection she shared with Adam if her gift hadn't brought them together, even while they tried to remain apart. Her affinity had helped her to save Michael and reclaim a new voice after she'd suffered tragedy and loss.

Malachi would never stop. He had been raised and trained by a monster. He would never rest until Michael—a boy with affinity *and* Brimstone blood— was under his control. She couldn't allow that. Ezekiel was right. Not that it was a privilege to send Malachi to the same place Reynard had been sent, to face whatever punishment waited on the other side of death, but he was right that it was her responsibility.

Adam's focus was on the daemon king he stood against. He didn't notice as she reached under her robes, shifting her backpack to the side so she could retrieve the daemon king's blade. Only when she stepped past him did he realize she intended to do what Ezekiel had ordered.

"No," Adam said. "You don't have to do this."

"Someone does. This compound is only a place. What does it matter if this castle falls? He will only rise to build another and another. Michael will never know peace. He'll never be free," Victoria said. "And neither will you."

"You don't have to give me peace with your blade, Vic. You have given me peace with your song," Adam said.

But the temporary stay of Malachi's execution that their words had given him also gave the evil monk an opportunity to break free of the daemon king's grasp.

His robe tore as he jerked away and Ezekiel was left with drab material in his hand as Malachi leaped toward Victoria. His body slammed into her with such force that they both fell to the ground. The air was knocked from her lungs by the landing and the weight of the big-boned monk on top of her. The blade she'd clenched in one hand flew from her stunned fingers as she coughed and choked and tried to suck in air.

Malachi's hands closed around her throat, making the urgency for oxygen even greater. She bucked. She punched and kicked. But her vision blurred and her muscles weakened. Malachi squeezed tighter and tighter. The reddened face above her was contorted with madness. The rest of the world was hazy and indistinct.

But as haze began to turn to black around the edges, Malachi's hands jerked and relaxed. His whole body stiffened, and he cried out as blood bubbled from his lips to trickle down his chin. Victoria gasped for air and reached for her crushed throat while Malachi tumbled to the side. He landed facedown. The daemon king's blade protruded from his back. It was buried to the hilt. Only seconds had passed, but it seemed an eternity.

"*I* give *you* peace, Victoria D'Arcy. I hope you'll give me your heart in return," Adam Turov said. He had retrieved the daemon king's blade from the ground and he'd plunged it with such force into Malachi's back that he'd instantly stopped the monk's heart.

But as her vision cleared, Victoria could see that something was wrong. Adam swayed on his feet. Blood burgeoned across his chest, soaking his shredded shirt in a sudden deep red flow. There was no sizzle. There was no smoke. She struggled to her feet and scrambled to reach him, but when she reached to take his arms he fell to his knees, taking her to the ground with him. They faced each other knee to knee and he reached for her face as she tried to keep him from slumping to the side.

"What is it? What happened?" Victoria asked. Her voice was a hoarse scream.

"One of my men loosed an arrow when Adam jumped to help you. He thought to protect me. He didn't realize Turov was trying to save you—my precious daughter." The daemon king had come to stand beside them. He towered over them, an ancient, dangerous creature who loved her and her son.

But his love often brought death.

"The Brimstone. It can save him. It's saved him so many times before," Victoria said. She wouldn't cry for Adam because there was no need. The burn behind her eyes was unnecessary. She blinked against it. And blinked and blinked. Because Adam's hands had slipped from her face to hang limply by his sides, and he finally slumped to the ground. She wasn't strong enough to keep him upright. She looked up at the daemon king. He was diamond-faceted and her face was wet with tears. No. No. No. There was no reason to cry.

"Victoria, he has no Brimstone in his blood. The requirements of our bargain were met when he delivered Malachi into my hands. I gave him back his soul. He is no longer bound to me," Ezekiel said.

"He's dying," Victoria said.

Her gut clenched in worse pain than her throat, as if merciless hands she couldn't see squeezed the life from her with Adam's every wheezing breath. She could see the arrow now. Daemon arrows had iron shafts and gleaming black feathers that looked like they came from raven's wings.

"Allow Michael to come to me once a year until he reaches the age of majority. At that time, he will be free to choose to inherit my throne or follow another path. It will be left to him. Allow this and I will save Adam Turov," Ezekiel proclaimed.

The earth stilled. Smoke slowed to a stop above them, hanging in the air like suspended sooty clouds.

"Adam is redeemed. He isn't damned anymore. I don't want the Brimstone back in his blood. Even if it means I have to say goodbye," Victoria protested. She had lowered herself to the ground beside Adam. His eyes were closed and his face was completely relaxed. For the first time, he looked softer than stone.

"I can save him without claiming his soul. Even for a daemon king, there are bargains that can be made, No one is too powerful for compromise or sacrifice," Ezekiel said.

As Victoria lay beside Adam she thought about her son. She thought about the Burn that had almost consumed him because she couldn't prepare for a process she didn't understand. If Malachi hadn't kidnapped him, Sybil could have helped her through it, but Victoria knew the daemon nanny needed to get back to her own life at l'Opera Severne. As Adam faded further and further away, she thought about Grim and how Michael joyfully rode the hellhound as if he was a pretty pony. She thought of her son's laughter as they disappeared into the nothingness of traveling in between worlds.

He was a half daemon who could grow up to be a prince. Was she protecting him by turning her back on his stepgrandfather, or was she keeping him from a throne he had a right to choose or refuse? She'd lived such a dark life that she'd wanted to protect him from every shadow, but Grim was living shadows and Michael loved him with all his toddler heart.

Maybe she should embrace the shadows too. Just enough to survive.

"I accept," Victoria said. "I accept."

The pause was complete now, but it lasted longer than she expected. Her head grew light because her lungs didn't function as the universe stilled to record the daemon deal in its darkest recesses.

She looked up at the daemon king when she heard him murmuring words that sounded Latin. He spoke too softly for her to understand what he said. He'd said even daemon kings still had bargains they could make. To whom did he speak? With whom did he bargain? Who had the power over Adam's life and death that they would temporarily give to the daemon king in return for something else?

When the world spun again, the earth trembled beneath them and choking clouds of smoke rolled, but Ezekiel ignored it all. He dropped to one knee and pulled the deadly arrow from Adam's back. A warrior's cry erupted from Adam's lips, full of fury and pain. Victoria reached for him as Ezekiel rolled Adam toward her so that he could access the wound left from the arrow's removal. She placed her hand on Adam's cheeks and looked into his pain-dimmed eyes.

"Your blood is cleansed of the Brimstone. Elena doesn't have to worry about your soul anymore," Victoria said.

She could tell it was an effort for Adam to speak, but she didn't try to stop him. If Ezekiel couldn't save him, she needed to hear his beautiful Russian accent one more time.

"It was my isolation that worried her," Adam said. He

coughed, but when he had swallowed he began again. "She accused me of living in the cage the prince had put me into even after the door had been opened."

"She knew about your work to save the children?" Victoria guessed.

"Yes," Adam said.

"She didn't linger to save your soul. She lingered to keep you company," Victoria said.

Adam nodded. No longer able to speak. His eyes had closed. She could feel him fading away. Victoria began to hum the same bayou lullaby that had saved her son. Soft and low. He no longer had Brimstone blood, but he was the Russian firebird and she was his nightingale. His eyes fluttered and opened. Their eyes met as the daemon king sliced across his own wrists to allow his blood to trickle in a steady stream onto Adam's wound.

She held him as he jerked and cried out against the burn. She cried out with him because in cutting his flesh the daemon king had released his hold on his scorching power and her pain matched Adam's. The scent of scorched flesh and ashes rose into the air.

And Adam passed out in her arms.

His collapse caused her heart to stop. She pressed through the paralysis of the scorch to touch his lips. Her heart began to pound again when she detected the slightest inhale and exhale from his mouth.

"We will help you carry him to safety before the mountain devours the monastery," the daemon king said. "What Michael has set into motion I cannot stop."

One of his men was binding his wrist to halt the flow of blood. Others rushed forward to lift her and Adam. One of the Loyalists wasn't capable of rushing anymore. As she was carried toward the gate, she saw him lying on the ground. His bow beside his limp hand. The daemon king's punishment for mistakes was swift and without mercy. An ominous shiver trailed its icy fingers down her spine.

Chapter 23

Once they were out of the compound, they hiked to a clearing on the mountainside where dozens of children of various ages sat on rocks and in the grass. Loyalist daemons mingled among them. Daemons were passionate creatures who often hid their deepest emotions beneath stoic facades, but the children seemed to be responding to cool kindness rather well, considering what their lives had recently been. Victoria's anger rekindled when she saw the children's injuries. Triage was taking place. Many of the children had been beaten or bound by the Order of Samuel. Her anger eased when she saw hardened daemon warriors become nurses to the weak and injured.

The daemon that had carried her out of the compound set her down near a young girl who was painfully thin. Her rib cage showed at the tattered neck of her rough robe. Her head had been shaved. There were cuts and bruises over older cuts and bruises on her arms and legs. But she flashed Victoria a white smile and held out part of a crust of bread she'd been gnawing.

"Thank you, but no. You have it all. Please," Victoria said. The hungry child didn't have to be told twice.

Another daemon arrived with Adam thrown over his shoulder. He took care to bend and lay his burden down beside her on the grass. She expected Adam to be unconscious, but he raised himself to a sitting position.

"We need to question all of them to find out where they're from so we can return them to their families," he said after he had taken in his surroundings. "Who got them out of the castle?"

Victoria would never forget the dark, barely materialized form of Grim leading the children to safety. They had followed the hideous hellhound as a savior compared to the devils that had held them prisoner.

"Grim saved them. I think he was probably searching for Michael among them, but whatever his motives they'll have a monstrous hero to remember," Victoria said.

"He came out of the shadows," the little girl said. She had heard them and once she swallowed her last bite she revealed what had happened with Grim in the keep. "At first we were afraid, but then he came to each one of us and he didn't bite or growl. He only whined. When the keep began to quake, he disappeared, but then he came back. He bit the chains and they snapped like they were made of plastic. Those that could helped to untie the ones who were bound with rope. Some of the little ones had to be carried. But I walked all by myself."

The ground had continued to tremble the whole time they spoke. No more daemons or children came from the compound. She and Adam hadn't been the only adults carried from the collapsing structure. There was another clearing separated from the children by a phalanx of Lucifer's Army that hadn't softened into nurses. They stood on guard between the two clearings as monks from the Order who had survived the battle were dumped on the ground. There weren't many. And judging from the expressions on the daemons who guarded them, Victoria surmised that the monks who had died were the lucky ones.

Suddenly, a great rumble shook the mountaintop. She looked toward the keep to see the castle cave in on itself completely. She imagined the fissure had opened to the point that it could swallow the keep above it. Moments later, the wall surrounding the compound also collapsed inward and disappeared. Smoke and roiling dust exploded into the sky like a mushroom cloud and then was pulled back down into the earth, as if the imploding monastery had created a vacuum as it disappeared into the mountain.

As the dust and smoke cleared, the children raised a cheer much stronger than their collective condition should have allowed. The cry was joyful and triumphant in direct proportion to the suffering they'd endured. Adam reached for her hand as he stood. He was already moving as if he'd never been injured at all. Ezekiel's miracle has caused Adam to heal. She was sore and exhausted and didn't reject the help as he pulled her to her feet. After all, she hadn't been healed by Ezekiel's Brimstone. The cuts and bruises she'd suffered from falling debris still stung.

But she'd never felt better in her life.

She felt like singing a new song. Her years singing opera had sustained her during a dark time, but she no longer missed the role of Juliet. Tragic romance was overrated. There were happier songs to sing.

"My people can help get these kids back to where they belong," Adam said. He squeezed her hand and leaned down to press a firm kiss against her lips before he moved away toward the daemons who were trying to help the children.

Victoria watched him walk—tall and strong and every bit the warrior, the vintner, the businessman and the Russian firebird all rolled into one extraordinary man. He'd saved himself by saving others. He'd resisted revenge and focused on justice and salvation. He would always have blood on his hands and scars on his back, but he was the one who had turned those scars into an angel's wings.

And she had nearly betrayed him.

Now that he no longer had Brimstone in his blood, would their connection remain or would her affinity tear them apart? Wanting to sing a new song and actually being able to successfully do it were two different things. She would always be blessed and cursed by Samuel's Kiss. If she wasn't an opera singer or an unwilling blood-hound for the Order of Samuel, what would she be?

Chapter 24

The vineyard was beautiful in the moonlight though not a single rose blossom remained on the bushes and vines throughout the gardens around the main house. They had returned to Nightingale Vineyards to find an explosion of rose petals all over the estate. Every petal from every rose had been scattered on pathways and in the grass and on the trees in a profusion of scarlet, crimson and a deep ruby that was nearly black. Esther told them there had been no storm or wind to account for the phenomenon. She had gone to bed on a still night and had woken to a riot of color all over the grounds.

Victoria strolled down a petal-strewed pathway and breathed deeply of the sweet, rose-scented air. She sang softly under her breath, making up the words as she went along. She'd already filled a notebook with lyrics. She'd made a few phone calls to professionals she'd met over the years. Once Michael arrived in Sonoma, she wanted to be prepared to begin a fresh new chapter in their lives.

She wasn't yet sure about how Adam Turov fit into her plans.

"Your singing still calls to me," a familiar voice interrupted from behind her on the path.

She paused and turned to see Adam's silhouette— so tall, so strong—backlit by moonlight so she couldn't see his face.

"I wasn't sure. I walked away from the house so I wouldn't disturb you just in case," Victoria said.

Her affinity could still detect the faintest glow of Brimstone in his blood, a remnant she recognized from when John Severne had won back his soul. Once you've faced damnation, you're never innocent again. Adam Turov would always be more than an ordinary man. He would carry a long and complex history with him for the rest of his life and all the experience that came with that, plus he'd always have just a touch of daemon fire in his blood.

But his magnetism went deeper and richer than that for her. She was drawn to him. The man who had saved hundreds of lives. The man who had saved her by helping her to reach her son so she could save him. The man who took her to the edge and caught her when she fell. He burned bright. Not because of Brimstone, but because of the strength of will he'd used to fight damnation and reclaim his soul.

He stepped closer and closer to her, but she couldn't move. She should continue walking or shift to the side so he could pass. She did neither. Within seconds, they were toe to toe. She looked up at his face, which had now come into the beams of hazy light from a crescent moon in a cloudless sky. He still had the Turov bone structure, with chiseled cheekbones and an angular jaw that would have made a male model envious, but his jaw was no longer clenched against her. His eyes were gray in this light, but they gazed at her directly with no shadowed secrets.

"I was so focused on the burn that I never realized what a weight flowed in my veins. I must have gotten used to it over the years so I didn't realize what an actual physical burden I carried along with the mental ones. Knowing you're damned. Trying to do what's right all the same. Failing miserably to resist a kiss you know you shouldn't savor," Adam said.

He lifted a hand to press a strand of her hair back from her face and then his hand lingered. He brushed her cheek with his thumb while his fingers rested lightly in her hair. "My physical burden has been lifted. But my mind is still troubled. I want to do what's right for you. Your affinity is drawn toward Brimstone blood. I find myself damned even though I've regained my soul because I need to let you go, and yet I still crave your taste and your touch. Does your song still draw me? Oh, yes. I feel as if I'll burn for you always. Brimstone or not."

He leaned to kiss her and she opened her lips for his tongue. She reached to hold around his neck because her knees seemed iffy about the challenge of keeping her on her feet. He'd seemed hesitant, but her response raised a groan in his throat and his hands came up to her back to crush her against him. She didn't protest.

A slight breeze blew up around them, stirring the rose petals at their feet. Adam drew back and opened his eyes to look around. Victoria did the same. The breeze continued swirling the petals all around the garden in gentle whirls. And then as soon as it came the breeze died down and faded away.

"I think we have my mother's blessing," Adam said.

"We've been blessed from the start in spite of affinity and Brimstone, not because of it," Victoria said. "You need nothing else to seal the deal with me, Adam. The question is whether or not you're prepared to be with a woman who has a half daemon prince for a son, a daemon king as a stepfather and an ability that will always bring daemons into your life." She couldn't help it. She held her breath as she waited for his reaction. She'd always been different. Some would say cursed. She could never be an ordinary vintner's wife. If he wanted to leave behind the warrior, he might want to leave her behind as well.

"There's a traditional bargain couples enter into when they want to be together—'til death us do part. I want to make a deal with you, Victoria D'Arcy," Adam said.

In the moonlight he suddenly looked like a temptingly handsome devil. His lips were curved into a wicked smile. His dark hair gleamed where moon-kissed light gave way to shadows.

"To have and to hold from this day forward," Victoria replied.

The world kept spinning. The universe didn't pause, but for one second she could have sworn that the petals that fell from the trees after the breeze were suspended in the air behind them.

"Only if you promise to sing for me." Adam leaned to tease the words against her lips.

"Only if you promise to burn for me," Victoria said.

"I can guarantee that won't be any problem at all," he replied, and this time when he pressed his mouth to hers, whether or not the world paused didn't matter at all.

Epilogue

Michael played in the garden near a cellar where vegetables used to be grown. To a casual observer, he played by himself, tossing tennis balls into the shadows. Victoria knew there was only one tennis ball and it seemed to inexplicably vanish and appear in different places as if there were more balls because the shadows had teeth.

Adam stood nearby. He'd had his turn. Michael had dutifully played catch with his stepfather, using the two battered vintage gloves and a faded baseball that now lay at Adam's feet. He'd laughed and enjoyed every minute, but he'd also been eager to play with Grim who had waited patiently for the tennis ball to be thrown his way.

She'd turned back to watch them for a while—it was always a pleasure to watch Michael play in the sun and her husband's dark hair gleam. She'd also grown very fond of Grim since the day he'd saved the children and her son from the Order of Samuel when the castle fell.

His size and teeth and uncanny abilities would always make her nervous. He was a hellhound after all. But she'd learned to love him, shadows and all.

She'd spent the morning writing in her notebook on a bench near the garden where Michael played. Now, Adam turned and waved. He'd known she hadn't walked away yet even though she hadn't made a sound to distract him. Their connection was deeper than ever. Charged by love and closeness with only a hint of Brimstone. She smiled in response and turned toward the path that would lead her to the cottage.

Since Michael had come to Nightingale Vineyards, there had been a flurry of changes. Adam Turov was a very wealthy man and he spared no expense for his people. She'd discovered he was even more lavish with his family.

A large room in the main house had been renovated into a perfect little boy's bedroom, complete with a tree house bunk bed. For now, Michael slept on the bottom and his faithful guardian slept on the top. She imagined that would change as he grew. To match the tree house, the walls had been painted with a sunny outdoor mural featuring more trees and grass and a bright blue sky with white fluffy clouds. Every time she entered the room to tuck Michael—and Grim—in at night, she thought about Gideon telling her that Adam had given him the sun.

He'd tried to give Michael the sun too.

She always chuckled whenever Grim fully materialized in the Huck Finn atmosphere of the bedroom. Other children worried about the monster under the bed. Michael had a monster as a faithful companion and he never seemed to worry about anything.

If occasionally she worried for him, it was a mother's

prerogative. Never mind that her worries were a little bit darker than most.

She strolled down the path with her notebook tucked under her arm. The roses were blooming again. Adam was already planning the first crush. It was hard to believe more than a year had passed since they'd defeated Malachi. She came around a curve in the pathway and walked through the arbor tunnel she'd first strolled through with Adam months ago. Sunlight penetrated the thick climbing roses only in sporadic places. She walked through sunlight, then shadow, then sunlight again until she reached the other side. The first song she'd recorded had been about finding light in the darkness.

When she stepped into the cottage clearing, she noted that the sod had taken root and was growing well. The workmen had repaired all the damage they'd done with their equipment as they'd converted the cottage into a recording studio. Tangled Vine was the name of her label. They'd left the exterior untouched. It still looked as if the entire building was made of climbing roses. But inside was a technical marvel with everything she needed to record her new songs.

She walked to the stoop where dried cherry blossoms had once terrified her on a dark night and opened the unlocked door. The skeleton keys now hung in Esther's kitchen where the firebird tea service was kept in a cabinet and brought out on special occasions.

Elena Turov's sitting room was no longer a shrine.

The Russian fairy tale book was on a shelf in Michael's room along with many other titles, some vintage, some new.

She always felt a tingle of excitement when she entered the studio to work, but this time she found the daemon king on a tall stool near her soundboard. She was

out of practice. The tingle was a reaction to Ezekiel's
Brimstone blood. He had it tempered and shielded, but
her affinity detected a hint as their proximity increased.

"You have been busy," Ezekiel said.

It was the first time she'd seen him in casual clothes.
His effect wasn't diminished. A black T-shirt and lean
denim jeans paired with narrow, square-toed black ox-
fords didn't disguise his hardness or the age that shone
from his eyes. They were very dark blue. So dark that
his irises blended into his pupils at times when he turned
his head from the light.

"He's only three. It's not time," Victoria said.

"Although our agreement says 'every summer.' I'm
not here to claim him. He's doing well with you. Your
affinity is helping him through his Burn. I don't want
to disrupt that," Ezekiel said.

Victoria forced herself to step into the cottage and
close the door. If any daemon screamed disruption it
was Ezekiel. She'd seen him glow with Brimstone as
he "disrupted" as much as he could. Granted, she'd also
seen him save Adam's life with the Brimstone from his
very own veins.

"He is doing well," she said as she placed her notebook on the soundboard. She'd managed to approach
him as if he was a normal stepfather come to call.

The daemon king rose and moved away from her.
For the first time, she realized with shock that he wasn't
wearing Lucifer's wings. He wasn't diminished. He was
still powerful and regal, but she did wonder at the ab-
sence of his mantle.

"I'm sorry. The wings were not without residual
power. They shielded me somewhat. Your affinity is
painful to me now. A reminder that your mother is
gone," Ezekiel explained. He took another chair across

the room. As soon as he settled into it, it resembled a throne in spite of its actual form.

"Why did you come here without them?" Victoria asked. She didn't want to know. She wanted him to leave. She wanted to lose herself in song for a few hours before dinner and then she wanted to play with Michael until bedtime.

"I bargained with heaven to save Adam Turov. It was a strategic mistake. Of course they asked for Lucifer's wings. He defied them. He's gone. They see his wings as a tribute they deserve. I saw it as a high price I was willing to pay…for you, for Michael, for an honorable servant," Ezekiel said. "Adam Turov saved me long ago. In exchange, I held his soul as I helped him defeat the Order of Samuel. But even though that bargain was complete, I found I could not watch him die while you wept."

"You are a king without a crown," Victoria said.

"One day, Michael will retrieve Lucifer's wings. Until then, I'll hold what we have wrenched from the Rogues with my own two hands, no wings required," Ezekiel said.

He raised two clenched fists and his conviction sizzled the air. Victoria had settled onto the stool he'd vacated, but she rose in response to his emotion. The potential for scorch in his company always made her nervous on top of his designs on her child.

"He has a choice," Victoria said. "He'll always have a choice."

"This I have promised to you, but I have no control over heaven and what they might require," Ezekiel warned.

He stood and moved toward the door. She was always surprised when he didn't vanish in a puff of smoke or go up in flames and disappear. Instead, he opened her cottage door and stepped into the sun.

"There's no one else I would have chosen to parent my heir than you and Adam Turov. I look forward to Michael's visits," Ezekiel said before slowly closing the door.

She forced herself to work for a few hours, but then she headed to the main house for much-needed company and rest. The daemon king's visit was only a reminder that there were always shadows, even when she walked in the light. Michael had come in from the vineyards where he had finished his game of catch to ride with Adam on an inspection tour. He loved the ATVs and they'd purchased a special booster seat and helmet so he could ride them safely.

He bubbled with news about what he'd seen while she ran his bath and placed him in a sudsy tub. Grim stood nearby as transparent as smoke. He would supervise the bath while she freshened up in her room just down the hall.

"I'll be back. Wash between your toes," she ordered.

Michael giggled when she squiggled a soapy finger between his toes just before she left. She was pretty sure Grim rolled his eyes.

She walked into the master bedroom to find a large white box on the bed. It was tied with a crimson satin ribbon.

"I thought this would never arrive and then I thought you'd never finish in the studio to come and find it," Adam said. He rose from a chair in the corner and came to take her in his arms. She leaned into his embrace with more gusto than he was expecting. "What happened?"

he asked, always on alert. She was glad to have the warrior to lean on.

"Ezekiel came to call," she said against his chest. His whole body stiffened in response. "He's gone now," she reassured him. "He only came to…well… I think he's lonely."

"Does this mean we've joined the sandwich generation?" Adam said.

He tried to cheer her and it succeeded. She laughed and pulled back from his arms.

"Yes. I think it does," she replied. "Early and in the darkest way imaginable. We'll be busy taking care of Michael and his unusual stepgrandfather. Avoiding the latter as much as possible!"

"We'll have to deal with him eventually," Adam warned.

"That's what I'm afraid of. We've dealt with him enough already. Daemon deals can't be trusted. I know that. But I keep having to make them. I'm afraid Michael will too," she said.

"Well, considering he is half daemon, I'd say he's going to make his fair share of deals in his lifetime. Our job will be to raise him to make honest ones," Adam said.

He tugged her back toward him and lowered his face to kiss her lips. The gentle connection instantly flared to something hotter than he'd intended. Their tongues danced and Victoria forgot all about the daemon king.

It was Adam who broke the kiss and pushed her toward the bed.

"I've been waiting too long for this to be distracted. Open it," he ordered.

Victoria reached for the satin ribbon and pulled it free. She lifted the lid of the box and placed it to the side on the bed. Inside the box mounds of golden paper shimmered. She carefully parted the folds of gilded tissue until she came to the treasure that nestled beneath them.

She'd once gone to a ball with Adam in a dress that resembled the firebird from his Russian fairy tale. But the dress she pulled from the box was as different from the firebird as night and day. The skirt was made up of white, jagged layers of silk edged with gray satin slashes that upon close inspection turned out to be in a feather design. The bodice was also gray silk with soft tufts of downy white feathers as sleeves.

Adam had disappeared while she gasped and sighed over the gift. By the time he came back into the room, she had shed her clothes and pulled the silk dress onto her naked body. She wasn't at all surprised that it fit her like a glove. The design was all Sybil. Her creations were always a fantasy sewed with a love that had been touched by shadows. And they always fit perfectly. Adam had ordered the nightingale dress, but it had to have been Sybil who had sewed it. No one else could have captured the power and the vulnerability of Victoria's new music with thread and shimmering fabric. The dress was a nightingale at night, but it was also Victoria's song. She'd sent the daemon seamstress her first recording. It had to have inspired the dress.

She turned to see another surprise. Adam had come back into the room in a tuxedo. The perfectly tailored suit was black with a slim modern cut, but his vest was brocade and Slavic in color and pattern. She could see the firebird illustration worked into the colorful design. Another Sybil creation. Dark and light and gorgeous. The firebird brooch glittered on his simple black ascot.

Elena Turov had worried that her son would someday be alone. Victoria's eyes burned, touched by a mother's eternal love. She had the same hopes for Michael. That one day he'd find someone who could handle his unique heritage of fire and song. He was different, but if there was one thing she'd learned about daemons it was that their love burned fiercer and hotter than a mortal man's.

One day her son would love and the world would burn.

Adam spoke and her full attention was brought back to the handsome man at her side. Not quite mortal. He'd lived too long for that designation and his love was fueled by a spark the Brimstone had left in his veins.

"I thought at this year's gala I would be the firebird and you would be the nightingale," Adam explained.

She had rediscovered her song. He was burning brightly and free. She'd never heard a more perfect idea.

He stared at her intensely with the same appreciation he'd showed the first night she'd arrived at Nightingale Vineyards, but it was enhanced by all they'd shared together since then. They'd braved Malachi's darkness. They'd defied the fires of hell. She suddenly knew that nothing they faced in the future would be too much for them to handle if they were together.

His arms were ready when she stepped back into his embrace. He held her close against his chest. She could hear the steady beat of his heart. But even better than that, she could feel the warmth of his reclaimed soul.

* * * * *

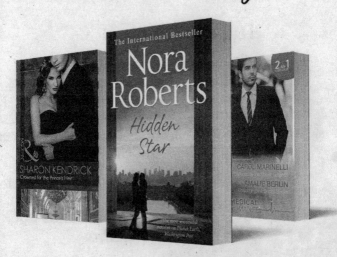